Cuthbert Bede

Glencreggan : Or, a Highland Home in Cantire

Vol. II.

Cuthbert Bede

Glencreggan : Or, a Highland Home in Cantire
Vol. II.

ISBN/EAN: 9783337160043

Printed in Europe, USA, Canada, Australia, Japan

Cover: Foto ©Andreas Hilbeck / pixelio.de

More available books at **www.hansebooks.com**

GLENCREGGAN:

OR,

A HIGHLAND HOME IN CANTIRE.

BY

CUTHBERT BEDE.

Illustrated with Three Maps, Eight Chromolithographs, and
Sixty-one Woodcuts, from the Author's Drawings.

IN TWO VOLUMES.

VOL. II.

LONDON:
LONGMAN, GREEN, LONGMAN, AND ROBERTS.
1861.

CONTENTS

OF

THE SECOND VOLUME.

———

CHAPTER XVIII.

CHAP. XIX.

CHAP. XX.

GROUSE-LAND.

CHAP. XXI.

STILL-LIFE, AND HIGHLAND DAINTIES.

CHAP. XXII.

CANTIRE BUCOLICS PAST AND PRESENT.

CHAP. XXIII.

HIGHLAND FARM-HOUSES.

CHAP. XXIV.

HIGHLAND COTTAGES.

CHAP. XXV.

ON THE ATLANTIC SHORE.

CHAP. XXVI.

COMMON OBJECTS ON AND OFF THE SEA-SHORE.

CHAP. XXVII.

MUASDALE; A WATERING-PLACE — IN CLOUDLAND.

CHAP. XXVIII.

KILLEAN — A SCOTCH KIRK AND SABBATH.

CHAP. XXIX.

LARGIE.

LIST OF ILLUSTRATIONS

TO

THE SECOND VOLUME.

CHROMO-LITHOGRAPHS.

WOODCUTS PRINTED AS PLATES.

(Drawn on the wood by Mr. J. Willis Brooks. Engraved by Branston.)

WOODCUTS PRINTED IN THE TEXT.

MAP.

GLENCREGGAN.

CHAPTER XVIII.

CANTIRE'S MONARCH OF MOUNTAINS, AND ITS LEGENDS.

A Highland Parish. — A native Poet. — Barr Glen. — Beinn-an-Tuirc.
— What is a Mountain ? — Hieland Hills. — Local Rhymes. — View
from the Summit. — Legend of the Wild Boar. — Fingal compasses
Diarmid's Death. — Diarmid a Victor. — Diarmid a Victim. — The
One-eyed. — Versions of the Legend. — Ossian. — Legend of Robert
Bruce. — A friendly Goat. — Bruce and the Beggar-man. — A Dish
at a Pinch. — How to obtain an Answer to a Question. — Friends
in need. — Highland Hospitality. — Bruce and Mackay. — A royal
Bargain royally fulfilled. — Another Version of the Tale.

HERE is abundant variety in the landscape
that I am endeavouring to sketch. It
might be said of the parish in which Glencreggan is situated, as Christopher North
said of his own native place (only for " loch " we must
read " sea "): " It was as level, as boggy, as hilly,
as mountainous, as woody, as lochy, and as rivery a
parish, as ever laughed to scorn Colonel Mudge and his
Trigonometrical Survey." And this applies to the

general features of the landscape, which, in its details, is much as follows.

The hill-side falls sharply from our feet into a valley (high above the sea) along which, in an easterly direction, runs a good road from the village of Barr for some four or five miles, communicating with several farm-houses on the Glenbarr estate. A few yards on the other side of the road is Barr river, hurrying on in its downward course towards the sea, over rocky fragments and ledges, and, for the most part, fringed and overhung with trees and hazel bushes up to its source. It is fed by many tributary streams, the chief of which flows from Loch Coiribh; but the main source of Barr River is Loch Arnicle, a wild and lonely loch at the western foot of the mountain Beinn-an-Tuirc.

A local poet, who has not much of the fire of Burns, or the ancient Scalds, thus celebrates the lochs of Cantire : —

> " The many lakes that stud Cantire,
>   No man would grudgingly admire,
>   But spare an hour for to retire
>   And take a view,
>   Which would his frame with health inspire,
>   And strength renew."

The same poet — whose success in verse is not equal to his good intentions — has also tuned his strings in praise of the glens of Cantire : —

" Cantire's glens perfume the air
  With roses sweet, and gowans fair;
  Their fertile sides, and crystal streams,
  Dress'd with the sun's life-giving beams,
    Delight the heart and eye.
      A walk then on the field
      Would health and vigour yield —
    A feast of joys supply."

Barr Glen is cultivated throughout its whole extent, and has extensive sheep pasturage on either side. In this cultivated tract, farm-houses and cottages are dotted about near to the road side, leaving the hills to loneliness and heather. The river runs along the valley far below us; on its further side the hills again rise to a considerable height. They range from right to left, terminating five miles from us in Beinn-au-Tuirc, near to whose base the shooting-party this morning commenced their day's sport.

Beinn-an-Tuirc is the most considerable hill in Cantire, being 2170 feet above the level of the sea, and only 306 feet lower than the Paps of Jura; but as it does not rise abruptly from its base, but towers out of a confused mass of lofty hills, it appears of less altitude than other mountains that are its inferior in height, but are better seen from standing alone. It has also been omitted in the tables of the Scotch mountains and hills, which give various altitudes down to that of Arthur's Seat, which is 823 feet above the sea.

Why, this nameless hill on which we are now seated is much higher than that; and yonder hill on the other side of the Barr Glen is still higher!

What is a hill, indeed; and what a mountain? at what altitude does a hill end and a mountain commence? in fact, at what altitude does a rise of ground become a hill? In the flat fen counties of England, it takes a very small proportion of earth to be dignified with the title of a hill. The Cambridge man when he lionises his country cousins, shows them the Gogmagog Hills; and they look over the gently rising fields to which he is pointing, and strain their eyes in the vain expectation of seeing a blue range worthy of the name of hills. The Cambridge man makes a tour, ascends Mont Blanc, becomes a member of the Alpine Club, and scorns the Grampians as mere hillocks. While, in a land of mountains like the Highlands, what would be a mountain in lowland counties, dwindles to a hill. Thus, that young Scotch minister who is one of our most accomplished and genial essayists says, " I am writing north of the Tweed, and the horizon is of blue hills, which some Southrons would call mountains."*
And Christopher North, speaking of his boyhood's home "among moors and mountains," says, "mountains they seemed to us in those days, though now we believe they are only hills. But, such hills! undu-

---

* Recreations of a Country Parson, p. 126.

lating far and wide away, till the highest, even on clear days, seemed to touch the sky, and, in cloudy weather, were verily a part of heaven." And Mr. Baillie Nicol Jarvie thus sums up the catalogue of items that constitute Highland scenery: — "These Hielands of ours, as we ca' them, gentlemen, are but a wild kind of warld by themsells, full of heights and howes, woods, caverns, lochs, rivers, and mountains, that it wad tire the very deevil's wings to flee to the tap o' them." So we may come to the conclusion that "the Hieland hills," if not mountains, are very good representations of them; and that we may better understand the 2170 feet that go to make up the altitude of Beinn-an-Tuire (*Beinn* or *Ben*, as we may remember, denotes a hill of the largest scale) we may call to mind the heights of the two greatest hills that a Londoner would first meet with on his travels northward; viz. the Malvern hills (Worcestershire Beacon) 1444 feet; and the Wrekin, 1320 feet. It was these "Hieland hills" that enabled the Scotchman to vanquish the Englishman with whom he was disputing as to the superiority of his native country in every respect over England. "But you must at any rate allow," said the Englishman, "that Scotland is smaller in extent than England." "By no means," was the reply; yours is a flat country, ours is a hilly one; and, if all our hills were rolled out flat, we should beat you by hundreds of square miles."

As Beinn-an-Tuirc is the monarch of mountains in Cantire, he demands of us a due recognition and special notice; so, while I am busied with my paint-brush in endeavouring to represent him as he appears to us from this Glencreggan moor, let me tell you what I know concerning him. The local poet, from whom I have just now quoted, has crowned him with mortal verse, in stanzas commencing thus : —

> " Delightful task 'tis to ascend
> Cantire's hill with a true friend;
> A page of nature's book to spy,
> When calm and cloudless is the sky.
> A great expanse of sea and land
> Stretches sublime from where we stand;
> The ocean wide, a mighty sheet,
> Spreads out the concave vault to meet."

The mountain is upon the estate of Torrisdale, in the parish of Saddell, whose minister, the Rev. John Macfarlane, thus describes the view from its summit. "From no point of the same altitude in the country is the view more grand, extensive, or picturesque. In the foreground (to the east) is the island of Arran; to the south, the Frith of Clyde, the Craig of Ailsa, and the Irish Channel. From the Point of Corsil, in Wigtonshire, the eye can range along the intervening counties, until arrested by 'the lofty Ben Lomond.' Hence the transition is easy to Ben Cruachan and Ben More, in Mull. To the north-west is the Horizon line of the Atlantic, presenting portions of its blue surface through the openings of the different islands with which it is indented, from Mull to the Giant's Causeway. In this range are embraced portions of seven Scottish and two Irish counties, and the circuit is supposed to be little less than 300 miles."

The name Beinn-an-tuirc signifies "The Mountain of the Wild Boar," and the Cantire Highlanders tell the following legend in explanation of the name.* Once upon a time, when this mountain was partly clothed with great forests, there lived among them a wild boar of enormous size and strength. He ravaged the country, wandering about for prey, and killing every man and beast that he met. For miles off he could be heard whetting his terrible tusks against the stately oaks, and people were afraid to pass that way, and had to drive their cattle to other pastures. The great hero Fingal came to Cantire, and was told of the wild boar's ravages. Among his brave men there was a mighty hunter named Diarmid †, of whom Fingal was jealous

---

* There is no account of this, or of any history attaching to the mountain, given in the "Statistical Accounts of Scotland," or other books in which Cantire is mentioned.

† Keefie of Gigha carried off Diarmid's wife, and was slain by him. See chap. xiv.

and wished to be rid; so to him was committed the dangerous task to slay the boar. Diarmid accepted the task with joy, and set out for the mountain. He entered the oak forest that then grew at its base, and soon got upon the track of the boar. He followed it through the brushwood and the thick hazels that gave to Caledonia its name *, and presently heard the boar crunching the bones of a bullock. Diarmid sprang upon him with his spear †, but it broke off short in the wild boar's chest, and the beast, maddened with pain and savage anger, rushed upon him. Diarmid stept lightly aside, and the boar, in his blind fury, dashed his tusk against the hard trunk of an oak. Diarmid was instantly upon him with his sword, and plunged it in his bristly body up to the very hilt, and the boar rolled over and died. Diarmid blew his horn and obtained help, and they dragged the dead body of the boar to the tent of Fingal, where there was great

---

* This, however, is a doubtful etymology; for though Caledonia is said by some to mean "the land of hazels," which grow there in such luxuriance, yet others would derive the word from *Na Caoillaoin*, "the men of the woods;" and the *Deucaledones* has the like signification. Tacitus is the earliest author who uses the word *Caledonii*.

† The readers of " Ossian's Poems " may call to mind the strife of the two kings, Culgorm and Sucandrolo, who jointly killed a boar, and then, like modern shooters with a bird, each laid claim to the honour of the deed. They quarrelled over it, and ended the dispute by a war.

rejoicing at the deed, and many shells * were quaffed in honour of Diarmid.

But there were many among the followers of Fingal who envied Diarmid his victory over the dreaded wild boar, and the great Fingal himself was enraged to see him return alive and successful; so, while some were preparing the pit with smooth stones, in which to roast the boar, others were speaking aside against Diarmid, and Fingal was revolving in his mind how he might best rid himself of the man who had so aroused his jealousy at his brave deeds. Then came there one to Fingal and said, "It is not wonderful that Diarmid hath slain the boar, for the boar had no power to hurt Diarmid." Then Fingal demanded how that might be; and was answered: "Diarmid hath a charmed body; no sword or spear of man, nor yet the tusk or horn of beast can wound him, save but in one little spot." "Tell me that spot," said Fingal, "that I may wound him there! where is it?" "Upon his heel," was the reply.

Now the dead body of the wild boar was lying near, and Fingal and his followers went to view it, and to express their wonder at its huge size and great length.

---

* In olden times the Highlanders drank from shells, a practice, indeed, which is not quite extinct in the present day. Thus it is in "Ossian's Poems" that a banquet-hall is called "the hall of shells," and the host, "the chief of shells;" while the wine-drinking is poetically termed "the joy of shells."

Then Fingal called Diarmid to him and complimented him on his prowess, and bade him measure the boar with his feet, to see how long the monster was. Diarmid was barefooted; but he stepped on to the head of the boar, and so measured it with his feet from the head downwards, the strong bristles yielding to his tread. Then Fingal bade him measure the boar again by treading backwards against the grain. Diarmid did so; but the stiff bristles were no longer pressed downwards, and they pierced his heel; and Diarmid bled to death. It was in this manner that the people of Cantire were rid of the terrible wild boar, and that Fingal compassed the death of Diarmid; and in memory of the monster whom he slew the mountain was called *Beinn-an-tuirc*, or "The Mountain of the Wild Boar." It is said also of this Diarmid that he had but one eye, and was therefore called in Gaelic *Camshuil*, or "the One-eyed;" and that the Campbells are descended from him, and retain in their armorial bearings a boar's head in remembrance of his exploit. Their descent from this Fingalian Achilles is also denoted in their title of *Clann Dhiarmaid*, "the children of Diarmid." *

* Mr. Campbell tells us of a namesake who "believed that Diarmaid, the Irish hero, was his ancestor, and his own real name O'Duine. He spoke of 'his chief MacCalain,' and treated me with extra kindness as a kinsman. 'Will you not take some more?' (milk and potatoes).

The Achillean invulnerability of Diarmid is worthy of notice.* The legend, at least so far as I have been informed, does not tell us how Diarmid's body was brought to its invulnerable state, but simply that it was so. Mr. Campbell, in his "Popular Tales of the West Highlands," briefly refers to the legend thus: "The boar was the animal which Diarmid slew, and which caused his death when he paced his length against the bristles; the venomous bristles pierced a *mole in his foot.*" † So that this would appear to be a different version of this portion of the legend. Mr. Campbell again speaks of the legend at the close of his second volume (p. 473). He first quotes Dr. Smith, of Camp-belton. "' DIARMAID. — This poem is generally inter-larded with so much of the ursgeuls, or later tales, as

---

'Perhaps we may never see each other again. Are we not both Camp-bells?'" — *West Highland Tales*, vol. i. p. 34.

* The reader who wishes to see how many Highland legends and fairy tales can be traced to a mythological source, and appear in sundry forms among different peoples, can scarcely do better than refer to Mr. Campbell's volumes; and more particularly to the chapter entitled "Highland Romances and Superstitions," in the fourth volume of Macculloch's "Highlands and Western Isles," a book to which Mr. Campbell does not refer, although he goes over precisely the same ground as that so well trodden by Macculloch in the chapter just mentioned. But Mr. Campbell has brought to his task a large share of that varied information and reading of which Macculloch gives so formidable a list, as being necessary to him "who may undertake the office of a Highland Grimm " (vol. iv. p. 322).

† Vol. i. Introd. p. xci.

to render the most common editions of it absurd and extravagant. But the fabulous dross of the fifteenth century is easily separated from the more precious ore of the ancient bards.' Of part of the same story of Diarmaid, Mrs. MacTavish writes in 1859 : 'A *dan* or song which I heard an old ploughman of my father's sing very near sixty years since. He had a great collection of tales and songs, and often have I stood or sat by him in winter when kiln-drying corn, or in summer when building a peat-stack, listening to what was to me so fascinating in those days. And then follows the story of how Diarmaid was killed by pacing barefooted against the bristles of a boar which he had killed, and the lament of Diarmaid's love, and the music to which it used to be sung ; and this same story of Diarmaid and the boar was sung to me by Alexander Macdonald, in Barra, in September, 1860, together with other long Gaelic poems: and whatever may be thought of Macpherson's collection (*i. e.* Ossian's poems), this at least is genuine old poetry, and still known to many in the Highlands.' " Mr. Campbell also says in another place: " I know not how many cairns are supposed to contain the bones of the wild boar whose bristles wounded the feet of Diarmaid when he paced his length against the hair." * The mountain of Sliobh-ghoil, in South Knapdale, is one of these places,

* Vol. i. p. 40.

and is visible from Beinn-an-tuirc. The Fingalian heroes had as many burial-places as Homer had birth-places.

Mr. Campbell tells us that he copied Dr. Smith's note on "Diarmaid" from some manuscripts belonging to the Highland Society, to which he was permitted to have access. He also transcribes from the same source the "advertisement" to "MS. poems collected in the Western Highlands and Islands by Dr. John Smith," which agrees in part with the introductory observations on the Gaelic poems, printed at pp. 126—130 of Dr. Smith's "Gaelic Antiquities." * This is a quarto

---

* "Gaelic Antiquities: consisting of a History of the Druids, par-ticularly of those of Caledonia; a Dissertation on the Authenticity of the Poems of Ossian; and a Collection of Ancient Poems, translated from the Gaelic of Ullin, Ossian, Orran, &c. By John Smith, Minister at Kilbrandon, Argyleshire. Edinburgh, 1780." Mr. Campbell men-tions Dr. Smith's "book on Gaelic poetry" (vol. i. p. 20), and says, "he condemns the 'urskels' as 'later tales' unworthy of notice, pro-bably because they were different from the poetry of which he col-lected so much." This statement, however, is taken from that manu-script "advertisement" belonging to the Highland Society. In the printed book Dr. Smith speaks at some length of the great assistance he had derived from "the traditional tales or *sgeulachds* which always accompany and explain the old Gaelic poems, and which often remain entire when the poems themselves are reduced to fragments." He also says: "The style of these tales is highly figurative and poetical, and the words and ideas so well arranged that they take the most lasting hold of the memory and imagination: insomuch that they are frequently to be met with where the poems are beginning to be rare" (p. 129). Dr. Smith also gives an account of his labours in collecting,

volume, published before Dr. Smith went to Campbelton
and obtained his degree. The poems are fourteen in
number, and are among those which "had escaped the
inquiries of the able and ingenious translator of Ossian,
whose researches were more chiefly confined to the
more northern parts of the Highlands." One of the
poems narrates the "Legend of Diarmid and the Wild
Boar;" and although it differs considerably from the
version of the story which I have already given, and
transfers the scene of the exploit to the mountain of
Sliobh-ghoil, in northern Argyleshire, it may be interesting to quote it here, and it will probably be new
to the reader; but as the poem occupies sixteen pages
of a quarto volume, it has been thought best to transfer
it to the Appendix, to which place I beg to refer the
reader.

So much for Beinn-an-tuirc in the olden days of
Fingal. But it has also a later history, in which there
is likewise a very strong flavour of the legend. It re-
lates (of course!) to that other Scottish hero, Robert

"from different quarters, as many editions as possible" of the old
Gaelic poetical tales. This task occupied him for ten or twelve years.
He collected the tales through the medium of several correspondents
in the Northern and Western Highlands and Isles, and also "by oral
recitation;" and he gives the names of thirteen persons who were his
chief helpers. In short, he pursued precisely the same plan as that so
effectively carried out by Mr. Campbell nearly a century after. Dr.
Smith's labours have not been sufficiently recognised.

Bruce, of whom there are quite as many romances told as were ever narrated of Fingal; and, as we saw when we were off the coast of Arran, the two heroes often run in couples. The following is the local legendary tale of Robert Bruce and Beinn-an-tuirc.*

In the days when King Robert Bruce was a wanderer, and was hiding himself like a hunted partridge on the mountains from the murderous Southrons, who had set a price upon his royal head and strove to take him dead or alive, he came to Sliobh-ghoil, that mountain in South Knapdale (North Argyleshire) nearly thirty miles due north of this spot, plainly visible from most parts of Cantire, and, by some, pointed out as the scene of Diarmid's death. On that bleak mountain the hunted monarch passed a cheerless night. He was well-nigh spent out with fatigue and hunger; and to add to his distress the night was bitterly cold. He would probably have perished had not a goat come to him and laid herself down beside him. She suffered him to refresh himself with her milk, and she kept him warm all the night through. It was in grateful memory of this that when he "en-

---

* The latter portion only of the legend, *i. e.* that relating to Mackay of Ugadale, is told in Smith's "Views of Campbelton." It is not mentioned in the other works that relate to Cantire. I owe this legend to Mr. Macintosh of Campbelton.

joyed his ain agen," he made a law that forbade anyone to poind (or pound) a goat.

Refreshed by his night's rest and the goat's milk and
warmth, the Bruce came on to Cantire the next morning. On his way he met a beggar-man. The King
was very hungry by this time, and he asked the beggar-
man if he had any food. He answered, that he had
but a little barley-meal. The King said that it was
very good; and they went to a spring of water, where
the King took off his shoe, and moistened the meal
in the heel of the shoe. Then he made a hearty meal
of it, and said, in Gaelic: —

> " Is maith an còcair' an t-acras,
>   'S mairg ni tallach air a' bhiadh,
>   Fuarag corna a beul mo bhròige,
>   An lòn is fear a fhuair mi riamh ; "

which means, in English — " Hunger is a good cook;
it is bad to slight food; barley-meal brose out of my
shoe is the best food that ever I used." Then the King
came on towards Beinn-an-tuirc, and reached its eastern
side, where was the forest of Bunlaradh. It was a
most lonesome spot; but a man was there, and the
King asked him his name. The stranger instead of
answering put the same question to the King, who, of
course, would not disclose himself. So, as neither
would answer, they drew their swords, and forthwith
fell upon each other. They fought desperately for

some time, for both were equally expert; till at length they became exhausted, and sat themselves down to rest. When they had got fresh breath, they set-to again; and again had to pause from exhaustion. A third time they renewed their contest, and a third time had to cease from it quite exhausted. Then said the King: "This is pitiful work that we give ourselves, alone, and in this dreary place. It will answer no good end, even if we should kill each other. Tell me your name, and I will tell you mine!" "Agreed," replied the stranger. "I am Robert Bruce!" said the King. "And I," replied his adversary, "am General Douglas!" Now General Douglas was one who had espoused the cause of Bruce, and, like his monarch, a price had been set on his head by the English, and this had made him a fugitive like the Bruce. So, when these two friends in misfortune knew each other, they threw aside their swords, and fell upon each other's necks, and embraced and kissed each other; so they went both of them together out of the forest of Bunlaradh, down to Ugadale near the eastern shore.* There was a farm there, occupied by an honest man named Mackay, who happened to be entertaining some

---

* Smith, in his "Campbelton," begins the story here, making Bruce land at Ugadale from Loch Ranza, in Arran. The rest of the tale is made up from Smith's account, and that of Mr. Macintosh. General Douglas does not figure in Smith's version.

friends at a kind of merry-making. There they went, and Mackay received them with Highland hospitality, placed them near to the fire, and presented them with a quaigh of usquebaugh. Bruce declined it; but Mackay pressed him with a sort of hearty command, saying, " I am king in my own house." Mackay gave them comfortable beds to sleep on, and a substantial breakfast the next morning; after which, the King asked him to show them the way to the western coast of Cantire. Mackay went with them willingly, and took them up Beinn-an-tuirc. When they were on the top, the King could see the western coast of Cantire, so he would not take Mackay any further, but thanked him for his kindness and hospitality; and ended by telling him that he was Robert Bruce, and for the protection and assistance which he had afforded him, he would grant him any favour he would wish to receive, if he was ever successful in regaining his throne. Mackay replied that if he had the farms of Ugadale and Arniele for his own property he would be as happy as a king. So, the Bruce promised that when he wore his crown again Mackay should have the two farms. The spot where they stood upon the top of Beinn-an-tuirc is marked by a large stone, which is called to this day, "*Cross Mhic Caidh*," or "the Cross of Mackay." When they parted, the King told Mackay to come to him in Edinburgh, when he saw a fire blazing on a certain hill in

Galloway. Then they went down from Beinn-an-tuirc, on their several ways.

Mackay looked long and anxiously for the signal-fire, especially after the tidings had reached him of the great battle of Bannockburn. At last he saw the beacon, and hastened to meet the King. The Bruce recognised him, and kindly entertained him, and made him a gift of the lands which he farmed, giving him the title-deeds of Ugadale and Arniele, to be possessed by him and his heirs for ever. They are still in the possession (it is said) of George M'Neill, Esq. of Ugadale. Before Mackay left, the King offered him a goblet of wine, but Mackay declined it; whereupon the Bruce said that he must drain it, for that *he* also was now " King in his own house."

Such are the popular tales that are told in connection with Cantire's " monarch of mountains." But this Cantire legend of their popular hero King Robert Bruce would appear to be but another version of a West Highland story told by Major-General Stewart in his " Sketches of the Highland Regiments." * James I. (of Scotland) had endeavoured to suppress the feuds of the Highland chief; and Donald Balloch, a kinsman of the Earl of Ross, made several descents on the west coast of Scotland. " To check these devastating invasions, the Earl of Mar, who commanded at Harlaw,

* Vol. ii. p. 456.

accompanied by Allan Stewart, Earl of Caithness, son of the Earl of Athole, marched with a considerable force to Lochaber; and in August 1428 lay at Inverlochay, a place celebrated both for its ancient castle and the different battles fought near it. Donald Balloch had good information from his scouts; and learning that the Earl of Mar, neglecting the necessary precautions of an experienced and brave commander, as he had shown himself at Harlaw and in the wars in Flanders and the Low Countries, where he commanded large armies in several campaigns with great military talents and success, or, perhaps, trusting to his numbers and despising his enemy, kept no night-guard or outposts, Macdonald landed from his fleet of galleys, and, at midnight, attacked the King's troops so unexpectedly, that they were totally routed with great slaughter. Of this number was the Earl of Caithness, and Mar escaped with difficulty. Retreating through the mountains to Braemar, he was two days without food, when he met with a man herding some cattle. This man had a small quantity of barley-meal, which he gave to the unfortunate commander. He mixed the meal with a little water in the heel of his shoe, and greedily swallowed it. Lord Mar told the shepherd, that if ever he required assistance to repair to Kildrummy Castle, where he would meet a grateful friend. The shepherd soon appeared at the castle; he was kindly received by

Lord Mar, who settled him, rent free, on a small farm well stocked, declaring that the handful of barley-meal and water in the heel of his shoe was the sweetest morsel he had ever swallowed. This afterwards became a proverb in the Highlands, something similar to *Hunger requires no sauce.*"

CHAP. XIX.

ON THE MOORS.

Inhabitants of Heather-land. — Gnats and Midges. — Recreations. — Eccentricities of Midges. — A Sketcher's Miseries. — Queer Head-gear. — The venomous Beast. — Mice and Moles. — A Curiosity in Natural History. — The Mole and the Campbells. — A Mountain Burn — Its Birth and Career. — Trees in Heather-land. — The Lady of the Woods. — The Rowan-tree. — Beeches and Wytch Elms. — The Berry Family. — Ferns and other Plants. — Bog-cotton, the Cana of the Poets. — Eagles. — Ornithology of the District. — Natural History of the same. — Scenery of the Moors. — Maps on Boulders.

By the time that I have come to the end of my legends of Beinn-an-tuirc, I have placed upon my sketching-block that last shade of purply-blue with which, in harmonious conjunction with other colours, I have endeavoured to represent him as he now appears to the modern descendants of Fingal and the Bruce, shorn of his forest clothing and his terrible wild boar, but shaggy with heath, and his sides seamed by mountain torrents. But only a portion of my landscape is yet completed. Sit with me awhile, yet a little longer, in the grateful shade of this great boulder, and close beside this fern-

hung, musical burnie, while I fill-in the many little
details of my sketch of heather-land.

We are exceedingly fortunate in being able to sit
here in perfect peace and enjoyment, without being

OUT ON THE MOORS.

irritated beyond endurance by the bloodthirsty attacks
of swarms of midges and gnats. What shooters and
sketchers with sensitive cuticles have often to go
through upon a Scotch moor, in the broad sunlight, can

only be equalled by what is savagely endured during
the darkness of night by the unhappy occupants of a
foul Highland lodging. Christopher North has devoted
one hundred and ninety pages of his " Recreations " to
the subject of "the Moors," in which he has treated
them with all his great power and minuteness, though
with his usual discursiveness and offensive egotism ; and
yet in those one hundred and ninety pages there is
not one word about gnats and midges. In one passage,
it is true, where he is combating the notion that the
moors are solitary, whereas they teem with animal life,
he says: " Your great clumsy splay feet are bruising to
death a batch of beetles. See that spider, whom you
have widowed, running up and down your elegant leg
in distraction and despair, bewailing the loss of a husband, *who, however savage to the ephemerals, had always smiled sweetly upon her.* Meanwhile, your
shoulders have crushed a colony of small red ants,
settled in a moss city beautifully roofed with lichens —
and that accounts for the sharp tickling behind your
ear, which you keep scratching, no Solomon, in ignorance of the cause of that effect. Should you sit down
—we must beg to draw a veil over your hurdies, which
at the moment extinguish a fearful amount of animal
life — creation may be said to groan under them ; and,
insect as you are yourself, you are defrauding millions
of insects of their little day." Beetles, spiders, and

ants; but not a word about gnats or midges, without which the true picture of a Scotch moor would not be complete. Certainly, such pests could not be classed among the " Recreations" of Christopher North, much more of a person with a southern skin. But, as the great Kit has swooped upon ants and spiders, why did he omit those more virulent enemies of man, the swarms of gnats and midges — unless, indeed, those Argyleshire moors that he was describing were free from the pest?

It is within the bounds of possibility, for, as entomologists will tell you, the habits of gnats and midges are exceedingly peculiar; and while they may be swarming on one spot, another more favoured spot, within almost a stone's throw, will be freed from their persecution. Mr. Weld describes this to have been the case in Caithness, where the midges were entirely absent from the banks of the Thurso, but swarmed on the Brawl moors in a way which he very graphically describes, and in such myriads, that lingering over luncheon was impossible to one not gifted with a pachydermatous skin; sitting down was out of the question, even standing still for a moment put the powers of endurance to the severest test; and it was very easy to believe in the tradition of the Persian army that besieged the city of Nisibis being put to flight by the mighty clouds of gnats which settled on them at the earnest solicitation of holy St. Jacobus.* Afterwards, when Mr. Weld endeavoured to sketch Ben Stack, in Sutherlandshire, he found it impossible to do so, for no sooner had he sat down than up rose millions of midges, which sent him " reeling down the craggy steep, half mad." †

Therefore I might account myself particularly fortunate in being able to sit and sketch for hours together on the Glencreggan moors, without being molested by a single obnoxious specimen of entomology. Hence my description of the South Argyleshire moors will resemble Christopher North's accounts of those of North Argyleshire, in this one particular — it will not contain any gnats or midges ; for they did not make themselves sufficiently apparent to me to call for any particular notice or anathemas. Thus my little illustration of one of the pleasures attendant upon sketching in the Highlands was not founded upon any personal and uncomfortable recollection, but nevertheless truly depicts a very common occurrence, and one which, while it drives artists to the verge of frenzy, also compels them to adopt mosquito-curtain veils and other extraordinary head-gear, partially protected by which shrouding they may paint under difficulties. One of Mr. Leech's inimitable sketches in " Punch "

---

* Two Months in the Highlands, pp. 81, 82.
† Idem, p. 265.

will doubtless be called to mind, where two artists in the Highlands are thus represented with their heads wonderfully done up in gnat-defiers, in which are glazed eyelet-holes and a mouth-piece, through which a sanatory pipe may be smoked. And the present

ONE OF THE PLEASURES OF MOORLAND SKETCHING.

writer, too, exhibited in the same publication the mode in which the ingenious Mr. Flyrod, when out fishing, protected his face from the insects, by covering his head with the net-work of his landing-net; only it unfortunately happened, that when Mr. Flyrod had a run, the handle of the landing-net, which stuck out like a pigtail behind him, caught its hooked end in a bough, and nearly strangled its owner, whom a great fish was tugging up-stream.

If we are to dread anything as we sit here on this Glencreggan moor, it will not be a wild boar from yonder Wild Boar's Mountain, whose only wild animals now-a-days are a few roes and rabbits, many hares and badgers, polecats and weasels, and (it is said) a wild cat or two — but it will be the venomous adder, which (together with the harmless ring-snakes and slow-worms) will be found basking in the sun on these moors, and sometimes attaining a length of more than two feet. It is quite as well, therefore, before we make a long *sederunt* on a Highland moor, to first inspect the ground for snakes that " mean wenom," like those that Mark Tapley encountered in his Transatlantic Eden.

I was quoting from Christopher North just now concerning the non-solitude of a Scotch moor, when deserted by other human beings than yourself, but teeming with animal life, zoology, entomology and ornithology. Pursuing his subject, he says: " A man among mountains is often surrounded on all sides with mice and moles. What cozy nests do the former construct at the roots of heather, among tufts of grass in the rushes, and the moss on the greensward. As for the latter, though you think you know a mountain from a molehill, you are much mistaken; for what is a mountain, in many cases, but a collection of mole-hills?" Professor Wilson wrote this sentence on a moor in North Argyleshire; and it is very remarkable, that, at the time when he penned it, it would have been utterly inapplicable to the moors in South Argyleshire; for, except within a few miles of Tarbert, there was not a mole to be found throughout the whole of Cantire. The author of the "Statistical Survey" of the country eighteen miles south of Tarbert, says: "The mole has not as yet made its appearance in the parish; but having several years ago passed the narrow isthmus of Tarbert, it is gradually progressing to the south, and will in all probability ere long overrun the whole peninsula of Kintyre." But he adds in a foot-note: "Since writing the above, the mole has advanced into the parish. It is a very singular circumstance in the natural history of the mole, that it travels by the hills and colonises the sterile districts before it attacks cultivated land." This was published in 1843.

This fact may certainly be classed among the "Curiosities of Natural History." The mole has done its best to take the place of the extinct animals, such as wild boars and wolves, which are said to have been formerly prevalent in Cantire, having their abiding-

places in those forests whose traces are still to be seen
in many a morass. The tradition of the Highlanders
in Cantire regarding the mole connected its non-ap-
pearance with the existence of the clan Campbell. The
moles were to drive the Campbells before them and
take possession of their estates; and when the moles
had reached the Mull, not a Campbell would remain
throughout the length and breadth of Cantire. Such
was the tradition and prophecy; and though never a
mole was seen till about twenty years ago, yet they
have spread through the district with amazing rapidity
from Tarbert to the Mull, but have altogether failed to
drive the Campbells from Cantire. When the prophecy
matched the mole against the Scotchman, the prehen-
sile powers of the latter were not taken into consideration.

But while you are listening to these curious " zoo-
logical recreations" touching moles and midges, I am
working away at my water-colour drawing, and endeavouring to place on paper the counterpart of the
landscape before us. What can be better for my purpose than our immediate foreground? Here before us
is one of those many little glens that seam the hill-
sides; and down it leaps one of those numerous burns,
or streamlets, that find their way to Barr River, and
will presently mingle their pure water with the salt
waves of the Atlantic. The burnie takes its rise in a

black peaty hollow on the hill top, where there is one
of those innumerable mountain-tarns, whose dark slug-
gish waters creep around islands of moss-hags and
tumps of rushes. When it issues from thence it filters
through mosses a yard or so deep, and only betrays its
presence by yonder line of greenest verdure. Then it
makes its first appearance in the world of sunshine,
and tumbles over a bank, or, in the more poetical
words of Burns,

> " White o'er the linn the burnie pours ;"

and makes a tiny waterfall that plashes musically into
as tiny a basin, girdled with plumes upon plumes of
feathery ferns. The heather-bells, pink and white
and crimson, are intermingled with the ferns; and the
thick mossy turf rounds off all the edges of the peat
banks, so that nothing is hard and sharp and angular
save the bits of granite that the stream has washed
clear ; and the belted bees are making a pleasant murmuring about

> " Those easy-curving banks of bloom,
> That lent the windward air an exquisite perfume."

Here and there the burn is so narrow and burrows so
low that the banks nearly close over it. Its waters
look a dark brown that is nearly black, where they
show the peaty channel, and where its banks fall away
and suffer it to broaden out into a little two-yard wide

river, with the projecting rocks for stepping-stones.
Then it loses itself under ground again, with its

"Low murmurs filling mossy dells;"

and dances into sight, tripping down a stony slope in a
way that shows that the pure mountain air has favoured
its muscular development. You will remember Tennyson's beautiful simile, where he speaks, in "Enid,"
of

"Arms, on which the standing muscle sloped, —
As slopes a wild brook o'er a little stone,
Running too vehemently to break upon it."

This Glencreggan burnie shows us the justice of the
simile; for where it trips down that stony slope it
seems like the muscular arm of some mountain giant,
whose skin is as white as a maiden's. Then it runs on,
now amid rocks, and now amid turf and fern and
heather, until it takes a waterfall leap into yonder
birch coppice in the valley, where

"The braes ascend like lofty wa's,
O'erhung wi' fragrant spreading shaws."

The trees are but scanty in heather-land, except where
the shelter of the glens has afforded them a snug place
to flourish in. The species that we then meet with are
the oak, ash, mountain-ash, hazel, birch, wych-elm,
alder, Scotch fir, and larch; but the plantations are but
few, and the landscape, in its general aspect, is barren

of wood. On the other side of Beinn-an-tuirc, woods of fine old forest timber are still to be met with.

The birch (next to the Scotch fir) is one of the most characteristic trees in Highland scenery. It has been well said by a late writer * : " Those who are familiar with our mountain scenery will acknowledge how much of its romantic beauty is derived from this most grace-ful, airy tree, so appropriately styled by Coleridge ' The Lady of the Woods.' In every situation its presence is felt as adding a charm to the scene, whether waving on the brow of the cliff, with its light transparent form seen quivering against the sky, or down on the shore of the broad loch, to which it forms a most harmonious foreground. . . . . The weeping variety is the one that prevails in the mountain districts of Scotland and Wales. It may be remarked that in ascending our loftiest mountains the birch is the last tree that we miss on our upward path, for it continues with us to heights far above the level at which even the Scotch fir disappears." The elegant shrub called the dwarf-birch also grows in boggy places in the Highlands. Strips of birch bark twisted together make the High-lander's torch. His favourite " Rowan-tree " is the mountain-ash, which he deems mighty against the powers of witchcraft and warlocks. The writer whom

* "Our Woodlands, Heaths, and Hedges," by W. S. Coleman; a delightful book.

I have just quoted says: "Between the trim suburban garden and the grim Highland steep there is, doubtless, a vast constitutional difference; so that, in general, an object harmonising with the one would seem to be totally discordant with the other: yet the mountain-ash oversteps the difficulty, and with easy grace accommodates itself to either situation. But ornamental as it is to the villa, we fancy there are few who would not prefer it in its native locality as a wild mountaineer." Of another favourite tree of heather-land, the larch, Major-General Stewart gives some curious particulars.

"The larch is now spreading over the whole kingdom, and has proved a valuable acquisition to the produce of many barren moors in the Highlands, where the climate is found more favourable for this species of pine than in the plains. The wood is of excellent quality. The Atholl frigate, built entirely of Atholl larch, is expected to show that it will prove a good substitute for oak in ship-building. The larch was accidentally brought to Scotland by a gentleman whom I have had occasion to mention more than once. Mr. Menzies, of Culdares, was in London in 1737, and hearing of a beautiful pine shrub recently imported from the Alps, procured four plants: he gave two to the Duke of Atholl, which are now in full vigour at Dunkeld, and may be called the parents of all the larch in the kingdom; he gave a third to

Mr. Campbell, of Monzie, and kept the fourth for himself, which was unfortunately cut down forty years ago. It had then been planted forty-five years, and had grown to seven feet nine inches in circumference. The Duke of Atholl's plants were placed in a green-house at Dunkeld, where they did not thrive, and were thrown out, when they immediately began to grow, and quickly showed the consequence of being placed in a proper climate. The Duke of Atholl sold a thousand larch trees of seventy years' growth for 5000*l*. If they had been planted and grown regularly, they would not have covered more than nine Scotch acres of the light soil on which they thrive best, allowing twenty-two feet square for each tree, more than ample space for the larch." *

Cantire can boast of magnificent beeches. Some we have already noticed in the Glenbarr plantations, and we shall see a fine wood of them on our road to Tarbert, on the eastern side of the loch. Notwithstanding what Gilpin says to the contrary, the beech is one of the most picturesque trees that we have; its smooth, shining, silvery-grey stem (like the under side of a willow leaf) affords a grateful study to the painter, especially when it is dappled o'er with clinging moss and lichens.

* Sketches of the Highlanders, vol. i. Appendix, p. liii.

The true elms of Scotland are —

"Wych-elms that counterchange the floor."

Their branches are more spreading and pendulous than the English elm, which in Worcestershire is indigenous, —and is seen in such profusion that it has obtained the name of "the Worcestershire weed."

There is a family of shrubs in heather-land that are heath-like in their appearance, and grow in tufts among the heather,—

"Mid muirs and mosses many O!"

and on which the grouse and moor-fowl feed. The leading members of this Berry family are named crowberry, cowberry, cloudberry, bearberry, blaeberry, bilberry, and cranberry, whose brilliant fruit-clusters form the choice food of grouse-land, and whose creamy waxen blossoms and fresh green foliage may be seen intermixed with the heather at elevations of 4000 feet above the level of the sea.

I have spoken more than once in general terms of the beauty and luxuriance of the ferns of heather-land. They deserve more particular mention, for in this district there is a good and varied field for the botanist. *Imprimis*, the *Osmunda regalis*, the pride of British ferns, is scattered in frequent patches among the common bracken, more especially in the neighbourhood of Beinn-an-tuirc. There the botanist may profitably go to gather

" Fair ferns and flowers, and chiefly that tall fern,
So stately, of the Queen Osmunda named;
Plant lovelier, in its own retired abode,
On Grasmere's beach, than Naiad by the side
Of Grecian brook, or lady of the Mere,
Sole-sitting by the shores of old romance."

Beside ferns of the *Lastræa* tribe, we shall also find the pretty *Cystopteris dentata* and *fragilis*, the *Hymenophyllum Wilsoni*, the elegant *Polystichum lonchitis*, the graceful " lady-fern," and the Green and Black Maiden-hair, which last-named fern the old Highland dames sometimes boil down into a tea, and warrant it a good remedy for coughs and colds.

When we get down to the sea-shore we shall see the plants that are peculiar to that locality; but up here in heather-land we find several species that will repay the botanist for the search. The bur-marigold (*Bidens tripartita*) grows abundantly on the mossy ground. Some of the larger St. John's wort (*Hypericum Androsæmum*) is found among the wooded cliffs. In the salt marshes there is the water drop-wort (*Ænanthe pimpinelloides*), and in the peat-bogs and tarns on the tops of the moors, the resort of the wild duck and her brood, there is the white water-lily (*Nymphæa alba*) in abundance. And among the quagmires and heathy morasses we shall find patches of the Cana, or " bog-cotton," to whose white feathery down Ossian likens the breasts of the " high-bosomed Strina-Dona:"

" If on the heath she moved, her breast was whiter
than the down of Cana." *   Indeed, the simile is by no
means an uncommon one with a " minstrel of the north
countrie." In Macpherson's " Melodies from the Gaelic,"
for example, the enraptured lover asks —

> " O, what is fairer than the Cana
>   Waving in the breeze,
> When summer laughs in flow'ry pride,
>   And verdure clothes the trees?
>   My Mary's snowy neck and breast,
>   By many a lurking Cupid press'd,
>   Are fairer than the downy Cana
>   Waving in the breeze."

The same idea is elsewhere used ; and in one poem the
complexion of the young lady is compared to the Cana
and mountain-ash berry, which are the rose and lily of
heather-land : —

> " Her cheeks were like the rowan red,
>   Her neck was like the Cana fair."

And in a farewell to the " Braes o' Laggan," the poet
sings : —

> " Fare ye well, ye spreading mosses,
>   Waving with the Cana's plume."

This beautiful plant, which is sometimes also called
Cannach, abounds in the Highland mosses. Its blossom
forms a spherical tuft about the size of a common wal-

* *Cath-loda,* Duan the Second.

nut, of a white downy substance like cotton, which is supported by a slender rushy stem about a foot high.

What bird is that winging its high flight towards yonder hill? Can it be an eagle? "aiblins not." Such destruction has been dealt towards them, that they are now rarely to be met with in these parts.* Yet John Macallum told us that he saw one not many weeks since, but soaring too high for him to get a shot,—a very happy circumstance. But though a rare visitor, the eagle is not yet extinct; and the golden eagle, the common or white-tailed eagle, the rock eagle, and the osprey or sea-eagle, are still to be seen in this part of heather-land. The ornithology of the district † also comprises the merlin ‡, kestrel, sparrow-hawk, gos-hawk, buzzard, hooded crow, carrion crow, raven, Cornish chough, magpie, cuckoo, grey owl, barn owl, brown owl, and many smaller birds, such as blackbirds, thrushes,

* "Not one fowler of fifty thousand has in all his days shot an eagle. That royal race seems nearly extinct in Scotland."—*Recreations of C. North*, vol. i. p. 92.

† The ornithology is given on the authority of the Rev. D. Macdonald, and the Rev. J. Macfarlane. Their complete catalogue comprehends upwards of one hundred various birds that visit the district around Glencreggan.

‡ The merlin will sometimes hover round the sportsman, and "has been known to strike down a wounded grouse considerably larger than himself, within range of gun, and, without compunction or delay, quietly commence tearing up the prey." —*Letters from the Highlands*, by James Conway (1859), p. 55.

linnets, goldfinches, fieldfares, wrens, tomtits, yellow-hammers, reed-sparrows, wheatears, whincats, swallows, sedge-warblers, wagtails, blackcaps, larks, &c. Of birds that may afford sport to the shooter, this district supplies the following :—Black-game and grouse, partridges, woodcocks, snipe, golden plovers *, landrails, curlews, rock and wood pigeons, wild geese, wild swans, solan geese, wild ducks, mallard, teal, widgeon, herons, cormorants, and various kinds of gulls, puffins, auks, guillemots, &c. The pheasant does not seem to do well here, and is only met with in small numbers in places (as at Largie) where great pains have been taken to induce it to breed. The quail is only an occasional visitant ; and the bittern, which old people remember as a common bird, is never, or but very rarely, seen,—owing, probably, to the better drainage and improved agriculture of the district. It is also said that the red grouse have diminished in numbers from the same cause. There are some birds, too, such as the nocturnal goat-sucker, which are plentiful on the eastern coast of Cantire, and are not found on the western.

The lochs and tarns of our heather-land, for the most part, teem with trout in all their variety, but

---

* I "have often heard in this country of an old Scottish act of parliament for encouragement to destroy the green plover, or peewit, which (as said) is therein called the *ungrateful* bird; for that it came to Scotland to breed, and then returned to England with its young to feed the enemy." — *Letters from Scotland* (1754), Letter VII.

there are no char, pike, or perch. The salmon and salmon-trout keep to the rivers. The salmon, as I have before mentioned, are not caught above twenty pounds in weight. Otters often make their way up to these moorland lochs at a time when approaching family cares warn them to seek a sequestered home, and there remain until they are able to take their little family down to the sea-side. Stoats, weasels, polecats, and martins also make their dwelling on these moors, and doubtless cause many anxious moments to the rabbits and hares and the young mothers of the grouse tribe. Thus it will be seen that Christopher North's protest against the solitude of moors is not without foundation.

By this time I have completed my sketch of heather-land, having painted-in those many details that make up the wide landscape. Here are the ferns, the heather, the burnie, the coppicing, the winding line of trees that mark the course of the deep burrowing Barr river, the level road up the valley through Barr glen, the long ranges of hills overtopping and overlapping each other, and Beinn-an-tuirc in the distance. One or two white farm-houses, with slated roofs, are seen in the valley, and by their neat and cared-for appearance show that the present proprietor of the Barr estates is improving the property in the spirit of the age. We also see on the opposite hill-side, some scattered cottages, with their whitewashed walls and dark thatch, from which rise tiny columns of smoke. The black patches near to them are peat-stacks, built with little bricks of peat, as we see in the fens of Lincolnshire and Huntingdonshire. Here and there we see evident morasses and quagmires, where there are moss-hags and tumps of rushes and bog-cotton, and where the verdure is of the greenest. Well-cultivated corn-fields lie down in the valley between the heathery hills, and there is many a little

> "Meadow gem-like chased
> In the brown wild;"

like that seen by Enid and Geraint after his fight with the three bandits—where the softly-rounded sheep, and the tiny shaggy oxen make moving spots of colour and light. And among the red-brown moors of heather-land, there are also many irregular patches of pasture that give diversity to the hues of the hill-sides — plots of green turf that have been so closely nibbled by the sheep, that not a daisy is to be seen upon them, so that they present

> "A look that is sheepish, and what in most ways I call
> An appearance that's certainly most lack-a-daisycal."

A conspicuous feature of heather-land may be remarked in

> "These mossy rocks,
> These lichen'd stones, all purple-tinged with blue;" *

---

* D. M. Moir.

the great boulders that are scattered here and there
over the moors, on whose white and shining sides the
lichens have mapped green and yellow continents as
fanciful in form as Scotland herself. They contribute
famously to those "bits of foreground" that delight
the sketcher's heart; and while they afford us sermons
in stones, also show us maps on boulders.

CHAP. XX.

GROUSE-LAND.

Highland Herd-girl. — Her pastoral Charge. — Not cowed by Bulls. —
Highland Cattle. — Stots and Kyloes. — Rosa Bonheur. — Highland
Raids. — Winter Beef. — A sharp-witted Lad. — Highland Rams. —
Auld Hornie. — Scotch Mulls. — The Collie — His Attainments and
Duties — Some wondrous Anecdotes thereupon. — Shooting. — Game-
Bags. — True Sport *versus* Battue Slaughter.— Gentlemen not Game-
keepers. — The Pleasures of Grouse-shooting. — St. Grouse vin-
dicated. — The Fox-hunting of shooting.

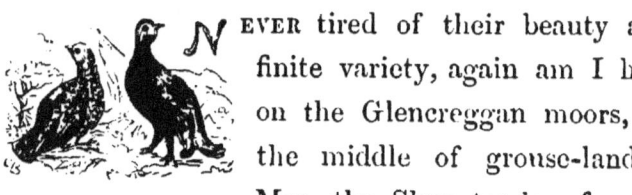 EVER tired of their beauty and in-
finite variety, again am I high up
on the Glencreggan moors, and in
the middle of grouse-land, with
Mac, the Skye terrier, for a com-
panion. The shooters are out again to-day, and I have
my usual gun and bag in the shape of pencil and
sketch-book.

Here is a lassie herding cattle, a very bonny lassie
too, bare-footed, of course, and very short-petticoated,
but *mirabile dictu*, not bare-headed. Like Christopher
North's Girzie, " she is what is delicately called *a*

strapper, rosy-armed as the morning, and not a little of an Aurora about the ancles." Indeed, there is plenty of muscle, as well as colour, about them; they are not at all of the strawberry-and-cream-complexioned school like that Gleaner of Mr. Frith, but have very positive and vivid reds and oranges on their surface, that show they have been exposed to the sun and wind from their earliest years. Her cheeks are much the same, and prove her to be no child of the pale-faces, and (like the majority of the Argyleshire peasants) she looks more of the gipsy, or Spaniard, than a Scot; for her eyes are large, dark, and deeply-fringed, and her hair is of the hue of the raven's wing, as the rhymers say. A loose bonnet of white calico, a looser jacket of pink calico, and a dark petticoat, complete her wardrobe as exhibited to the world. If this maid of tartan-land wore tartan, Burns' lines would correctly describe her petticoat and its longitude :—

> " Down flowed her robe, a tartan sheen,
>   Till half a leg was scrimply seen ;
>   And such a leg ! my bonny Jean
>   Could only peer it ;
>   Sae straught, sae taper, tight and clean,
>   Nane else cam near it." *

But she has only the leg without the tartan. She has her wand of office—a long stick—in her hand, and she

* The Vision.

is lolling about in an extremely natural and *dolce far niente* style, on the soft grass amid the blooming heather. Thus I sketch her, and she does not shrink

HIGHLAND HERD GIRL.

from the ordeal. Jenny Macallum, she tells me, is her name, and she has "nae been drawit afore." But she is nothing loth to be *drawit* now; so with a genuine blush, rising superior even to the sunny colouring of her cheeks, and also with some genuine vanity, she stands up that I may sketch her in a perpendicular, instead of a horizontal, attitude. Certainly, one might have a worse subject for the pencil than this Highland herd-girl, from the crown of her head, or bonnet, down to the bare soles of her feet, so fearless of the hard bent, and rough roots of the heather.

A little conversation is carried on the while, though with some difficulty, not only from mutual bashfulness, but also from mutual inability to understand each other's speech. Jenny tells me she can't read, she has "had nae larning," so she has no chance of whiling away the time by a perusal of the last fashionable novel. She bides up the brae, she says. And what does she do all day? "Just tends the beasties." She does her duty, in short, and let us hope she gets a fair day's wage for a fair day's work. Her pastoral charge is over about thirty oxen, and two or three bulls, great, swarthy, long-haired fellows, with sharp horns and wicked eyes, who, when Mac and I came suddenly upon them, looked so remarkably as if they ought to have been labelled " dangerous," that we considered discretion to be the better part of valour, and beat a hasty retreat to the knoll where Jenny was lying. She was not afraid of them, not a bit! and when one of those big black bulls was evidencing a tendency to roam to

further pasture, the lassie speedily ran after·him (Mac
and I ready to take to our heels if he came our way),
and with voice and action, but above all, with hearty
thwacks of her oaken staff, compelled him to return to
his appointed spot. Hither to some part of the moor,
where there were irregular patches of grazing-ground
amid the heather — she brought her beasts at early
morn; and here, through the long day, she kept them
together, and then at dewy eve took them back to their
farmstead.

Not only on the Glencreggan moors, but elsewhere
in the Highlands, we saw many very small children
thus engaged in tending cattle; but probably there
were no bulls in their droves. The oxen were of the
small Highland breed,— those stots, or kyloes, with
whom Rob Roy was wont to do such a good business,—
mild-eyed little gentlemen, who in their rough, shaggy
coats looked like so many door-mats or carriage-rugs,
and altogether innocent of foray and black-mail. They
were placable enough; and, so that you did not prevent them from eating, you might pull, or poke, or
stroke them as you liked, without the smallest provo-
cation being felt or shown. The innumerable droves
of these small Highland cattle that one sees out on the
moors and hills, are by no means a detraction to the
picturesqueness of the scenery. What with their wild
look and general shagginess, no less than from their

diversity of colour,—for their coats show every possible variety of hue that can be made up of white, black, red, brown, grey, and yellow-ochre,—they are in singular harmony with the moorland landscapes wherein they make so conspicuous a feature. In Tartan-land they are " the cattle upon a thousand hills;" for throughout the Highlands, wherever there is a hill, you may feel sure there will be some scores of Highland cattle.

What companions Rosa Bonheur must have made of them ere she could have represented them with such wonderful fidelity ! Her affection for them, indeed, is well indicated in her portrait, where she leans so con-fidingly on the neck of one of her favourite kyloe models. A few favoured ones were taken back with her to France, as her *compagnons de voyage;* and no doubt she found them very intelligent fellow-travellers, and worthy of her repeated study. Her pictures of them, and her equally faithful delineations of the landscapes in which she first painted them, transport the spectator to the very heart of the Highlands. The magic wand of her brush can raise up all the spells of the scene, and place before our eyes the moors of Scotland with their shaggy verdure and shaggier denizens. In none of her kyloe pictures has she done this with a greater degree of illusion than in the wonderful picture of the " Highland Raid," exhibited during the past summer (1860). The scene is laid late in the year, when the heather is dead

and brown, and the steaming herd of shaggy bulls and
kyloes are coming towards us through the heavy, misty,
rain-charged atmosphere, wet, dirty, mud-splashed, wet-
nosed, and *audibly* bellowing. Wonderfully true and
powerful was this picture, painted with such a free, and
dashing, and masterful hand ; wonderful in every respect,
more especially when the picture was compared with
its Spanish *pendant*, equally truthful and powerful,—
where all is glaringly sunny, broiling hot,—shadows
dark and sharp, road white and dusty, sky intensely
blue. It was quite a relief to turn from Holman Hunt's
more wonderful than pleasing picture to Rosa Bonheur's
misty Scottish moor and dirty bellowing kyloes.*

The Cantire kyloes have, in olden time, played their
part in many a Rosa Bonheur " Raid," in which they
have formed the *creach*, or plunder. It would seem
that beef was considered as great a Christmas necessity
in Cantire as it is in England ; and, when November
came, certain raids were accustomed to be made, which
resulted in a supply of Christmas beef. The foggy
season of the year, additionally severe in Scotland,

* Flat heresy, no doubt, to express such an opinion. But, to my
mind, Hunt's picture will be more acceptable as an engraving, where
its miraculous minutiæ of detail may be studied with greater relief to
the eye, and where plain black and white will somewhat tone down the
elaborately-washed and enamelled countenances and limbs of the figures,
and will take off the gloss of unworn newness from the dresses, all of
which have evidently just left the loom and embroiderer.

enabled the marauders to carry on their carrying-off designs with the more completeness. The kyloes that were driven off and destined to death were termed *Feoi 'lgheamhruidh,* or "winter beef." *

There is a tale told of three men who lived near to each other in a sequestered glen in Cantire, who made a joint-stock partnership in these November forays for winter beef. One of the three died out of the partnership, leaving the two survivors to carry on the trade. When they had gone on their annual November trip, the widow of their late partner was bemoaning her destitute state, and lamenting that she had now no person to supply her with winter beef, when outspake her son, a brave lad of twelve, "Do not weep, mother! I shall soon be grown up, and then you will not want; and it may be that I can supply you this same year with the *feoi 'lgheamhruidh.*" With that he took down his father's gun, loaded it, and went away. He was aware of the errand on which his late father's partners had gone, and he knew the road by which they would return, . so he concealed himself behind a bank and lay in wait for them. The night came on, and at length, by the light of the moon, he saw them drawing near, and driving before them a fine fat cow. He waited till they came underneath him by the bank, and then bang

* There is a Gaelic proverb, "There are long horns on cattle in mist."

went his gun over their heads. Away they ran in a
terrible fright, leaving the cow to shift for herself. As
soon as they had cleared away, the brave lad came from
behind the bank, and led the cow by a roundabout road
to his mother's shieling; and very glad was she, and
very proud was he when he pointed to the cow and
said, "Mother, you shan't starve *this* winter. Here is
your *feoi 'lgheamhruidh!*"

The Cantire marauders were not content with making
raids upon their neighbours; for it is said that they
often went further a-field, and extended their freeboot-
ing expeditions to their brother Celts in some of the
glens in Ireland. These raids were conducted on a
grand scale; the men were strongly armed to repel
resistance, and were attended by the pipers, considered
so indispensable to blowing them on to victory. There
is a Cantire legend that, in one of these Highland raids
on Irish ground, their piper was friendly to the Irish
women, and that he played a tune called *A mhnalhan
nan ghne gu'r millc dhuibheirigh,*—" Ye wives of the
glens, 'tis time ye should rise!" The women were
sharp enough to take the hint, and, by the time the
freebooters had swooped upon them, had driven away
the cattle to a place of safety.*

* Sir W. Scott, in "The Two Drovers" in "The Chronicles of Canon-
gate," has given us a very minute account of the Highland herdsmen,
and their peculiar fitness for the drover's trade. Sir E. Landseer has
depicted them in his "Highland Drovers departing for the South."

What with these Highland kyloes and the immense flocks of horned Highland sheep (which have depopulated many places and driven thousands of emigrants to distant lands), the Scotch cattle are like the Scotch landscapes, remarkable for their picturesqueness. Wordsworth's " Ram " will be called to mind : —

> " Most beautiful,
> On the green turf, with his imperial front
> Shaggy and bold, and wreathed horns superb,
> The breathing creature stood."

" STRANGE THINGS COME UP TO LOOK AT US! "

They certainly look magnificent fellows, and withal have a touch of the terrible in their horned heads and black faces which, when unexpectedly presented over the side of a rock right in the face of a nervous sketcher, may tumble him from his camp stool with a sudden accession

of horrible memories of " Auld Hornie," and the verses of Burns thereupon. Their horns are very large, massive, and twisting, and are greatly used for " Mulls,"— that is, receptacles for snuff. Indeed, the head and horns often form one *mull*, the horns being left for ornament and tipped with silver, while the interior of the skull is fitted up for the rappee, the lid being on the top of the head, and made of silver and cairngorms.*
The spoons and other instruments that pertain to a well-appointed mull depend from the head by a chain, like a lady's *chatelaine*, and the whole affair forms into an expensive ornament that is peculiarly national. The prevailing stock of sheep on the Cantire moors consisted of the black-faced breed (said to be originally imported from Moffat), and, as a large proportion were horned, a goodly number of mulls might be furnished by their " wreathed horns superb." The small breed of the old white-faced Highland sheep, whose flesh was considered so tender and delicate, and whose wool was so superior in quality, is now said to be extinct. Landseer, and other animal painters of Highland scenes,— but more particularly Ansdell,—have made Englishmen familiar with the aspect of these black-faced, horned sheep.

Nor must the claims of the collie-dog for picturesqueness and sagacity be forgotten; although his master was

* See sketch in vol. i. chap. v. for a mull of this description.

by no means that picturesque and theatrical-looking personage that certain artists had led me to anticipate. For example, the accompanying sketch of a "Scotch Shepherd" is taken from an etching by no mean artist (W. H. Pyne), published in a work that professes to give the costumes of the inhabitants of Great Britain.*

THE SCOTCH SHEPHERD OF FANCY.

In the original plate, which is coloured, the gentle shepherd wears a coat of scarlet tartan, and a plaid and philabeg of green. He holds in his hand a mull, shaped like a scorpion, while a liver and white-coloured dog, of

* "The World in Miniature; England, Scotland, and Ireland," by W. H. Pyne. 4 vols., with 84 coloured engravings, Ackermann, 1827.

no particular breed (unless it be that of the thorough-bred mongrel), meditates a sneeze.

But the real Collie, with his long silky coat, bushy tail, and intelligent head, is a far more picturesque quadruped.

The Scotch shepherd's dog is no more like the English sheep-dog than Monmouth is to Macedon, and is as much its superior in value, intelligence, and beauty

THE SCOTCH SHEPHERD OF REALITY.

as a high-born Scottish lassie is to a Hottentot Venus. His attainments and duties have been never better described than by the late Mr. Gisborne; and as his account is remarkably clever and lifelike, and so well delineates what one is constantly seeing from day to day in the Highlands, I think I cannot do better than quote it, instead of treating the reader to "poorer parritch" of my own.*

* The passage occurs in the graphic description of "A Falkirk Tryst," in Mr. Gisborne's four "Essays on Agriculture." He was

"To any inquiry of a Scotch shepherd as to the race of one of his faithful ministers, you would receive the answer, 'Hout! he is jist a collie!' But this designation is far too indiscriminate, for it is applied equally to the malapert animal which, at the sound of your wheels, rushes from every black hut, and, having pursued you for a few score yards with his petulant yaffle, gives his tail a conceited curl and trots back to inform the family that he has driven you off the premises. Far different is the sheep-dog. Whether employed in driving on the road, or herding on the hill, his grave and earnest aspect evinces his full consciousness that important interests are committed to his charge. When on duty he declines civilities, not surlily,—for he is essentially a good-tempered beast,—but he puts them aside as ill-timed. At an early age the frivolity of puppyism departs from him, and he becomes a sedate character. At home he shares his master's porrich; lies on the best place before the fire; suffers with complacency the caresses of the children, who tug his ears and tail, and twist their little fingers into his long coat; and, without inviting familiarity from a stranger, receives him with dignified courtesy. When accustomed

---

remarkably well qualified to write on the subject of Highland and Lowland sheep-farming, and his opinions may be accepted as those of an authority; while he treats his subjects so clearly, and with such power, originality, and humour, that even by a non-agriculturist his "Essays" may be read with the fascination of a romance.

to the road he will, in his master's temporary absence, convey the flock or herd steadily forward, without either overpacing them or suffering any to ramble; and in the bustle of a fair he never becomes unsteady or bewildered. But the hill or moor is his great theatre. There his rare sagacity, his perfect education, and his wonderful accomplishments are most conspicuous. On the large sheep-farms a single shepherd has the charge of from three to six or more thousand sheep, varying according to the nature of the country and climate. In performing his arduous duties, he has in ordinary seasons no assistance except from his dogs. Those shepherds who have studied political economy introduce the principle of division of labour into their kennels. When on the hill they are usually accompanied by two dogs: of these, one is the driving out and the other the bringing in dog. To the first he points out a knot of sheep, and informs him by voice and action, that he wishes them to be taken to a distant hill. The intelligent animal forthwith gathers the sheep together, and acts according to his master's instructions. By similar means he informs the second that a lot of sheep, on a distant hill, are to be brought to the spot on which he then stands; and with equal certainty they are shortly at his feet. To either dog he indicates the individual sheep which he is to catch and hold. The eagerness and impetuosity with which the dog rushes at the neck of his captive would lead you to suppose that the poor animal was in great danger. Nothing of the sort. The dog follows Izaac Walton's precept, and handles him as if he loved him. The hold is only on the wool. The sheep stand in no habitual terror of the dog; though within a few yards of him, the elder will quietly chew the cud, and the younger shake their heads and stamp with their feet, provoking him to frolic or mimic war. We have spoken here simply of the daily occurrences of the sheep-walk—milk for babes—for we fear that the more staggering, but not very ill-authenticated, instances of canine shepherding, with which we might fill our pages, would prove too strong for southern stomachs."

I certainly witnessed some " instances of canine shepherding " that *were* staggering. For example — in one of these flocks of thousands, where the shepherd called his sheep by their own names and knew their individual faces, and where he walked before his flock in a way that most forcibly realised the Scripture scenes of shepherd-life, he would say to his dog, Go into the flock and fetch me out so and so, mentioning many names. Whereupon, the dog would dart into the flock, and single out here one, and there another, until he had got together a certain number of sheep. Of course I had to believe that they were the very sheep designated by the shepherd; but, at any rate, it was curious that the dog should fetch them from various parts of the flock. What the shepherd wished me to believe was, that his dogs knew the names and faces of the sheep as well as he himself did; but he told me that only two of his dogs would do this. Whether or no he was humbugging me (I forget what is the equivalent word in Tartan-land) I must leave the reader to decide.

On another day the same shepherd found that about two hundred of his sheep were missing. He searched for them with his dog till nightfall, without success. I was with him when he came back. He explained to the dog — with similar words and manner that he would have used in addressing a fellow-being — that the sheep *must* be found, and that he (the collie) must manage the business as best he could. With that he dismissed him. The collie answered with an intelligent look and wag of the tail, and bounded away into the darkness. The next day the shepherd renewed his search, but neither sheep nor collie were to be seen. In the afternoon the shepherd had reached a distant moor, and heard every now and then the faint barking of a dog. Guided by the sound, he advanced up a glen that narrowed at its farthest extremity into a small plot of ground, guarded on every side but one by lofty rock-walls. There, at the outlet, was the faithful collie, giving signal barks, but not daring to stir from his post; and there, before him, hemmed-in by their rocky fold, were all the sheep. Not one was missing. This glen was between four and five miles from the spot from whence the flock had wandered.*

This same collie showed his nationality by evincing a particular weakness for milk; and (among many other performances) he had been taught to help himself to his dainty beverage in the following way. First he took (with his teeth) a saucer, or plate, from the table, and placed it on the floor. Then he reared himself with his fore-paws on the table, and, by the aid of his teeth, took the milk-jug by its handle, and carried it down to the saucer; and then, with the milk-jug still held by his teeth, he poured out the milk into the saucer. This was the most difficult part of his performance, as it obliged him to hold his head on one side with extraordinary care, and with an agonised expression that would have gone to Landseer's heart; for if poor collie spilt one drop of milk in the process, he was forbidden his dainty. But he had brought his performance to that degree of perfection that a failure and disappointment of this kind were very rare.

But let us leave collies, and sheep, and cattle, and our Highland herd-girl; and walk on a little further into grouse-land. The Skye terrier, who is our companion, is leaping among the heather, scarcely able to

* A like circumstance is recorded of the Ettrick Shepherd's dog, "Sirrah."

keep his head afloat over its blossoms, and is " putting
up " grouse and black-game, with all the ardour of a
keen sportsman. There they go in a level flight, with
a whir-r-r-r! their glossy blue-black plumage gleaming
like metal in the fierce sunlight, and their crimson
moons flashing vividly as they stretch out their necks
with a hoarse cry. They have reason to thank Mac
for driving them from their lair, or by this time
they might have been food for powder; for here come
the sportsmen.

They are having good sport to-day. Besides dealing
with black-game and grouse, they have paid a visit to a
lonely tarn, lying far away in the hollows of the hills,
on whose black and solemn waters, half-full of reeds
and rushes, the wild-duck and teal do love to congre-
gate, and from whence they fly out in streaming lines
that assume a wedge-like figure. Christopher North
would have made sad havoc with them with his muckle-
mou'd Meg; and there is one at least of the present
party who would do the same. They have also passed
some boggy places, where the woodcock and snipe have
presented to them those long bills which they have endeavoured so promptly to meet.

Altogether they have made good bags, although not
such as would cut a good figure in a newspaper para-
graph, or compete with the wholesale slaughters of
battue shooting. There is plenty of game on these

moors, but there is also plenty of walking and hard work required for their shooting. Therefore the daily average and the grand total at the end of the season, while they satisfy the true sportsman, will not present any very exaggerated display of arithmetical numbers. The bad weather must also be taken as a very serious set-off against the number of birds; for what avails any amount of game if the Scotch rains and Scotch mists shall succeed each other, with the unvarying monotony of the steak-and-mutton-chop and mutton-chop-and-steak dinners of a country inn? We have already seen what the weather is like at Glencreggan: it is often "varra coorse;" and this "coorseness" must be set on the *per contra* side, when the subject of shooting and the prevalence of game in this portion of grouse-land is taken into consideration. By universal consent — indeed, it was a fact sufficiently proved by figures, — our host at Glencreggan was *the* shot of the party; and his best day's sport, in one day, in that season (1859) was eighteen-and-a-half brace. In the season of 1860, however, which was at first a remarkably good one, the figures were higher; and, in the first three hours of the first day's shooting, eighteen brace fell to " the master's " gun *; and in the first nine days, 156 brace, besides hares, snipe, &c. The weather

---

* One of Purdey's guns. The eighteen brace were bagged with forty-one shots.

at that time was all that could be wished ; and though
the season in England had been so remarkably wet,
yet it was agreeably the reverse in Cantire, where the
crops were looking famously.   But October brought a
change ; and high winds and "coorse" weather was
the rule, and a tolerably fine day the exception ; so that
in three weeks there was only two days' shooting on
the Glencreggan moors.   As a matter of course this
considerably diminishes the game-book's grand total for
the season, although its numbers on certain days may
be large.   The " saft days " were the best friends that
the birds had.

But what says Christopher North? — " We do not
admire that shooting-ground which resembles a poultry-
yard.   Grouse and barn-door fowls are constructed on
opposite principles, the former being wild, and the
latter tame creatures, when in their respective perfection.   Of all dull pastimes, the dullest seems to us
sporting in a preserve.   The sign of a lonely way-side
inn in the Highlands ought not to be the Hen and
Chickens.   Some shooters, we know, sick of common
sport, love slaughter.   From sunrise to sunset of the
First Day of the Moors they must bag their hundred
brace.   That can only be done where pouts prevail,
and cheepers keep chiding ; and where you have half-
a-dozen attendants to hand you double-barrels *sans*
intermission, for a round dozen of hours spent in a per-

petual fire. Commend us to a plentiful sprinkling of game, to ground which seems occasionally barren, and which it needs a fine instructed eye to traverse scientifically, and thereof to detect the latent riches. Fear and hope are the deities whom Christopher in his sporting jacket worships, and were they unpropitious, the moors would lose all their witchcraft. "A gentleman," says this authority, "ought neither to shoot like a gamekeeper or a bagman, neither kill or miss every bird; but, true to the spirit of the Aristotelian doctrine, lean with a decided inclination towards the first rather than the second predicament. If we shoot too well one day, we are pretty sure to make amends for it by shooting just as much too ill another; and thus, at the close of the week, we can go to bed with a clear conscience. In short, we shoot like gentlemen, scholars, poets, philosophers as we are; and, looking at us, you have a sight

> ' Of him who walks in glory and in joy,
> Following his dog upon the mountain side.' "

A later writer, speaking of the Caithness moors during the season of 1859, echoes Christopher North's opinion, and says:—" And now the sporting reader will be impatient to know the nature of our bags, for this is the true test of the quality of preserves, whether land or water. Well, our chief, who kept the game-books very accurately, tells me that our sport averaged fifteen brace of grouse per day per gun; but besides grouse, the bags always contained snipe and hares, and occasionally wild ducks and plover. These figures look, it is true, very insignificant by the side of those startling returns which the Scotch papers love to parade of the slaughter perpetrated on certain moors. But I agree with Christopher North in not admiring any shooting ground which resembles a poultry yard, preferring that requiring skill and good dogs to discover the latent riches. Fifteen brace of grouse, as the result of a day's shooting, should satisfy any man; it is right, however, to add, that this number was only obtained by hard work, and that our party shot to so late an hour in the evening, that when we had driven home and changed our clothes, it was generally ten o'clock before we sat down to dinner." * This was not the case at Glencreggan, where the dinner-hour was rarely delayed to a later hour than seven; for, where there are ladies in the case, gentlemen sportsmen must do their best to be punctual. Thus the opportunity was not afforded them, of shooting on their way home at a late hour in the evening, when the birds were settling for the night, even if they had considered it sportsmanlike to do so.

* Weld's "Two Months in the Highlands," p. 83. "If at the end of the day I could produce six or seven brace of grouse, they were hardly earned and duly prized." — *Recollections of a Fox-Hunter*, by "Scrutator" (1861 p. 279.).

There they go! They take their range down the
valley, and give the dogs the wind.   A puff of smoke,
a sharp crack or two from the guns, answered by dull
echoes from the opposite hill, and then I see the beaters
pick up the fallen birds, or take them from the dogs'
mouths.   It is a pretty sight to watch the dogs working, and doing their work so quietly, while they obey
the slightest motion of the hand — for grouse are some
of the shyest of game birds, and talking and noise
must be kept as far away from the well-regulated
grousing-moor as from the scientific whist-table.   And
there are so many other things that tend to the pleasure
of grouse-shooting, beside the delight in watching the
working of the dogs — the novelty of the scene, the
purity of the air, the invigorating exercise, the excitement of the sport, and the calling into play so much
judgment and skill — that one cannot wonder at the
sport obtaining such a hold on British sportsmen, or at
the twelfth of August being looked forward to as a day
that exalts St. Grouse to a far higher estimation in the
human mind than many a less-known saint whose name
is marked in the Romish calendar.

Nor, although Maxwell should pooh-pooh grouse-
shooting as an "operation so common-place, that none
but a cockney would find novelty in its detail," * can I
wonder that one who has often trodden the moors, and

* Wild Sports of the West, Letter XIII.

there done his sportsman's duty, should write thus en-
thusiastically on the subject : — " There is no department of the chase, wherein the gun is used as the instrument of capture, that approaches, much less equals,
it in the quantity of excitement, and of positive enjoyment it affords its followers. The tawny tiger, it is
said, once having tasted human blood, thirsts for it
evermore, and thereafter is dissatisfied with ignobler
prey ; the modern shooter, it is *known*, once having
rejoiced in a perfect day's grousing, from that day forward places it highest among his affections, sets a lesser
value upon all other kinds of fowling, and naturally
seeks occasion for renewing the pleasure as frequently
as he may, in future." Another writer calls grouse-
shooting " the fox-hunting of shooting," from its wildness of scene and game, and its greater excitement over
partridge shooting. It has also been called " the aris-
tocracy of shooting," from the expense attendant upon
its pursuit, so that it has been said that he who engages
in all the cost of moors and their many *etceteras,* will
have to pay a guinea per head for his grouse.

The denizen of Glencreggan grouse-land is red and
fine. The Argyllshire grouse are larger, but not so
dark as those of Perthshire. " The West Highlander,"
says Mr. Colquhoun, " is a beautiful rich red, and very
large," while those that abound in the corn districts of
Lanarkshire, Renfrewshire, and the Lowlands, are " a

very light brown, borrowing a tint from the stubbles on which they delight to feed. . . . . All these birds are so light in colour, as more nearly to resemble partridges." And Mr. Colquhoun adds this interesting observation :—" But, let us take the mountain from top to bottom, and admire the wondrous care of the Divine appointments. The ptarmigan, the colour of its snowy summit in the winter time, and of the grey granite rock in summer; the grouse, lower down, exactly like its own red-brown heather in the autumn; while the partridge, which subsists upon the little patch of corn that skirts the moor, has the yellower shade of the stubble on its wing."

CHAP. XXI.

STILL-LIFE, AND HIGHLAND DAINTIES.

Old Rudd. — Illicit Stills. — Moonlight, Mountain-dew, and Daylight.
— Clishmaclaver. — A Fight with the Gaugers. — The big Judge. —
The Excise. — Suppression of Smuggling. — A Smuggler's Profits. —
Christopher North's Opinion. — The Worm i' the Bud, and the Still.
— Spoiling the Egyptians. — The Sportsman's Return — How to pack
Grouse. — How to heat it, and eat it. — Dinner Dainties. — Haggis
and singed Sheep's Head. — Salmon. — A rare Entertainment. — An
Ogreish Proposition. — Scotch Sweets. — The Sleep of a Grouse-
shooter.

THE shooters are working round to another beat, and
here comes old Rudd with two dogs coupled. He has
to take his station here for a time, and then to shape
his course according to circumstances. His game-bag
is already pretty full, and Atlas-like, he is glad to rest
from his load. He eases the shoulder-straps, and flings
himself down on the short grass beside the heather,
while his dogs tug at their couples with excitement, as
they watch their comrades leaping among the heather
in the valley below us, and *Mac* goes round to the

game-bag and sniffs its contents. Old Rudd's short pipe is soon lighted, and in full operation. When on duty, he forbears this relaxation, out of deference to the gentlemen.

"Well, Rudd! what sport?"

"Eh, well! pretty sport. The master's doing bravely."

"That's a fine covey that the dogs have just flushed."

"Eh, they're just naught but cheepers! the puir bodies o' dowgs ken nae better."

No more did I, it seemed; so I changed the subject. "They tell me, Rudd, that there used to be a whiskey-still or two out on these hills."

"Eh! they tell'd ye that?" and old Rudd turned round upon me with a very shrewd look.

"Stills that never troubled the government. And they tell me that you used to take a great interest in these *moonlight* matters." The term "moonlight," I should observe, was applied to the illicit whiskey, in contradistinction to that which paid duty, which was termed "daylight."

"And they tell'd you that as weel?" said old Rudd, as he puffed away at his short pipe, and watched the shooters down in the valley.

"Yes! and they even went so far as to say, that at one time you could have given me a much better glass

of moonlight than the drop of daylight that this would
purchase." And I handed to him a shilling.

"It'll jest whet me thrapple!" said old Rudd. But
it opened his lips. "There was a still just hereabouts,"
he said, "doon yon glen — bigget in the hill-side, and
covered up wi' turf and heather. Ye might pass close
beside it a hunnerd times, and never clap eyes on it. I
went there one day to see a friend. Me friend kep it,
you understand!"

STILL-LIFE IN THE HIGHLANDS. — "STILL I LOVE THEE!"

"Perfectly! and you, very naturally, took an interest
in your friend's property."

Old Rudd made the nearest approach to a wink that
politeness would permit. "Varra weel! so I went.
But me friend was not there, you understand; he'd gone
out, maybe."

"Gone to market, probably."

"Aiblins he had. So it was my thought to help him
on wi' his work a bit, and to work I went, and I was
getting on beautiful, when they came upon me."

" Who were they? the excise gentlemen ? "

" They were two chaps as ought to have known better," replied old Rudd, whose Celtic peculiarities of language I am quite unable to reproduce on paper, and whose speech the reader must suppose to be flavoured with those words like " thocht, nicht, droukit, inkle, chiel, cantie, drumlie, mou', tocher, carles, and kimmers," over which we stumble and stagger in a perusal of Burns. " I'd just step'd outside the still, and there they were. I ken'd them weel, and what they wanted. ' But,' said I, 'have ye come for a little clishmaclaver?'" (which Mr. Rudd explained to mean idle talk). "'No,' says they; 'we've not come for clishmaclaver, but for work, and we've caught you nicely. We thought that old cow had smelt something in the wind.' It was the grain ye see," said Mr. Rudd, parenthetically, "that the auld beast had smelt when it was distilling, and it had draw'd her to the spot, and the gaugers followed her. 'Well,' says the one, 'we must trouble you to walk wi' us.' 'Not if I knows it,' said I, and I hit him under the lug, and knocked him down. Then the other chap ran at me, and I knocked *him* down. Then the first chap picked himself up, and I knocked him down again ; and the other chap picked *him*self up, and I knocked *him* down. Then they both picked themselves up, and I knocked them both down."

"Why, you must have been born for an auctioneer, with such a talent for knocking down."

Old Rudd grinned grimly. "And I should ha' got clean away, only the cowards had called out murder, and used all manner o' sich dreadful language, and two other chaps had come up to help 'em."

"And then, I suppose, *you* were knocked down?"

"Well, something like it. Anyways, they fell on me and mauled me, and took me off; and, what was worst of all, broke the beautiful still all to pieces, and wasted the wash all among the heather in the most sinful way. And then I went afore a big judge, and the big judge gave me twelve months."

At this interesting stage of the narrative a whistle, and a movement among the shooters down in the valley, gave the policeman-like signal to Mr. Rudd that he must "move on there!" So he put out his pipe, tightened the shoulder-straps of his game-basket, and gathered himself on his legs. "I should just like," he said, "to catch the big judge out on these moors! I'd— here *Don, Lady,* come along wi' ye!" and away he went with the impatient dogs, who were with difficulty restrained by the coupling-leathers.

So let this be a warning to that judicial authority before whom Mr. Rudd may have been forced to appear (owing to the ties of friendship and circumstances over which he had no control), supposing him to be as keen

a sportsman as Lord Chief Justice Campbell, — not to
venture for a day's grouse-shooting on the Glencreggan
moors with Mr. Rudd for a beater.   It is evident that
when Burns penned the line,

" Freedom and whiskey gaug thegither,"

he had not Mr. Rudd and his " twelvemonth " in his
eye.

The original of this picture of " Still Life " was
painted not very many years ago ; and, even up to this
present day, a few illicit stills are said to be in existence
in the Cantire Highlands.   But such cases (even if they
now exist) are supposed to be exceedingly rare ; and
smuggling of all kinds has been almost suppressed by
the vigilant exertions of excise officers, aided in the
discharge of their duty by the crews of revenue cutters.
At one time smuggling was a chief employment of the
fishermen and crofters, more especially during the
winter ; and many daring encounters are recorded to
have taken place between the government officers and
the Cantire Highlanders.   Of the latter, the most desperate were the Skipness men, on the eastern coast of
Cantire, with whom it was no uncommon exploit to
overpower a whole crew of cuttersmen, then to carry
off their oars and tackle, and coolly to set them adrift
in their own boats.

Since the year 1821, emigration has done much to

thin the population of Cantire; and this, together with
the more active exertions of the government for the
suppression of illicit distillation, put an end to many
private stills, as well as to much smuggling. The
progress of education, the influence of resident gentry,
and the greater facilities for procuring articles of consumption, are also causes which have assisted in this
work. The cottar who can grow his little plot of barley
or bear can turn it to better account by taking it to
Campbelton, and disposing of it in an honest way, than
if he risked it in the manufacture of illicit whiskey.
The palmy days of smuggling in Cantire are over, and
now-a-days it could scarcely pay a man to be dishonest
in this particular ; and thus the powerful argument of
£ s. d. is brought to bear upon the question in a way
which results in good.

But prior to the year 1821 the smuggling trade was
very lucrative, and a majority of cottagers and day-
labourers in Cantire (so says a very trustworthy authority), supported large families by the profits of
smuggled whiskey. In those palmy days a professed
smuggler could clear his ten shillings a week after all
his expenses were paid, and this sum enabled him to
keep a horse and a cow. A wife was an indispensable
portion of his stock in trade, and early marriages were
very frequent. Their trade demoralised them in many
ways, notwithstanding that Christopher North writes so

eloquently in defence of smuggling and of illicit stills, and represents the maligned Highland smuggler as a sober and sedate character, and says that, "without whiskey, the Highlands of Scotland would be uninhabitable." * So old Rudd would doubtless say : and it is highly probable that the greater portion of the inhabitants would say the same. We have seen, however, in the case of the head-keeper at Glencreggan, that a man may inhabit the Highlands of Scotland, and flourish therein on nothing stronger than spring-water; but " aiblins " he was the exception to prove the rule. Yet, according to Christopher North, the pursuits of a Highland smuggler must be reckoned among those ingenious arts which soften men's manners, and do not permit them to be brutal; but what line of argument could be expected from one who can say: " An evil day would it indeed be for Scotland, that should witness the extinguishment of all her free and unlicensed mountainstills ; " and, "There is no disgrace in getting drunk —in the Highlands." The same writer also says that, to the Highlander, whiskey is a cordial and a medicine. It was indeed so ; for, till very recently, whiskey in Cantire was considered a sovereign remedy for every disease.

---

* " Smugglers are seldom drunkards; neither are they men of boisterous manners and savage dispositions. In general they are grave, sedate, peaceable characters, not unlike elders of the kirk." — *Recreations*, vol. ii. p. 141.

In those days there was no more destructive " worm i' the bud " of Scotland's national health than the worm of the illicit whiskey-still. The maker of home-made whiskey had it always at hand, and had not to expend his " siller " in a drinking bout; the consequent temptation to perpetual tippling—or " cocking one's finger," as they epigrammatically term it — was enormous, and the morals of the Highlander were far from being whiskey-proof against his temptations.* Many a man, even of " strict principles," like Andrew Fairservice, could, like him, reconcile himself to cheating the revenue, as being " a mere spoiling o' the Egyptians," and could echo old Andrew's words : " Puir auld Scotland suffers enough by thae blackguard loons o' excisemen and gaugers, that hae come down on her like locusts since the sad and sorrowfu' Union; it's the part o' a kind son to bring her a soup o' something that will keep up her auld heart, and that will they, nill they, the ill-fa'ard thieves."

It will be somewhere about six o'clock in the after-

---

* George IV., when at Edinburgh, countenanced the illicit distillation by drinking "mountain-dew" in preference to "parliament whiskey." Miss Sinclair says: "One very small still was discovered in the Highlands last year, with the boiler buried beneath a stone gate-post, which had been hollowed out for the chimney; and another was detected within the precincts of a Roman Catholic chapel, where the priest connived at the trick, and sold whiskey under the name of ' holy water,' to a gentleman who mentioned the circumstance." — *Scotland and the Scotch.*

noon before the shooters will be back at Glencreggan,
and what a "bag" there is for the larder! Perhaps
thirty head of game, on an average, to each gun; and
this, not from tame battue shooting, but from down-
right hard and honest sport. There is game enough to
stock a poulterer's shop at Christmas time. The keeper
ranges them in files,—here a row of black-game, there
a row of grouse; here a batch of hares, there a few
ducks, it may be with a stray woodcock, and a few
"inconsidered trifles" as makeweights. When sufficient has been kept for the requirements of the house,
the remainder will be sent away as gifts. (N. B. no
vending of game at Glencreggan!) The greater part will
find its way to distant English counties, where, thanks
to steam-packets and railroads, it will be enabled to
make its appearance at dinner in a state in which it
will be impossible for it to walk off the table,—an
apocryphal feat which is often reported of "high"
grouse, eaten in southern English counties in the old
coaching days. Their good condition on delivery,
however, is greatly owing to the admirable manner
in which they are packed when they leave Glencreggan.
The boxes are made by Duncan McMillan at Barr, of
various sizes, to hold from three brace upwards. Each
bird is wiped dry and profusely peppered, — especially
under the wings and legs, — and then (sometimes)
wrapped up in paper. They are then laid in the box,

head to tail, in a row one deep, and the lid is nailed
down, and the box despatched to its destination. No
straw or heather is placed in the box, according to the
custom of some packers; indeed, heather from its heating properties is about the very worst thing in which
grouse could be packed.

How beautiful they look as they lie there in the
larder, in all their rich plumage, from the red-brown
of the grouse, to the metallic lustre of the black-game!
And, how very sentimental may a non-shooter grow
over them,

"Murder'd to make a *sportsman's* holiday,"

forcibly taken from their wives and little ones, and their
happy homes amid the purple heather, away away on
the mountain's brow! But, there's

" The tocsin of the soul, the dinner bell!"

It is time to dress for dinner, by which time all our
poetical hallucinations will have cleared away, and we
shall find ourselves doing ample justice to grouse soup,
and, afterwards, to grouse itself. Grouse! surely we
were never tired of eating it. Hot grouse, cold grouse,
grouse pie, grouse soup, come under whatever form it
may, still grouse was most acceptable; and, partly
from the hunger-producing effect of the mountain air
and the Atlantic breeze, and chiefly from its freshness
and absence of "high" mite-iness, grouse at Glen-

creggan was altogether a different thing to grouse in Worcestershire. We eat it at breakfast, we eat it at luncheon, and we eat it at dinner; and we were never tired of it.

Not that we were limited to grouse as an article of consumption; for the larder was always in a plentifully varied state, and the Glencreggan dinners were things to be remembered — pleasant at the time, and pleasant to look back upon — *dapes inemptas*. There is a Highland proverb which says, " Make a good breakfast, for you know not where you may dine ; " and at Glencreggan we secured the breakfast, although tolerably certain of the locality of our dinner-table, and its profusion of good fare. Besides the English cook, a genuine Scotch cook had been added to the establishment; so we were favoured with several national dishes, of which we might otherwise have been deprived. To a southron's eye, some of the Scotch dishes make a peculiar figure on the dinner-table. Haggis to wit; of which Christopher North has said that, if such a thing were to be found in a glen, no untravelled Highlander would be able to swear, conscientiously, whether it belonged to the vegetable-kingdom, or was a pair of bellows, or a newly-imported bagpipe !

Then, there was a Scotch hotch-potch, and Scotch barley-broth, and singed sheep's head, of which a

recent genial Scotch essayist has said, " The sheep's
head of northern cookery has not, at the first glance,
an attractive aspect; nor is the nutriment it affords
very symmetrically arranged; but still, as Dr. John
Brown has beautifully remarked, it supplies a great
deal of *fine confused feeding.*" * Of this dish, too,
Miss Sinclair tells us, that one English traveller thought
its preparation was confined to the singeing of the
hair, and declared his intention ever afterwards to
throw some burned wool into the soup to give it that
peculiar zest which he so greatly admired. Another
English traveller, a lady, and a woman of observation,
when she saw a singed sheep's head brought to table,
remarked, that she had noticed that the faces of the
sheep, when off the table, were also black. " Yes," it
was replied to her, " there is such a demand for sheep's
heads in Scotland, that the farmers are obliged to keep
them ready singed." " What made ye sae late?" said
Mr. Jarvie to Frank Osbaldistone. " Mattie has been
twice at the door wi' the dinner, and weel for you it
was a tup's head, for that canna suffer by delay. A
sheep's head ower muckle boiled is rank poison, as my
worthy father used to say; he likit the lug o' ane weel,
honest man!"

Of course our table was well supplied with salmon,
salmon-trout, and trout. Old inhabitants of Shrop-
shire and Worcestershire can still remember the days

* Recreations of a Country Parson, second series, p. 72.

when Severn salmon were so cheap and plentiful that,
one of the clauses in the indentures of an apprentice
bound his master not to give him salmon more than
three days in the week! Something like this appears
to have been the case in the Highlands a century ago;
for the author of the " Letters from Scotland" says,
" The meanest servants, who are not on board wages,
will not make a meal upon salmon, if they can get
anything else to eat. I have been told it here, as a
very good jest, that a Highland gentleman who went to
London by sea, soon after his landing passed by a
tavern, where the larder appeared to the street, and
operated so strongly upon his appetite that he went
in; that there were, among other things, a rump of
beef and some salmon. Of the beef, he ordered a steak
for himself; but, says he, ' Let Duncan have some
salmon.' To be short, the cook who attended him
humoured the jest; and the master's eating was eight-
pence, and Duncan's came to almost as many shillings."
Elsewhere, the same writer tells us of a horrible mode of
cooking salmon at Inverness, on great occasions, when
the judges are entertained on circuit, and the freedom
of the corporation presented. " The entertainment is
salmon, taken out of the cruives * just by, and imme-

---

* These were the wears. The rails of the cruives had to be made of
a certain width, to permit fish of a certain size to pass up the rivers.
See Pennant's "First Tour," p. 117.

diately boiled and set upon a bank of turf, the seats
the same, not unlike one of our country cock-pits; and,
during the time of eating, the heart of the fish lies
upon a plate in view, and keeps in a panting motion
all the time, which to strangers is a great rarity." For
the credit of humanity, it is to be be hoped that it *was*
a rarity, and that such a sight could be witnessed at no
other place.

The price of salmon in towns, this author tells us,
had been one penny per pound; but by a regu-
lation of the magistrates, had been raised to twopence, which was "thought by many to be an exor-
bitant price." A fowl cost twopence or twopence
halfpenny, and was dear at the price; for the hens
were so miserably thin that you might have cut up
one with the breast bone of another. When they
had any oats given them, the individual oats were
counted out to them. A hungry stranger at an inn
was one day set down to one of these starved chickens,
and expressed his dislike to it, whereupon the landlord
placed before him a piece of fine salmon, saying, "If
you do not like the fowl, what do you think of this?"
"Think!" replied the guest; "why I think it is very
fine salmon; and no wonder, for that is of God Almighty's feeding; but I suppose if you had the feeding of it, it would have been as thin as this fowl."

The Scottish pronunciation plays sad pranks with

our English tongue; for it converts a duck into "a duke," a fowl into " a fool," and a moor-fowl (or grouse) into " a mere fool;" which will account for the old English gentleman's horror, in the accompanying sketch, at the Scotch waiter's ogreish proposition. This, however, is merely an imaginary sketch; but history presents us with a genuine example, which could scarcely

English Tourist in the Highlands. " Waiter! what can I have for dinner?"

Highland Waiter. " Weel, what wad ye wish? we can cook ye a fool, or a duke, or a mere fool!"

be improved by any flight of fancy. A Scotchman was giving evidence at the bar of the House of Lords in the affair of Captain Porteous, and telling of the variety of shots that were fired on that unhappy occasion, was asked by the Duke of Newcastle, what kind of shot it was. " Siccan as they shoot fools wi'," was the reply. " What kind of fools?" asked the Duke. " Why, dukes, an sic kin' o' fools!" was the answer. Of course the man referred to " fowls " and " ducks."

Of Highland peculiarities, among the sweets that made their appearance at the Glencreggan dinners may be mentioned the Scotch pancakes, and the very excellent light pudding known as " Panferry," the receipt for which Miss Acton would do well to procure.

One cannot wonder at a grouse shooter thoroughly enjoying a good dinner, or a sound night's rest, and sleeping that sleep, which

> " Could snore upon a flint,
> While drowsy sloth finds a down-pillow hard."

And we had an amusing example of this, which, for the time, made a sensation. Among the company staying in the house was a lady with her "grown up" son and daughter. The son had to return to England before his mother and sister, and was to be aroused at six o'clock on a certain morning in order that he might drive to Campbelton, to meet the Greenock steamer. After a farewell day on the moors, during which he had done great execution on the grouse, and had satisfactorily proved that the motto of "Floreat Etona" had lost none of its power by the bracing air of Glencreggan, he had retired to rest, with orders to be called at six. At that hour the faithful butler knocked at his door, and knocked, and knocked again. No response from Etona. Louder did the butler knock and shake the door; not a sound was to be heard, not even a snore. The door was locked on the inside, and so also was the outer door of the dressing room, which opened upon the lobby; the windows afforded no facilities for escape, and it was clear that Etona must be in his bedroom still — yes! *very* still. The butler began to get alarmed. He did not like to rouse the house; but the time was getting on, and the occupant of the room ought to be getting up; and yet there was not the faintest sound to be heard within, either of motion or of *life*. Dreadful thoughts filled the butler's brain, and, inspired by them, he hammered at the door, and shook, and rattled it, with a total disregard whether it alarmed the household or no. Which of course it did. Presently appeared the mother and sister, full of alarm, as may be imagined; then the master of the house, also full of alarm. All knocked at the door, individually and collectively; and then listened breathlessly for the slightest sound or murmur from within. Not a word came to cheer them; even a sigh or a groan would have been a relief; while a snore would have been esteemed as the lifting off of a weight of anxiety. After an anxious and very serious consultation, it was determined that force must be applied. A poker was procured, and vigorously handled by the head of the house. With a crash the door was burst in, and the anxious group peered into the room.

And what did they see? Etona turning round in his bed, just aroused from sleep, and, as his eyes encountered the unlooked-for apparitions, drowsily inquiring, " Hallo! what's the row? is it six o'clock? "

And the simple explanation of this scene (which sounds like fiction, but which, nevertheless, is pure fact) was, that he had been kept awake the first part of the night by a window that *would* rattle (it faced the Atlantic, where a storm was brewing); and, to the rattle of the window, the roaring of the Nor'-wester, and the ceaseless dash of the Atlantic breakers, had at length sunk to rest, and had slept the sleep of the grouse-shooter.

CHAP. XXII.

CANTIRE BUCOLICS PAST AND PRESENT.

A Farm-house. — English Associations connected with the Word. —The Highland Farm-house. — Tastes differ. — Highland prejudice against Pork. — Fingal and Ossian ate Pork. — Three pleasing Features in Cantire. — Rents and Soums. — A Time of Scarcity. — Blood-cakes. — Servants' Wages. — Farm Leases. — Rotation of Crops. — Enclosures. — Soil. — Sea-wrack for Manure. — Sheep-farming. — Agricultural Implements. — The Caschrom. — Harrowing at the Horse's Tail — Creels. — A strong Man. — The Braidh. — The Quern. — Present State of Agriculture in Cantire. — Condition of the Farmer and Labourer.

LEAVING the mansion and the moors, let us now pay a visit to the farm-houses and cottages in the near neighbourhood of Glencreggan, and look a little into the past and present condition of agriculture in Cantire, in which we shall be able to find other matters of interest besides dry statistics and blue-book records.

At the mention of the word farm-house, the English reader places before his " mind's eye " a pleasing picture of a two or three-storied house, more or less gabled and half timbered, old fashioned and picturesque, irregular and roomy — with a front-yard, and a back-yard, and a straw-yard, and a fold-yard, and a stack-yard, and ever so many yards — and a garden and orchard, and big barns and granaries, and rows of cow-houses and stables, and hovels, and sheds enclosing a square, paved two or three feet deep with golden straw, where the half-smothered cattle are feeding out of picturesque little pent-houses; and a confused medley of crowing cocks, cackling hens, cooing pigeons, gobbling turkeys, and grunting pigs; and a pond with ducks and geese; and rows of majestic stacks, like giant bee-hives, or little parish churches minus tower or steeple; and an old cart-shed, overshadowed by a great walnut-tree; and a big sheep-dog mounting guard on a horse-block; and, perhaps, a noble screen of elms to shelter the farmstead from east winds; and indoors the large paved or quarried kitchen, with its fireplace, that might almost roast an ox, and its oak tables and benches, and highly-polished chairs, and the dresser, and the rows of shining plates and mugs, and the eight-day clock, and the corner cupboard, and the strings of onions, and the home-cured hams and flitches, hanging like banners, and far more useful, even if not quite so ornamental; and the best parlour, and the dairy, and, in short, all the other places so comfortable and cleanly; all this mingled mass of pleasing items form themselves into

the picture that appears before the "mind's eye" of
an Englishman, at the word farm-house.

Now if the English reader will have the goodness to
dismiss this picture from his gaze, he will be able to
study the counter-part picture of a Highland farm-
house with a less prejudiced mind. To an Englishman
a farm-house is usually the centre of an aureola of
golden joys and solid comforts; and doubtless, so far
as all practical results are concerned, a Highland farm-
house is the same. Yet, if fulfilling the same ends,
with how different an outside show does it accomplish
its purpose! I visited more than one farm-house in
Cantire, and though I could not speak too highly of the
friendliness and hospitality of the people, yet their
homes, and ways, and manner of life were certainly as
far removed from our English notions of the farmer's
home, as is a palace from a cottage. Many of the
farm-houses on the Glen-barr, Largie, and other estates, where the proprietors are resident, and attend to
the comforts and wants of their tenants, have been
either rebuilt, or put into proper condition; but a large
proportion of farms in Cantire still remain in a very
sad plight, either from want of capital on the part of
the landlord, or from the poverty of the over-weighted
tenant, and may be seen in much the same state that
they must have presented a century ago.

Writing twenty years since, the Rev. D. Macdonald,

the then minister of the parish in which Glencreggan is situate, says, "The farmers, with a few exceptions, enjoy, in a reasonable degree, the comforts and advantages of society." I confess that I do not understand this sentence. Its meaning and force would depend upon what is meant by the word *society.* "They are, upon the whole, comfortably lodged, and well fed with wholesome and substantial food." Here again, all depends upon what is meant by *wholesome and substantial food.* As old Lady Perth said to the Frenchman, "Tastes differ, Sir; some folks like parritch, and some like puddocks"—*i.e.* frogs. And the Skye boy who was pitied by the English visitor for having nothing to eat but porridge, indignantly exclaimed, in defence of his accustomed food, "Would you have me quarrel with my *meat?*" And not so very long since, at a public meeting in Edinburgh, where the subject of discussion was the sameness and poverty of workhouse fare, it was shown that it was better and more varied than the daily food of the majority of the Scotch peasants. From which we come to Lady Perth's conclusion, that tastes differ; and that an English farmer would turn up his nose at the fare that would be considered wholesome and substantial by the Highland farmer. There is no doubt but what the latter class (in Cantire) are a very hard-working class of men, and that, in many instances, they live very poorly. On very sufficient authority I can say, that butcher's meat, or *flesh,* as it is termed, is very rarely seen at their tables, and that their food mainly consists of porridge made of oatmeal, potatoes and fish,—the " fish," however, being smoked herrings. Bacon is comparatively unknown; for although many of the farmers rear pigs, yet they are fattened for sale. Where pigs are reared, they are not allowed to go at large; they are invisible to all but the farmer's eye. The consequence was that, during the time I was in Cantire, I only saw one pig throughout the whole district; so that one might at first imagine that Cantire had been a colony of Jews * instead of Presbyterians and Protestants.

But although pigs (if searched for) are to be met with, though not commonly seen in Cantire, yet there, as elsewhere in the Highlands, exists a popular prejudice among the lower orders against pork, or swine's flesh. Sir Walter Scott refers to this in his notes to " Waverley," and says, " King Jamie carried this prejudice to England, and is known to have abhorred pork almost as much as he did tobacco. Ben Jonson

---

* Captain Moore, R. N., jocularly asked Dr. Wolff why there were so few Jews in Scotland? Wolff replied, " The Scotchmen are called Caledonians, which proves their Chaldean descent." " And this Dr. Wolff believes seriously; and the Chaldeans themselves say that three Jews are needed to cheat one Chaldean, which may be the reason why so few Jews are in Scotland." — *Dr. Wolff's Travels and Adventures,* vol. ii.

has recorded this peculiarity, where the gipsy in a masque, examining the king's hand, says,

'You should by this line
Love a horse, and a hound, but no part of a swine.' *

James's own proposed banquet for the Devil was a loin of pork, and a poll of ling, with a pipe of tobacco for digestion." † Lord Teignmouth mentions as a proof of the distinctness of race of the Orcadians, that they entertain no prejudice against swine, as the Western Highlanders and Hebrideans do. ‡ The author of the "Letters from Scotland" says, "I own I never saw any swine among the mountains, and there is good reason for it; those people have no offal wherewith to feed them; and were they to give them other food, one single sow would devour all the provisions of a family." He also mentions a case where the chief of a clan declined pork at a public dinner, and his followers did the same; but a few days afterwards, when the chief dined with him in private and was under no restraint, he ate it with a good appetite. Macculloch thus pleasantly and learnedly treats the subject:—"They may fancy

* The Gipsies Metamorphosed.
† Waverley, vol. i. p. 219.
‡ Vol. i. p. 276. Dr. Somerville, in his recently published "Life and Times," speaking of Scotch customs during the latter half of the past century, says, "Though pork was sometimes presented at table, few ate of it when fresh, and even when cured it was not generally acceptable." (p. 335.)

they dislike pork, if they please; but if they do, it is certain that Ossian was not a Highlander, and they must then renounce all claims to a descent from Fingal. Indeed, I think this argument against the Highland origin of Ossian's poems quite insurmountable; and if they really mean to prove their lineage and claims, I recommend them to take to pig meat as fast as possible. There can be no question that Fingal had a seat in Valhalla, with his father Trathal, and his grandfather Trenmor, and his son Ossian, and his grandsons Ullin, Carril, and Rhyno, voices of the days of old. It is equally certain that they breakfasted, dined, and supped upon the boar Scrymner, and that the goddess, Gna, was the housekeeper. To be sure it would be against the liberty of the subject to cram the modern Fingalians with this diet by force, as you do a sausage, particularly as Dr. Kitchiner considers forced meat unwholesome; but I think when once they have heard my theory, and Vallancey's, of their real origin from the Jews, a descent quite clear, they will hasten to remove the stigma by taking the pig into their embraces, and the office of a hog in the Highlands will no longer be that of a gentleman and a sinecurist. There must be some oblique and Mosaical parentage of this kind, because the pig (I never speak his name without respect) was highly favoured by the Welsh, and the Britons, and the Gauls, as well as by the Saxons and

Scandinavians — all brethren from whom our friends have so basely degenerated. Honourable must his state have been when he and his family are represented in basso relievo on the ancient British coinage." *

Thus although pigs *do* exist in Cantire, yet they so little obtrude themselves on the public gaze, that a casual visitor might leave the country without seeing a solitary porker; and the tourist in this part of the western Highlands might mention among some of its attractions these three pleasing features,—no turnpikes, no beggars, no pigs. Since the failure of the potatoe crops, it has been out of the power of the Highland labourer to keep his pig, and from the same cause some of the farmers have given up rearing them.

They don't know much in Cantire about the acreage of their farms, and describe them according to their rental. Thus when you ask a Cantire farmer what is the extent of his farm, he will tell you it is a two-hundred pound farm, or whatever its value may be. The rent has frequently to be determined more by the *soums* that the hill-pasture will keep than by the value of the arable land, the average rent of which is somewhat under a pound per acre. The *soum* is the keep of a milk cow, or two heifers, or three stirks, or ten sheep. But from the variable quality of the hill pasture it is

---

* Highlands and Western Isles, vol. iii. p. 339. See also Mr. Campbell's "West Highland Tales," p. 92.

extremely difficult to estimate its value: While some
of it in the glens is luxuriant and of great value, other
portions are not worth more than half a crown per acre.
The rents have been greatly raised during the last sixty
years.* In the time of the war with France farming
became very profitable; and, with the improvement of
agriculture and the drainage of marshy ground, the
soil was made more productive and remunerative.
During the Irish rebellion of 1799, when the Cantire
people lived in daily dread of a descent being made
upon their coast, the scarcity of food and the consequent rise in the price of provisions was very great.
Oatmeal was sold at the rate of five shillings the ten
pounds, Dutch weight; and when the oatmeal was
exhausted at Campbelton, and only barley remained, a
small quantity only was allowed to each family, who,
before they could receive it, had to procure a cer-
tificate from a magistrate stating the number of their
children. At this time the barbarous practice of bleed-
ing cattle in the spring, for the purpose of making
cakes of their coagulated blood, was not uncommon,
and was continued until some twenty years within this

* Sir John Sinclair estimated that the rental of Scotch estates, between the years 1660 and 1750, increased from two to three-fold. By
1770 it had doubled. By 1790 it had doubled again. By 1841 it had
again increased two-and-a-half times. Since the Restoration, therefore,
the land rental of parishes in Scotland has increased two thousand per
cent.!

present century.* The wretched beasts were so reduced
by it in strength, that it became necessary to lift them
up, and "being at the lifting" formed a part of the
farmer's business.

"The wages of farm-servants (says Mr. McIntosh of
Campbelton) were very low till about a hundred years
back, when they began to rise. It was much talked of
when the first servant girl got twelve merks† Scotch of
wages for six months, and able-bodied young men from
twenty-five to thirty shillings. They had other perquisites which increased their wages, such as a pair of
shoes and stockings, with some ground to grow a certain
quantity of flax or potatoes on." The little kail-yard
and the wretched cottage form the usual perquisites of
the Cantire labourers of the present day. They make
themselves very contented with their lot; and in cases
of emergency, when a neighbour has been reduced by
untoward circumstances to a state of privation and
poverty, they have often been known to contribute,
without any solicitation, a sum of money for his relief.
On every Sunday, too, they give their mite to the support of the church, and it is wonderful where they can
find the money to pay for the "drap o' whiskey."

The farms are commonly let on a nineteen years'
lease. Indeed the Duke of Argyle, who is the chief

---

* Lord Teignmouth so testifies. Macaulay refers to this practice.
† The value of a merk is 13s. 4d.

proprietor in Cantire, is prevented, by the provisions of the entail, from granting leases beyond this term. Sometimes, however, farms are let on a twelve or fourteen years' lease, and occasionally are let from year to year without any lease. The Rev. D. Macdonald writes as follows : — " In terms of leases, which are generally for nineteen years, the majority of landlords bind their tenants to follow a regular rotation of white and green crops, to sow grass seeds along with bear, and not to take more than two crops of grain from the same field in succession. But, except by such as are in easy circumstances, the above system is seldom adopted. A great proportion endeavour to study what they conceive to be their own interest and convenience, and are very reluctant to lose two successive crops. The natural consequence is that the succeeding tenant finds his farm so much exhausted and impoverished, that, in spite of all his efforts to improve his lands, his lease has nearly expired before he begins to reap the benefit of his expenditures. At the termination of the lease another tenant steps forward and outbids his offer ; or, should he be permitted to retain possession for an equivalent rent, the great increase discourages him, and holds out no temptation to expend more money upon his improvements. . . . . The heritors would not only improve the general appearance of the parish, but advance their own interest, were they to encourage farmers to enclose their fields, either by remunerating the tenant at the termination of his lease for improvements and expenditures, or by being themselves at the expense of inclosures and sub-divisions, and charging interest for the money expended to accommodate the farmer."

The most prevalent soil is a light loam ; in the immediate vicinity of the sea the soil is of a sharp and sandy nature. Potatoes are very largely cultivated ; and at one time the farmers chiefly depended upon them for the payment of their rent, as the Cantire potatoes were in great demand and had a good repute for seed. Barley or bear is cultivated to a great extent, together with oats, pease, and beans. The corn-stacks are made very much smaller than those which we are accustomed to see in England,—a circumstance attributable to the precariousness in the Scotch weather, and the apprehension of the corn heating if put together wet. The want of inclosures and subdivisions is a great obstacle to a regular rotation of crops, and many of the farmers are in the practice of ploughing more land than they can afford manure to keep in heart, and do not recruit, by pasturing, such fields as have been sown with clover or rye-grass. The sea-wrack, or wraic (*Alga marina*), furnishes an unlimited fund of excellent manure; and those fields in the near neighbourhood of the sea have been from time immemorial, without any cessation, alternately cultivated with bear and potatoes, and, except in seasons of long continued drought, had never failed to yield fair crops. But "by a too frequent application," says Mr. Macdonald, " the wraic acts as a caustic, pulverises and weakens the soil to such a degree as to nourish weeds of diverse sorts, particularly wild mustard — provincially sciloc." I saw them drawing the wraic on to the fields of barley, and spreading it about before they had removed any of the standing sheaves from the ground.

Although much ground has been claimed during the last half century, yet the arable soil bears but a very small proportion to the uncultivated and mountainous regions. The hill pasturage, however, has greatly increased in value and estimation since the introduction of the sheep-farming and cattle-grazing system ; and in some parts of Cantire the farmer has sacrificed everything to the system, and the depopulation of those parts has been the result. Emigration stepped in to the aid of the Cantire Highlander, who, from the want of any reasonable prospect of employment or support in his native land, was compelled to quit those hills and glens to which he was attached by the dearest ties.

The modern improvements in all instruments of agriculture have now found their way into Cantire, and threshing-machines and good ploughs are to be met with. Not long since, their ploughs were exceedingly cumbrous and most laborious to work, requiring

for this purpose, four horses to draw, and three men to
manage them ; one man to drive, another to guide the
plough, and the third to dress the furrows after the
plough.   Still earlier, the universal plough was the
caschrom or hand-plough, which is even now to be met
with here and there.   It is a kind of wooden plough-
share, with a curved handle, the share part being tipped
with iron, and a projecting piece of wood being placed

THE CASCHROM.

for the foot.   It is peculiarly adapted for the western
Highland soils, where the ground is encumbered with
protruding rocks, and where the soil is consequently
dispersed among them in an intricate manner.   Being
constructed to grapple with these difficulties, it is very
different in its character from the " breast-ploughs "
used in the English fens.   The *caschrom* was (and is)
greatly used in Skye, and was noticed by Dr. Johnson
in his Hebridæan journey.   He thus describes it : —
" The soil is then turned up by manual labour, with an

instrument called a crooked spade, of a form and weight which to me appeared very incommodious, and would, perhaps, be soon improved in a country where workmen could be easily found and easily paid. It has a narrow blade of iron fixed to a long and heavy piece of wood, which must have, about a foot and a half above the iron, a knee or flexure with the handle downwards. When the farmer encounters a stone, which is the great impediment of his operations, he drives the blade under it, and bringing the knee or handle to the ground, has in the long handle a very forcible lever." * The author of the " Letters " from Scotland in 1754, also describes the *caschrom*. Macculloch says, that it " is a far more powerful instrument than the spade, yet it is not so effectual in pulverising the soil. As far as is yet known, this primitive plough is confined to the Highlands; no traces of it at least have been found elsewhere, not even in India where the simplest draught-plough, formed merely of a crooked branch, is still in use. We might imagine the *caschrom* to have been the contrivance of man where the use of animals was unknown." †

So much for ploughing. The harrowing was on a par with it. The harrows (called *racans* or "clod-breakers") were heavy frames of wood, with stout

* Dr. Johnson's " Works," vol. viii. p. 301.
† Vol. iii. p. 209.

wooden pins fixed in them ; and, at an earlier period *, were tied to the horse's tail, without any sort of harness whatever, in a like manner to the Irish practice, as described to us by the lively author of " Paddiana ; " † and, when the tail (either by nature, or by that long service which must literally have proved more harrowing to the horse than the ground) had been so docked as to become too short of the purpose, instead of being considered exempt from this peculiar system of education at Harrow, the unfortunate beast's tail was artificially lengthened by twisted sticks.

Wheeled carts were vehicles rarely to be met with. In their place, they used wicker *creels*, which were slung across the horses' backs ; and, in this fashion, they took peat and other necessaries to their homes, and carried manure to their fields.‡ If they had a load which could not be divided, they placed it in the one creel, and counterbalanced it by placing stones in the other. Their potatoes were placed in sacks, and carried home on horseback. The labourers of that day were

* In use in 1754, according to Capt. Burt.

† In the two last chapters of the book, where (and also by Lord George Hill, in his " Facts from Gweedore ") it is adduced in evidence of certain peculiarities in the character of the Celt.

‡ The author of the " Letters from Scotland " says, that near Fort William, where the manure had been brought in this way, he saw the women " on their knees, spreading it with their hands upon the land, and even breaking the balls, that every part of the little spot might have its due proportion."

accustomed to lift heavy weights; and it is told of two Cantire Highlanders who were disputing as to their strength, that the one said to the other, "Put that sack of potatoes on to my back." It weighed four hundred pounds; but the man lifted it on to his back. When the man had got it fairly balanced on his back, he gave three hops on one foot, and then, throwing the sack from his shoulders, challenged his neighbour to do the like. But he declined the offer.

Each farm had a kiln to dry the grain. The form of their kilns was round, with a long oven on the outside, in which they had a peat fire, and rafters of wood over the kiln pot, covered with hair-cloth. These kilns often took fire. If they were at any time very short of meal, they would take in a sheaf of corn from the field or barn, separate the grain from the straw, and grind it with the *braidh* in a short time. The *braidh* was a round stone with a hole through the centre, in which was fixed a handle. The grain was placed upon a flat stone, and the *braidh* was turned round upon it, so as to crush the grain. It was, in fact, a hand corn-mill; and appears to have been the same as the *quern*, figured in Pennant's "Voyage to the Hebrides," and here copied. He says that it employed two pairs of hands four hours, to grind a single bushel of corn.* I need hardly remind the reader, that this Highland

* Pp. 281—286.

braidh, or *quern,* is precisely similar to the eastern hand-mill for grinding corn referred to in the Scriptures, and still in use in the Holy Land.*

Such was the rude state of agriculture, and agricultural implements, not a hundred years ago in Cantire. That there has been a vast improvement since then, is apparent everywhere; and that agriculture is, in most instances, at this present day, in an

THE QUERN [FROM PENNANT].

advancing state (especially where the landlords countenace and aid their tenants in improvements), I am assured by one who has a long knowledge of the country. But, that very much remains to be done is also painfully and obtrusively apparent; and the cases are neither few nor far between, where the farms and farmers are a century behindhand in improvement, and where the dwellings of master and man are alike opposed to cleanliness, comfort, and even common decency. As compared with even the lowest class of

* See Dr. Clarke's "Travels," vol. iv. p. 167, and his account of the custom still existing at Nazareth. It also exists in Lapland.

English farms and labourer's cottages, the majority of those that I saw in Cantire seemed to me to be miserably inferior in every way. The reader will be better able to judge for himself, by accompanying me to almost any farm-house and cottage in the near neighbourhood of Glencreggan ; but, before doing so, let me quote two authorities on the subject.

Lord Teignmouth says (and his words hold good at the present day), " The farm-houses are generally, throughout Cantire, old and poor habitations, far behind the general improvement visible in this part of the country. The entrance is usually through the byre, which is a continuation of the house in the same line ; the fire is placed on the middle of the floor, contained in a grate, either square or shaped like a bowl, and raised a little above the ground, a custom peculiar to Cantire. They are without lofts, probably as the country furnishes no poles, and are cold, as the thatched roof forms their only covering. There are some few farm-houses in the modern style, indicating the slow growth of improvement." *

Of the cottagers in the parish of Killean (in which Glencreggan is situated) its former minister, the Rev. D. Macdonald (who of course, had abundant opportunity of arriving at facts) thus writes : — " The most numerous class of the community are cottagers or day-

* Vol. ii. p. 388.

labourers, and the fact cannot be concealed that the
privations under which they labour are truly deplor-
able.   Three or four poor families frequently congre-
gate into one farm, live in wretched hovels, rudely
constructed without any mortar, one division of which
is occupied by the family, and the other converted into
a kind of byre, and often no partition in the hut to
separate the human from the brute creation.   They
hold their dwelling-houses from year to year, and the
tenants (who are their landlords) can dispossess them
at pleasure.   A rent of 4*l.* or 5*l.* sterling is exacted
for a house kept in bad repair, a small kail-yard, the
scanty pasture of a cow, and some ground for planting
potatoes in the outskirts of the farm.   Their meagre
diet consists of potatoes, sour milk, and when they can
afford it, a little oat bread and porridge.   Animal food
is a luxury in which they seldom indulge.   Such as can
salt a little fish occasionally use a change of diet.
Their sole dependence for payment of rent is upon the
earnings of their children, whom they hire out as servants through the district.   For the honour of human
nature it should be recorded, that their sons and
daughters would conceive themselves deficient in gratitude and natural affection, did they not reserve a portion of their wages to pay house rent for their parents.
For culinary purposes they sometimes use a species of
wild leek which grows among the rocks of the shore;

the juice of bogbean for rheumatism, and wild thyme for headaches. They also ascribe great virtue to the essence of ground ivy and centaury."

Such is the present state of agriculture, the farmer, and the labourer, in Cantire. Having now got their general condition pretty well before us, let us pay them a visit in their own homes.

CHAP. XXIII.

HIGHLAND FARM-HOUSES.

The Farm-house. — Where ? — Dirty approach. — Highland Milkmaid.
— On the Ground-floor. — An Interior. — Furniture and Tenants. —
Bare Legs. — Macbeth's Witch. — Mrs. Mac. — The Mon, puir Body !
— The Spence. — A Four-poster. — Pound-cake and Sherry. — Can-
tire Hospitality. — No Canny. — Extremes. — Oatmeal Bannocks. —
What are they like? — Milk, a popular Beverage. — Compulsory
Enjoyment. — How happy could I be with neither. — The romantic
Tale of the brave Girl of Barr Glen.

On approaching a farm-house in Cantire, our first
thought will probably be — Where *is* the farm-house ?
Surely, we feel tempted to ask, it cannot be this low
range of building of one story high? these must be
cattle sheds, bullock hovels, and the like, the outlying
buildings of the farm.   The farm-house, doubtless, is
over the hill side, and down in the glen.   But, no;
"yon's the biggin!" we are told; and this long, low
hovel, with its midden * and dirt-heaps, and kennels of

* *Midden.* Sir Thos. Dick Lauder suggests its derivation from
middle-in, "the *midden* being always *in the middle* of all rural premises

foul water, is really the farm-house of Mr. Mac-so-and-so.

"Hens on the midden, ducks in dubbs are seen." *

You must pick your way carefully; for although liquid manure may be a very useful thing in its proper place, yet it is not precisely that odorous compound in which we should prefer to bathe the boots that will afterwards bear us into the presence of ladies. Our approach, therefore, to the house, is distinguished by a succession of little acts of agility, which are more well meant than successful; and which, indeed, we soon find to be altogether acts of supererogation, for we presently pass to deposits of filth through which we must boldly pass with bated breath, though not averted eye. The approach reminds us forcibly of the farmer's dream of heaven; for, there are " such heaps o' muck!"

Here comes Mr. Mac's milkmaid, setting us the example how we ought to walk, by paddling through all the dirty messes with her still dirtier feet. They are naked of course, and are visible to some distance above the ankle; and very unpleasant is the prospect. They look much better in the sketch than they do in reality, as one cannot depict the encrusted dirt of weeks

in Scotland, so that unlucky visitors not unfrequently walk up to *the middle* into *the middle* of it." — *Legendary Tales of the Highlands,* vol. iii. p. 2.

* Allan Ramsay.

(it may be years !), nor if it were possible, would it be
desirable to do so. Mr. Mac's milkmaid is utterly
unlike the pictures that one sees of Highland milk-
maids on painter's canvas, and in the pages of illus-

HIGHLAND MILKMAID, AS SHE APPEARED BEFORE MY MIND'S EYE.

trated "gift-books." She is a gaunt and scraggy
middle-aged woman, "long, and lank, and brown," in
a large mutch cap — very much like Mrs. Gamp's night-
cap — with a blue gown, that shows her bare arms,

a handkerchief folded over her shoulders, and apparently no other article of attire. She does not elegantly poise her milkpail upon her head, but carries it in front of her, in a very unorthodox manner.

HIGHLAND MILKMAID, AS SHE APPEARED BEFORE MY PENCIL.

Here is more than one door in this long shed of bullock-hovels. Which is the one that will lead us into the immediate presence of Mr. or Mrs. Mac? Their neighbour (who is evidently a man for improve-

ment) has lately marked out his front door by painting
it a brilliant scarlet; but here there is no such ru-
brical guide whereby to direct our steps. We appeal to
the dirty milkmaid, and she points to the farthest
doorway. The door is open; we knock, and enter.
Everything is literally on the ground floor; for there
is no quarry, stone, brick, or board to tread upon;
nothing but the bare earth, worn into irregularities of
surface that afford so many channels and little stag-
nant pools for wet and filth. Lord Palmerston once
defined *dirt* to be "a right thing in a wrong place."
There is plenty of it here. Probably this is a passage
common to the byre and to the dwelling room. At
any rate the cow has been here; and yes! here she is,
in the room to the left. We are plunging on in mid
gloom down the earthy passage, and, on arriving at the
end, turn to the right, and find ourselves in the room
that constitutes the working centre of the establishment, and is, *ipso facto*, the farm-house.

A suffocating smoke pervades the room, and makes
your breath to catch, and your eyes to smart. It pro-
ceeds from the peat-turf, heaped on the fire, and
moulded into a red-hot cake. The fire is laid upon a
low brick hearth; over it hangs a gigantic cauldron
which might serve for Macbeth's witches, and in this
cauldron some culinary preparation — which, from the
noise, would proclaim itself of the bubble and squeak

genus — is steaming, and making the great pot-lid to dance a throbbing jig. The smoke, after making a complete tour of the room, finds its way out through a hole in the thatch that does duty for a chimney. Some fowls are strutting about the floor, scratching in the dirt, and scarcely heed our approach; but a collie dog advances, and sniffs at our heels with muttered growls. The side walls of the room are not so high as a grenadier, and the timbers of the pitched roof rest upon them, and are all laid open to view, together with the heather that forms the thatch. A pitched roof it may well be called; for the peat smoke has blackened it, as though it had been really pitched over, and the black timbers shine like japanned work. Two small windows in the low walls face each other, and through their smoked and dirty panes let a scanty light into the room. As a matter of course neither of the windows are made to open. On the third side of the room is the hearth before mentioned; and, on the opposite side, the whole extent of the wall, save a small space for a doorway, is taken up by a rudely-enclosed cupboard, divided into four parts, two above the other two. These four divisions, from the bedding heaped upon them, proclaim themselves to be the sleeping berths of the family; but how Mr. and Mrs. Mac, and their large family, male and female, and their servants are disposed of in these four cribs or box beds, is a delicate

question, which I do not commit the impropriety to
ask. A fowl is perched upon the edge of the one upper
crib, and looks as though she had been laying an egg
upon the pillow; and, for aught I know, there may be
a sitting hen in the dark recesses of the other crib.
Such furniture as there is, is of the homeliest and

rudest; there is the chest or "kist," and the wooden
press, called the ambry; and the only attempt at display
is in the garnishing of the old dresser with platters and
jugs.

As I enter the room, I find it tenanted (in addition
to the fowls and collie) by a bare-legged lassie, stout,

well-favoured, and auburn-haired; and by an old crone, who is squatted on a low stool on the other side of the hearth, and is hard at work at a spinning-wheel. From underneath her dirty white mob-cap her gray hair hangs coarse and dishevelled, and, in appearance, remarkably like the wool on which she is at work. Spinning may be a picturesque occupation, but it is certainly not a cleanly one; and the old lady looks as though she would be mightily improved in appearance by being treated to the old witches' remedy of a float in the horse-pond. As the barelegged damsel does not vouchsafe to introduce the old lady to me, and as I imagine (from her harmony with surrounding things) that she may be the mistress of the establishment, I put that query to the lassie.

" She's just a puir old body!" replies Barelegs ; and, vanishing through the opposite doorway, leaves me to the old lady and the cauldron. She looks me full in the face, and waggles her head at me in a very knowing manner. Looking from her to the witches' cauldron, I should not feel at all surprised if she thrust out her skinny arm and forefinger, and addressed me with " Thrice the brinded cat hath mewed !" in which case I should be prepared with my answer; but she only mutters something in Gaelic, which to me might as well be gibberish.

While I am thinking what a remarkably effective

head the old lady has, and am mentally taking her portrait for that scene of Macbeth and the Weird Sisters which I am intending to paint some day — when I have the time (to say nothing of the qualifications)—a woman comes in through the opposite door, wiping her hands, and apologising for being untidy. There is no apology requisite, however, so far as her personal appearance is concerned; for she is a neat, cleanly, ruddy-faced woman, in a blue petticoat, sufficiently short to reveal her white stockings and shoes — her feet thus giving visible tokens that she was the head of the establishment. As I advance to meet her, there is a rolling among the confused heap of bed-clothes on one of the upper cribs, and the apparition of a human bewhiskered face, with a tangled mass of black hair, rises from underneath a patchwork counterpane, and gazes upon me with a pair of dark, lack-lustre eyes.

"It's the mon, puir body; he's been sick the lang time, and nae looks sae buirdly," says the ruddy-faced woman, in answer to my startled look of inquiry. "The mon" of course is *the* man, *par excellence*, in Mrs. Mac's eyes—Mr. Mac, the head of the household.

But she soon leads me away to an inner room, of which she is visibly proud,—a room reserved for visitors, and high days and holidays, the *spence* or parlour. (I should inform the reader that Mr. and Mrs. Mac are "bettermost people," and that some of the neighbouring farmers had no such room.) The spence is a step higher than the other room; it has a boarded floor, a plastered ceiling, a good sized window (made to open) and a fireplace after the new and improved fashion, with a mantelpiece, on which are china ornaments of Uncle Tom and Eva, Prince Albert (a very startling bust), and a dog of doubtful species, — together with a shepherdess in a dress of sea shells, and a small basket made of card and ribbon. Over the mantelpiece is a looking-glass. There is a shining mahogany table, *ditto* chairs, *ditto* chest of drawers, on the top of which is a writing-desk, a large Bible, "Calvin's Institutes," "The Whole Duty of Man," "Boston's Fourfold State," "Alleine's Alarm to Sinners, and Saint's Pocket Book," "Baxter's Saint's Rest," "Pike's Early Piety," "Jenks' Family Prayers," and "Moore's Almanack." But by far the chief object in the room is an enormous four-post bed, reaching to the ceiling (not that it required to be very lofty to do that), and occupying the lion's share of the apartment. It is covered with snowy linen, and a smart patchwork counterpane, and looks as though it had never been slept in, and was not intended to be occupied—as, indeed, I found that it was not, except by extraordinary visitors on extraordinary occasions. As I look at the four-poster it becomes a matter of curious speculation to me whether this rival of the great bed of Ware is ever made use of at a family festival, by the

guests sleeping in it gipsy fashion, top and bottom,
stacked like bottles of wine, or game in a grouse-box.
There is ample room for this; and a bolster at the foot
of the bed lends force to the supposition. In the day-
time, doubtless, when they are keeping high jinks, they
use the bed as a great ottoman.

No one can be prouder of her *spence*, or more hospitable in it than Mrs. Mac. She flits about like a
busy bee,—she brushes imaginary dust from a chair, so
highly polished that I might shave myself before it, —
she rushes out of the room with a shrill "Jeannie, lassie!
be handy, noo!" sounded like a note of interrogation, as
are all Highland comments and commands,—she comes
back again, closely followed up by Barelegs carrying a
tray covered with a snowy cloth—(wherever can all these
clean things come from out of this dirty house?)—and
then, from a side cupboard in the *spence*, she produces
one of the richest of Scotch cakes (the plainest of which
are a trifle richer than wedding cake) and a decanter of
sherry.—Sherry? well, she called it by that name;
though its *bouquet* was curious, and its vintage doubtful. On these viands I am immediately set to work, in
spite of all protestations to the contrary; and my request for some of her beautiful bread and butter is altogether disregarded. Mrs. Mac will not be gainsaid,
and will take it as a personal affront, and a slight upon
Cantire hospitality, if I do not immediately fall-to at

the sherry and the pound-cake—in every square inch of
which I see a bilious headache. Being of a weak mind,
and in the presence of a woman who has evidently a
will of her own and will not be trifled with, I resign
myself to my fate, and munch this headachy stuff as
though I liked it; while Mrs. Mac watches every
mouthful in such a way that I am unable to accomplish
any feat of jugglery, by pocketing a piece, while her
attention is directed to another part of the room. No
sooner have I done than she insists on my beginning
all over again, and having another piece of cake and
another glass of wine, informing me that if I refuse she
shall consider me "no canny,"—and, as I am rapidly
sinking into a state of idiocy from the combined influences of the oppressive heat of the shut-up room,
the perspiring difficulties attendant upon holding a
conversation in an unknown tongue, and the unwonted
nature of my luncheon, I give way before the undefined
horrors of her threat; and taking the wine and cake as
rapidly as though they were themselves medicine, and
not the causes for medicine, I heartily bid Mrs. Mac
farewell, and, rushing through the other smoky room,
with a collective adieu to Barelegs, Macbeth's witch,
and the gude mon in his crib, plunge through the filthy
byre, and out into the fresh air and pools of liquid
manure.

Now while I sat in that neat and spotless room, in

the company of the clean and tidy Mrs. Mac, drinking
her curious sherry, and eating her rich cake (which had
been purchased at Campbelton at ever so much a
pound), I might have fancied myself anywhere else than
in the *spence* of a Highland farm-house, where almost
all besides, even if it did not suggest dire poverty, certainly manifested the extremity of dirt, untidiness, and
squalor. It was a contest of "fierce extremes." And
yet Mr. and Mrs. Mac were, as I have said, bettermost
people, and could afford to entertain their visitors with
such costly fare in this rich apartment. When I called
upon their near neighbours, they had no such *spence* in
which to receive me, nor could they offer me sherry
and pound-cake; though their hospitality and friendly
feeling were just as great and as warmly evinced. In
these cases, the refreshment offered was a glass of milk,
and a plate of oatmeal bannocks.

As for the bannocks, they are deal boards made easy,
and taste like a compressed mixture of bran and chaff.
They hurt the teeth, and cause a sensation in the throat
similar to what must be felt by any one who stands
open-mouthed before a winnowing machine when it is
in full work. As for the milk, it is not every southron
past the age of infancy, who is possessed of sufficient
bodily and stomachic power to drink a glass of it
before dinner without materially interfering with his
digestion for the remainder of the day. So that not

only in Mrs. Mac's, but also in the other cases, the hospitality degenerated into a bore—as, indeed, enforced hospitality always does. Compulsory enjoyment is apt to produce unsought-for effects. When, for example, the fond papa took his son for a day's jaunt into the country, and, catching him by the collar and shaking a big stick over his head, said, "Now, my boy! I've brought you out here to enjoy yourself; and, if you don't begin to do so at once, I'll give you the soundest thrashing you ever had in your life!" doubtless, the fear of the possible performance of this threat would somewhat damp the young gentleman's pleasure.

And so with these hospitable and friendly Highland farmeresses. You must either persistently refuse their pressing invitation to eat and drink what they have set before you, and so avoid that mysterious alternative of being thought " no canny," or else you must swallow the curious sherry and rich cake — an act of egregious folly that you would never dream of committing at home, not even with your own wedding-cake — or hurt your teeth with chaffy oat bannocks, and destroy your inward serenity for the remainder of the day by tossing off a glassful of new milk. How happy would you be with neither! and yet you do all this for the sake of not rejecting the well-meant hospitality of people you never saw before, and shall probably never see again, and for whom you certainly do not

care one brass button. But what easy fools some
people are !

One cannot be surprised at being offered milk in a
Highland farm-house, for it is a popular beverage with
adults in Scotland. You not only see it thus drunk in
private houses, but you meet with glasses of milk set
out on the refreshment stalls of the railway stations,
and in the best confectioners' shops in Edinburgh, Glasgow, and other large towns. Thus your way in Scotland is made into a milky way.

I will close this chapter with a legendary tale told
concerning a Cantire farm-house and its inmates in the
near neighbourhood of Glencreggan, which, in its dra-
matic character, surpasses the story of Mary the Maid
of the Inn. It is this :— Once upon a time, in Barr
Glen, on a wild winter's night, a farmer and his family
and servants were comfortably seated around a peat-
fire, when the wind was howling terribly around the
house and the drifting snow was clogging up the doorways. The farmer knew that his son and the servant-
girl were much attached to each other, but he would
not consent to their marriage. While they were all
sitting round the fire on that winter's night, he thought
of a plan by which the servant-girl could be got rid of ;
so he said that if, before the next day, she would bring
him a skull that was in Saddell Church, she should
have his son for a husband. The girl's love was so

strong for the young man, that she joyfully agreed to the proposal, although it was quite seven miles to Saddell, and the road thereto lay over Beinn-an-Tuirc. She knew the road well and all its dangers and difficulties even by daylight, which would now be immensely increased by the darkness of the night, the fierce wind and driving snow, and the slippery rocks and swollen torrents. But she did not shrink from the danger, and at once made ready and went on her way. The farmer took good care that she went alone, and that his son did not follow her.

The brave girl went over hill and glen, battling with the snow storm, and tracking her path with the greatest difficulty. She passed safely over the southern side of Beinn-an-Tuirc, and by midnight reached Saddell Church. Its door was open, burst open perhaps by the violence of the wind. She knew the place where the skull was kept, and she groped towards it in the dark. As she did so she heard a great and peculiar noise, made up, as it seemed, of loud moans. There was a trampling of light feet over the pavement, and she heard forms rush past her; then a moment's silence, succeeded by more mysterious moans and sounds. Terrified, but not disheartened, the brave girl kept her purpose steadily in view; and, groping towards the skull, seized it with both hands, and made for the church door. The trampling of feet and the moans continued, and the forms pursued her. Grasping the skull she gained the door, and pulled it to after her. As she did so she heard a rush against it; but she turned and fled. By daylight she had regained her lover's home, and, half dead with fatigue and excitement, placed the skull in the farmer's hands, and claimed the fulfilment of his promise.

The farmer was taken aback by seeing the girl, having hoped that she would have perished amid the snow and wilds. He would not believe that she had really been to Saddell, and taken the skull from the church on such a night; so he at once set out to Saddell with some of his men, expecting to be able to disprove the girl's tale, by finding the skull still in its place in the church. When they got there, and had opened the church door, they found within the building — not the skull, but a number of wild deer, who, having found the door open, had sought shelter from the violence of the storm. The girl had told him of the sounds she had heard within the church. Here was their cause; and much as he wished it otherwise, yet it was impossible for him to disbelieve her tale.

There was nothing for him to do but to yield with the best grace he might. He gave his consent to the match; and, to make assurance doubly sure, the lover took his brave girl to Saddell Church the very next day, where she replaced the skull in its old position, and they were married off hand.   And as some of the deer that had frightened her had been killed and cooked, they had a hearty wedding and plenty of good venison at the feast that followed.

CHAP. XXIV.

HIGHLAND COTTAGES.

Wretchedness of the Cottages. — Their Exterior. — Their Middens and Kail-yards. — The Interior of a Highland Hut, with Figures. — The Lassies and their Mither. — Bonnie. — Cottages a Century ago. — Dr. Johnson, Garnett, and Pennant's Testimony. — An unwashed Bridegroom. — A Mahometan Paradise. — Dr. Parkins's Theory of wholesome unwholesomeness. — Bother'd. — The Geography of Dirt. — Calvinism and Cleanliness. — Christopher North's poetic gilding. — Lord Palmerston's sound Advice. — Landlords to the Rescue!

IF the average farm-house in the neighbourhood of Glencreggan was as I have endeavoured faithfully to depict it, — and for this purpose I have by no means chosen the worst specimen — what were the cottages?

Not to mince matters, they were miserable cabins, so wretched and filthy, that if an English gentleman lodged his labourers in such places, he would be gibbeted in his county newspaper, and held up to deserved reproach. How can morals and decency be expected to exist (much less to thrive) in homes where the inmates are huddled together to sleep in one small hut, reeking with peat smoke and dirty abominations? Hitherto I had imagined such a state of things to exist only in the uncared-for wilds of Ireland. But, here in Cantire, cleanliness, comfort, and decency were equally as little provided for by the insufficient accommodation as in the Emerald Isle, and equally as much proclaimed the wretched condition of the Celtic labourer. It is for the landlord to take the initiative in these matters; the poor cottars must take things as they find them, and encounter the Sisyphean lot of endeavouring to make the best of what is intrinsically bad.

Here is a row of three cottages. The walls are of a dark brown, weather-stained hue, composed of rough stones and turf cemented with mud. To each cottage is a door and a little window about a foot square, not made to open. A similar window pierces the opposite wall at the back of the cottage; but the door is front door and back door combined. Round the outside of the doors and windows are traces of a band of white-wash — a common form of decoration in Highland cottages, the outside of the house (apparently) being the only portion of it thus favoured. The roof is composed of heather-thatch, laid over turf upon larch poles; and, unless you are of Tom-Thumb dimensions, you may stand without the cottage and touch its eaves with the Adam's apple in your throat. Of course there is no upper chamber; as it is at the farm-house, so it is here; every thing is on the ground-floor. A slight hump on the pitch of the roof directs our attention to the opening meant for a chimney. In some cases, especially where the thatch is old and the cottage exposed to the full fury of the Atlantic gales (on which account its walls are made of such thickness), the roof is kept from taking a fly through the air by heavy stones slung across it in rows by ropes, like " a row of curl-papers," as Dr. Johnson truly remarked; and certainly, in the slang sense of " thatch " for *hair*, this simile holds good. In front of the door is the *midden*, or family dunghill *; but there is here a marked distinction between the Celtic Highlander's home and dung-hill, and those of the Celtic Irishman, in the absence from the former of " the joutleman that pays the rent " —the pig. As we have already seen, there is no pig in Cantire, at any rate so far as the cottagers are con-cerned. Near to the dunghill is a black heap of peat-turf, their only fuel except a few sticks. Their small *kail-yard* garden is behind the cottages, walled in by large stones rudely piled together. A narrow road

---

* I have already, in a note to chap. xv., referred to the utter absence of all out-door accommodations. In turning over some of the volumes of the " Transactions of the Highland and Agricultural Society of Scot-land," I find that (at least in one case) the silver medal was awarded to the proprietor who had erected his " improved cottages " without any out-door accommodations; although the committee were informed they were " yet to be added." Many plans and elevations of improved cottages and farms will be found in the useful volumes of the " Trans-actions."

leads by the kail-yards to the croft, a patch of ground common to the three cottages, where the little square plots are so variously cultivated that they resemble a tartan pattern, produced for the benefit of Ceres herself.

Let us stoop our heads, and enter this first cottage. As soon as we step over the doorway, we are face to face with some rude boards that form the end of the cupboard where are the sleeping cribs. They form the one side of the room. Sitting on the edge of the crib, I sketch the interior of the hut. Those cribs are surely the "smoky cribs" to which King Henry referred *; for barely six feet in front of me is the fire-place, not upon the hearth in this instance, but bricked up, and containing a small grate, in which a peat fire is smouldering and filling the hut with an eye-smarting smoke. Over it hangs the universal cauldron, or kail-pot, and almost as much light streams from the chimney as through the small dirty windows. A table, two chairs, a low stool, a dresser with mugs and crockery, and a spinning wheel constitute the furniture of the room. Some peat for immediate use is piled in the right-hand corner; and strings of smoked herrings are suspended from the roof. The floor is the natural floor of the earth, in which a motherly hen is vainly scratching to discover something for her brood's dinner. The interior of the pitched roof is smoked as black as

* 2 Hen. IV. Act iii. Sc. 1.

was that of the farm-house. The wattled walls are uneven, cracked, and foul with dirt. The place feels damp and unwholesome, and even the peat smoke cannot conceal the shut-up froustiness and foul smells. But the Highlander seems to care for neither smoke nor dirt. To the latter he "gets manured," as the Malapropian gentleman remarked; and, as to the former, Hugh Miller testifies that "it takes a great deal of smoke to smother a Highlander," and Christopher North contends that it preserves him in health. In England it is different. There, a smoky chimney and a cross wife are put in the same category. Hotspur thought Glendower "worse than a smoky chimney," because he made himself so complete a nuisance.

Two little girls are the tenants of the room; and, though bare-legged and poorly clad, they look clean and decent, and of wholesome appearance,—a fact sufficiently accounted for by the circumstance of their being attendants at the Glenbarr school, from which they have just come. Very comely little lassies they are, with the national type strongly marked in their faces and the colour of their hair, — though many of the Cantire Highlanders (like Mr. Mac at the farm) have black hair and a swarthy complexion. The locks of the one are of that peculiar golden red, in which his Grace of Argyle takes a pride, and which seems to be ever accompanied with a clear and lovely skin:—

"'Tis a fair stripling, though a Scot;"

INTERIOR OF A WEST HIGHLAND COTTAGE, CANTIRE.

and a good subject for the pencil.   In fact, this " Interior of a Highland Hut, with figures," is precisely one of those subjects that, with a good *chiaro-scuro* effect, is so acceptable to the artist, and looks so well upon paper, while, in sober reality, it is all that is repelling. For, however correctly the forms may be sketched and the lights and shades painted, · yet it does not come within the pencil's province to depict the dirtiness of the dirt, or the smokiness of the smoke—and, I might also add, the foulness of the fowls; for very unpleasant evidences of the presence of poultry are liberally strewed (together with other abominations) over the floor, and even the beds.   These are the points that make themselves disagreeably apparent to the visitor, and which the artist cannot imitate if he would, and would not if he could—unless he were a stark and staring pre-pre-Raffaelite.   It is for these reasons that pen and pencil may not quite agree, and yet do their work faithfully.

Presently the mother of the children comes in, wet up to her waist with sea-water,—for she is a kelp gatherer : and she enters into an account of her labours, which, as I shall shortly describe them in their proper place, I will not here further touch upon.   But though she has a hard life of it and is miserably poor, it is with very great difficulty that I can induce her to accept a shilling or two for her children—my little models.

Like the Highland herd-girl, they have "nae been drawit afore;" and they are not a little surprised when

Highland Woman. "Thank the leddy for the siller, Jeanie. Eh!
ye're a varry bonie leddy!"

English Visitor. "Bony lady, indeed! nothing of the kind!
Impertinent woman!"

they can look at my sketching-block, and point to each other's likenesses with, "Ech! there's Jeanie!" and

"Ech, noo! there's Girzie, sae trig and cantie! Weel, noo, look ye there! the gentle's drawit the cootie fool." Which meant, that the gentleman had introduced the motherly hen into his sketch. For a fowl, as I have before observed, becomes "a fool" in the mouth of the Highlander; and their favourite laudatory adjective of *bonnie* is pronounced as though written *bony*. Thus when this good woman of the house pronounced my sketch to be *varry bony*, I understood her commendation; and when, after I had given her the silver and was leaving her house, she pronounced *me* also to be *varry bony*, I knew perfectly well that she did not refer to any reduced appearance of body that I might present, consequent upon the loss of flesh attendant upon climbing the Highland hills; although I could imagine a case where she might use this personal address in a way that would turn her compliment into an insult.

These Cantire huts seem not to have improved one whit for the last hundred years, but to remain in the same state as those described by the century-ago tourists, who thought as much of an expedition into the heart of the Highlands, as we should into the regions of Lake 'Ngami. Dr. Johnson thus speaks of the huts of his day:—"A hut is constructed with loose stones, ranged for the most part with some tendency to circularity. It must be placed where the wind cannot act upon it with violence, because it has no cement; and where the water will run easily away, because it has no floor but the naked ground. The wall, which is commonly about six feet high, declines from the perpendicular a little inward. Such rafters as can be procured are then raised for a roof, and covered with heath, which makes a strong and warm thatch, kept from flying off by ropes of twisted heath, of which the ends, reaching from the centre of the thatch to the top of the wall, are held firm by the weight of a large stone. No light is admitted but at the entrance, and through a hole in the thatch which gives vent to the smoke. This hole is not directly over the fire, lest the rain should extinguish it ; and the smoke, therefore, naturally fills the place before it escapes." *

"Their cottages," says Garnett, "are, in general, miserable habitations. They are built of round stones without any cement, thatched with sods, and sometimes heath ; they are generally, though not always, divided by a wicker partition into two apartments, in the larger of which the family reside. It serves likewise as a sleeping-room for them all. In the middle of this floor is the fire, made of peat placed on the floor, and over it, by means of a hook, hangs the pot for dressing the victuals. There is frequently a hole in the roof to allow the exit of the smoke; but this is not directly over the fire, on account of the rain ; and very little of

* Works, vol. viii. p. 240.

the smoke finds its way out of it, the greatest part, after having filled every corner of the room, coming out of the door; so that it is almost impossible for any one, unaccustomed to it, to breathe in the hut. The other apartment, to which you enter by the same door, is reserved for cattle and poultry, when these do not choose to mess and lodge with the family."*

"The houses of the common people," says Pennant, "are shocking to humanity; formed with loose stones, and covered with clods which they call *devots;* or with heath, broom, or branches of fir;—they look, at a distance, like so many black mole-hills." † Captain Burt describes these *devots* or *divets,* as slices of turf that served for tiling, and "if there happens to be any continuance of dry weather, which is pretty rare, the worms drop out of the *divet* for want of moisture; insomuch that I have shuddered at the apprehension of their falling into the dish when I have been eating." These accounts coincide with Sir Walter Scott's description of the huts at the clachan of Tully-Veolan: and they may be applied without any variation to the cottages near to Glencreggan.‡

* Tour, vol. i. p. 121.

† Scotland, vol. i. p. 131. See also an account of Highland huts in Knox's "View of the British Empire," and in Dalrymple's "Memoirs of Great Britain."

‡ The writer of a work (published January, 1861) who is well qualified to speak on this subject, favourably contrasts the cleanliness of the

Now how is it possible for much attention to be given to cleanliness or common decency in squalid huts like these, where the inmates are packed as close as figs in a drum, and where all healthy, physical and moral laws are set at defiance? Looking at their befouled interiors, one is inclined to believe in that Scotch traveller's tale of the expectant bridegroom, who presented himself in all his dirt before a spruce Edinboro' clergyman. "The marriage to take place directly!" exclaimed the horrified parson; "surely you mean, after you have washed yourself!" "I'm well eneuch!" was the reply. "But surely," urged the decent clergyman, as his thoughts flew to the bride; "surely you would not wish to be married in such a dirty state!" "*Me*, dirty!" cried the indignant bridegroom; "*me*, dirty! what if ye saw *her!*"

One of the promised joys of the Mahometan paradise was, that it would be filled with perfumes, like to the

"Odours of Eden, and Araby the blest."

West Indian negroes and their dwellings with that of the Scotch labourer. (See "Reminiscences of a Scottish Gentleman," by Philo-Scotus, p. 198.) In another work published at the same time, viz. "Lady Elinor Mordaunt," by Margaret Maria Gordon (*née* Brewster), will also be found a faithful picture of many West Highland cottages, with the "children growing up in the habits of savage life, because they have habitations of no greater pretensions to decency than the Esquimaux hut or the Indian wigwam" (p. 341). The many evils resulting from the bothy system and the immoderate use of whiskey, are also forcibly detailed.

If there were any faithful followers of the prophet, who dwelt amid such unwholesome stenches as those in which a Highland hut is steeped, how keenly must they have enjoyed the change to their sweetly-scented paradise ! And yet, according to Dr. Parkins' new theory, poverty, filth, and density of population are *not* unwholesome, or predisposing causes to endemic diseases. Contrary to all the theories of the Board of Health, accumulations of filth and of everything that can give out horrible stinks appear (from Dr. Parkins' statistics) to be anything but predisposing causes to disease ; and those who advocate the bothy system, and condemn the Highland labourer to his present dwelling and consequent condition, will be glad to fortify themselves with Dr. Parkins' crowning fact that, when the natives of Kamschatka and Russia, and the Greenlanders and Esquimaux crowd together in over-heated rooms during their long winter months, excluding every breath of external air and breathing a polluted atmosphere, they are almost entirely exempt from fevers and epidemic diseases; and it is not until they emerge into the pure air that that class of diseases is known. Such is the new theory of wholesome unwholesomeness !

But new theories are very hard to be digested. And when a Greenlander's hut in the middle of winter or a Parisian *abattoir* in the height of the dog-days, is represented to us as one of those health-giving places to which invalids should resort, we are reduced to much the same state of blank surprise as the old cottager found himself in the other day, when the curate had been laboriously and somewhat too learnedly, explaining to him the nature and conditions of faith — "Well," said the old man, when the curate had come to an end of his essay, " what wi' the railroads, and the telegraphs, *and faith*, I'm fairly bother'd! "

The " Saturday Review " said, that " To the investigator of calm mind and stoical nostrils, who enters upon his subject without any undue predisposition to nausea, the geography of dirt is a curious scientific problem;" and suggested that the distribution of dirt being as important a matter of investigation as the distribution of quadrupeds, Mr. Keith Johnstone should construct a map that should contain *isorypal* as well as isothermal lines. Primæval filth is being rapidly dispersed by the widening track of tourists; the " Review " therefore advised the compilers of guide-books boldly to mark out the odorous and inodorous hotels, so as to shame the hotel-keepers into cleanliness. Romanism and dirt are known to go together *; and it would seem that Calvinism and cleanliness are opposed to each other.

---

* " It is a strange but undoubted fact, that wherever a population is peculiarly Catholic it is almost always peculiarly dirty. Wherever the practice prevails of adorning the roadsides and street corners with little

Christopher North strives to hide the dirt of the Highland cottage by the glamour of a poetic halo, and to conceal its inodorous smells by the sweeter scent of "the honeysuckle stealing up the wall, and blinding, unchecked, a corner of the window, its fragrance unconsciously cheering the labourer's heart, as in the midday hour of rest he sits dandling his child on his knee, and conversing with the passing pedlar. And let the moss-rose tree flourish, that its bright blush balls may dazzle in the kirk the eyes of the lover of fair Helen Irwin, as they rise and fall with every movement of a bosom yet happy in its virgin innocence." This is a very dexterous method of leading us away from the matter in question and directing our thoughts to sweeter subjects. Not less ingenious and lapwing-like are his flights from the dirty cottage to "honest poverty, — strength of muscle and mind, — plain, coarse, not scanty, but unsuperfluous fare,— the future brightening before the steadfast eyes of trust, — the nook which hope consecrates to the future," &c. &c. All this is very fine, not to say highly imaginative, though in the

shrines and images, there your nose will not fail to discover adjuncts which sensibly modify the poetry of the scene. Wherever a Roman Catholic church is peculiarly alive with worshippers, it is generally also peculiarly alive with something else; and the Protestant visitor will carry off with him some entomological companions who certainly did not enter the building for the purposes of worship."— *Saturday Review*, Sept. 17, 1859.

" unsuperfluous fare," truth has crept in, and "the
steadfast eyes of trust" may denote that the inhabitant
of the cottage is (what is vulgarly called) "going upon
tick" at the village-shop or public-house. When,
however, Christopher North makes out that the Highland cottage is such a beatific abode that "the very
babe in the cradle, when all the family are in the
fields, *mother and all*, hears the cheerful twitter" (of
the sparrows making holes in the thatch) "and is
reconciled to solitude," * we feel that he is very much
in the position of the Old Bailey barrister who has to
defend Mr. Jack Sheppard from a charge of burglary
with violence, and astonishes the prisoner by describing
to the jury the home of his client's innocent childhood
as an *à fortiori* argument that it was impossible for
him to have been guilty of the crime with which he
was charged.

In fine, no poetical gilding or artistic chiaro-scuro
can avail to conceal the abject squalor and indecency
of the average West Highland cottage; and, until
landlords take up the subject in the way they ought to
do, as stewards of a trust committed to their hands, so
long must all other efforts to ameliorate the Highland
labourer's condition be fruitless, and the benefits derived from education and religious teaching be nul-

* This very improbable statement really occurs in Christopher
North's panegyric on Highland "Cottages."—*Recreations*, vol. i. p. 217.

lified. Mr. Stirling of Keir, and Mr. Scott Burns, in a paper read to the London Farmer's Club, in December last, adduced a great mass of evidence relative to the evils resulting from the bothy system in the Western Highlands; and a remarkable speech was made by Lord Palmerston at Romsey during the Christmas of 1859, and, in substance, was repeated in December 1860, in which were uttered many valuable truths concerning lodgings for the labouring classes, which Scotch no less than English landlords would do well to take to heart and act upon. The noble Viscount's argument was to this effect: — That a landlord ought not to look to the rent of the cottages on a farm reimbursing him for the expense incurred in building those cottages, any more than he would expect to receive rent for a farmhouse separate from the farm. That the cottages for the labourers are farm appurtenances, equally as much as the barns and buildings essential to the cultivation and stocking of the land. That land cannot be well cultivated unless the labourers are *well housed;* and, if the labourers have to trudge three or four miles to their work, they get physically exhausted, and the farmer does not receive his money's worth for the wages that he pays. That the weekly rent paid by the labourer is rather to impress upon his mind that he is earning the accommodation given to him, than from any idea that it is to repay the expense of erection.

That the carrying out of these propositions would be to the advantage of the farm; and that a farm that can be cultivated to advantage is worth more to a tenant.

This is good advice; and advice that a landlord may turn to his own benefit, as well as to that of his labourers. Except in certain cases, where a two-roomed cottage is adequately sufficient for the comfort and decency of the inmates, every cottage should have at least three sleeping apartments—one roomy one for the man and wife, and two smaller ones for the boys and girls.* There is an " Association for promoting Improvement in the Dwellings and Domestic Condition of Agricultural Labourers in Scotland," which has already been of service, and might be of much more. It sup-

---

* This subject has been again " ventilated " in the " Times " during the past autumn, by the well-practised and forcible pens of " S. G. O.," and others. An argument brought forward against the *three* (or even *two*) sleeping-rooms is, that you will thereby increase the evils which you seek to remove, by giving the cottagers an opportunity to take in lodgers; and that experience tells us that they will avail themselves of that opportunity. This difficulty, however, may be readily overcome (in all those cases where the landlord is prepared to do his duty) by the landlord's permission being first required before a lodger is permitted to be taken. The landlord (or his agent) would determine whether or no the circumstances of the case permitted of the second or third bedroom being sub-let to a lodger; and if a lodger was taken contrary to orders, the tenant should be dismissed. The gentleman to whom this book is dedicated has, during the past year (from the designs of the author), erected eight cottages, each containing three bedrooms, where the above rules are insisted upon and observed.

plies designs for Highland cottages; but the designs are somewhat too strictly confined to the present national characteristics of thick-walled cottages of one-story high, with bed-recesses in the living rooms. An infusion of English comforts and conveniences would benefit the designs, and still more the Highlanders.

Landlords, to the rescue! and do your best to put an end to the evils of the bothy system; and make your habitations for human beings at least as comfortable and commodious as your stables and kennels.

CHAP. XXV.

ON THE ATLANTIC SHORE.

Mushrooms and Sea Air. — Beallachaghaochan Cave. — A Mountain Stream.—By the sad Sea Waves. — Receding of the Sea. — Detached Rocks. — Their geological Character. — Their botanical Character.— The Blue Bell of Scotland — Its distinctive Marks. — Hairbell or Harebell. — A Spot for a Pic Nic. — Kelp Gatherers. — Manufacture of Kelp. — Wraic. — The Kelp Harvest. — Value of a Kelp Shore. — Vraic in Jersey. — Hard Work. — Herrings and Wraic.

A FIVE minutes' walk from Glencreggan brings us to the seashore and within the splash of the Atlantic breakers. Our shortest way would be across the down-like fields, and to scramble down the cliffs. If we follow this course we shall find evidences that would convict a late Saturday Reviewer of a mistake. " Mosses and mushrooms," said he, " shrink from the sea air." Here, nevertheless, are mushrooms in profusion, scattered all over the grassy downs, up to the very verge of the cliffs, and thriving in the Atlantic sea air. And very excellent were they, as the Glencreggan breakfast-table enabled us to testify. They shrank no more from the sea air at Glencreggan, than they do on the Freshwater downs.

But our best way to the beach, and, in the end, the most expeditious, is to follow the high road for a short distance to the right. Since this road left Barr Village, it has traversed the cliffs at a considerable elevation above the sea, and at a distance of about a quarter of a mile from the shore. Shortly after passing Glencreggan, the road is carried over a mountain stream that comes from the hills through a little glen planted with larch and fir, and passes in front of a miserable farmhouse. When the road has crossed the stream, it winds suddenly and sharply seawards down a steep descent, and round the face of a rock, which is the spur of the hills that follow the crescent shape of the shore towards the village of Meusdale. The high-road winds down to the shore, and thus continues, with but few intermissions, all the way to Tarbert, a distance of twenty-six miles.*

The rock I have just mentioned stands boldly out above the road, and in its base is a large cave, called Beallachaghaochan—for thus the name was spelt to me by a Gaelic scholar. Ballochagoichan it is called in Mr. Keith Johnstone's map of Cantire; and Bealach-a'-

---

* "Dine at a tolerable house at Barr, visit the great cave of Bealach-a'-chaochain near the shore, embark in a rotten leaky boat," &c. — *Hebrides*, p. 197.

chaochain by Pennant, who mentions it in the only
sentence that he devotes to that portion of Cantire
between Campbelton and Tarbert. The Rev. D. Macdonald, in his account of the parish, writes the word
Bealochachaochean; another proof of the difficulty that
there is in arriving at correctness in spelling the names
of remote places in the Highlands. This cave contains a spring of excellent water, without any visible
outlet.

The mountain stream, that I have mentioned, passes
under the high-road at a depth of six or eight feet, and
dashes down its ravine, whose rocky sides are lavishly
hung with ferns and adorned with heather and wild
flowers. It comes on musically towards the sea, dancing
down its water-breaks and " depth of flowery shelves,"
and is in itself so beautiful an object that we long to
transport it bodily to a certain garden in a far-off English county, where it would receive the daily homage of
admiration, instead of wasting its sweetness on this
desert air, where it has a thousand rivals in the thousand

> " Wild brooks babbling down the mountain side."

A rough cart-road follows the side of this stream,
and conducts us down to Beallachaghaochan Port, and
Bay.

In a sheltered nook under the sea-wall of cliff a
rude boat-house has been constructed, and here the

cobles or fishing-boats are run up in rough and stormy
weather. At present they are down on the beach; not
quite high and dry though, for the faint waves that
" o'ercreep the rigid sand "

> " Tap the tarry boat with gentle blow,
> And back return in silence, smooth and slow;"

as they did when Crabbe, the Parson Poet, watched
them on the Suffolk shore. Two children are at idlesse
in the boat, pulling up ropes and chains,— throwing
stones at the gulls as they dart down upon the waves
and rise and fall "like floating foam," — and singing
merrily all the time, like Tennyson's fisherman's boy
shouting with his sister at play, while the sea breaks
over the cold grey stones.

We are now upon the Atlantic shore. Let us turn to
the left towards Barr Village and Glenacardoch Point.
On our left hand rise the grassy cliffs, here and there
scarped with rock. Over the waves on our right, are
Islay and Jura, with their satellites.

> " The gentleness of heaven is on the sea.
> Listen! the mighty Being is awake,
> And doth with His eternal motion make
> A sound like thunder everlastingly."

The beach is rough with rocks of varied form and
size, between whose fragments " the cruel, crawling
foam " leaves its white patches. Not only here, but for

the distance of several miles along the coast, there is a
strip of greensward (in some places cultivated) between
the cliffs and the sea, which has been thus described :—
" In the immediate vicinity of the sea a narrow stripe
of low alluvial land, edged by an indented declivity,
bears evident traces of having at one period been occupied by the sea. The general belief among the aged
inhabitants is, that the sea is gradually retiring from
the land. In confirmation of this belief, the bank or
sloping declivity which forms the boundary of the level
land occasionally assumes a shelving appearance, and
in such places as the sea has encountered obstruction
from projecting precipitous rocks, they have formed an
irresistible barrier against any encroachment of the
ocean ; but, where no such interruption occurs, the
waves seem to have forced a passage farther inland.
Along the shore the remains of some rude circular
inclosures are still visible, which, from their appearance
and position, must have been at one period surrounded
by the sea."*

On the Atlantic shore, underneath Glencreggan, from
Beallachaghaochan Port to Glenacardoch Point, this
strip of alluvial soil is not cultivated, but remains a
greensward. It is evident from the nature of the
ground, which resembles the Undercliff at the Isle of

* The Rev. D. Macdonald's " Statistical Account of the Parish of
Killean."

Wight, that landslips must have occurred at some remote period; and, scattered over the soft turf, are
detached masses of rock, from twenty to fifty feet high,
and of varying dimensions, which have doubtless been
dislodged from the rocky ramparts above, and are now
set up on the green sward, like so many Titanic nine-
pins. It is at this portion of the western coast of
Cantire, according to Macculloch's geological map *, that
the secondary red sandstone touches upon the micaceous schist; though the leading geological features
only are marked in his map, and the small local details are necessarily omitted. Hugh Miller has described
similarly-placed rocks occurring at a more northern
part of the western coast of Argyleshire. At the feet of
the conglomerate cliffs " there stretches out a grassy
lawn, which sinks with a gradual slope into the existing
sea-beach, but which ages ago must have been a sea-
beach itself. We see the bases of the precipices hollowed and worn, with all their rents and crevices
widened into caves; and mark, at a picturesque angle
of the rock, what must have been once an insulated
sea-stack, some thirty or forty feet in height, standing
up from amid the rank grass, as at one time it stood up
from amid the waves. Tufts of fern and sprays of ivy
bristle from its sides, once roughened by the serrated

* Description of the Western Islands of Scotland, vol. iii. p. 63. See
Appendix, " Geology of Cantire."

kelp-weed and the tangle. It owes its existence as a
stack — for the precipice in which it was once included
has receded from around it for yards — to an immense
boulder in its base, by far the largest stone I ever saw
in an old red conglomerate." He had previously not
seen any that weighed more than two hundred weight,
and he comes to the conclusion that these detached
rocks were the sport of the fierce Atlantic tempests,
which had been the rough agents in moving them to
their present position.*

On every little rocky ledge and coign of vantage of
these Titanic ninepins there is a mingled mass of moss,
and fern, and wild thyme, and heather, and wild flowers,
worked into one of those mosaics of nature of which
Horace Smith says : —

> " Ye bright mosaics ! that, with storied beauty,
>   The floor of nature's temple tesselate."

The botany of these rocks on the Glencreggan shore
comprises the sea-cale, marine holly, crane-bill geranium,
creeping convolvulus, scarlet poppy, starwort, rose cam-
pion, St. John's wort, musk rose, bog pimpernel, sea
bind-weed, scurvy grass, maiden hair, celadine, and
others; while ivy clothes portions of the rocks with its
evergreen mantle.

Nor must we forget the Blue Bell of Scotland, which
is the heath-bell, or harebell (*Campanula rotundi-*

* Cruise of the Betsey, pp. 7, 9.

flora), a very different plant from the English hare-bell (*Scilla nutans*), dedicated to St. George, which has a thick, soft, brittle, hollow stem, while that of the Scotch harebell is as wiry and supple as a very Scotsman;

> "Red-haired, high-cheek'd, sly, *supple*, and a Scot,"

says *the New Timon*, in summing up the northern characteristics; and suppleness is a distinguishing mark of the Blue Bell of Scotland. No English harebell would ever have

> "raised its head
> Elastic from her airy tread,"

if Ellen Anyone had planted her foot upon it, notwithstanding the poetical fact that

> "A foot more light, a step more true,
> Ne'er from the heath-flower dash'd the dew."

The darker flower that, from its reflex leaves, gave to Homer and Milton alike the simile of "hyacinthine locks," loves shady and sequestered dells; while the paler cærulean flower delights in open, windy places such as this, where the wild blasts of the Atlantic breezes blow over it and hurt it not. Many poets have confused this point, drawing no distinction between the two flowers.* But Shakspeare, like Scott, studied

---

* "In the lone copse, or shading dell,
> Wild cluster'd knots of harebells blow."
> *Charlotte Smith.*

nature out of doors, and was a too close and pious observer of her wonders and beauties not to note the distinctive characteristics of the two flowers, and he compares Imogen's veins to the "azured harebell." *
Perhaps the word ought to be written *hair*bell, and the name derived from the bell-like flowers depending from the wiry hair-like stalk; whence Tennyson calls it "the *frail* harebell." But books give us a different etymology, and tell us that it is called harebell because it grows in places frequented by hares. Yet out here on these Titanic nine-pin rocks, set up on end on this stretch of green sward by the Atlantic shore, even the mountain hares would find it somewhat difficult to gain a footing on those tiny ledges and crevices, —

> "Where blue bells and heather
> Are blooming together." †

Burns speaks of the "little harebells o'er the lea," and there, indeed, the hares might sport among them; but these detached rocks are, for the most part, inaccessible even to the nimble Highland hares. The wealth of wild flowers lavished upon these lovely rocks reminded us of similarly garnished rocks in the most luxuriant part of that most luxuriant district between Bonchurch and Niton; but with this difference, — in which the

* Cymbeline, Act iv. Scene 2.
† Robert Nichol.

Highlands had the superiority over the Isle of Wight,—
that here at Glencreggan the rocks had the additional
charm of clumps of flowering heather. Mr. "Dirty-
boy" Hunt once painted for Mr. Ruskin a tiny picture,
into which he had conjured "a bit of Mont Blanc." *
What a full subject would one of these lovely rocks at
Glencreggan form for Hunt to paint, and Ruskin to
word-paint !

Here is a charming spot for a picnic. These detached
rocks, scattered over the grassy sward, divide it into a
series of natural rooms, all of which, in the language
of marine advertisements, "command an excellent sea-
view," though they fulfil this promise much better than
do the advertisements, the sea-view of which is frequently
a glimpse over and between your neighbour's chimney-
pots. But here "there is no mistake ;" here is the
Atlantic rolling in to our very feet and wetting us with
its spray; and as we gaze straight before us still we
see the Atlantic, and nothing but the Atlantic. We
could certainly picnic here with vast success. In this
room, "with rock-wall encircled," with the soft velvet
turf for our carpet, the blue sky overhead, the sea before
us, the heather and wild flowers perfuming the air, and
the grassy cliffs rising sharply behind us to shut us out of
sight of any inquisitive passers-by,—here would we dine

* One of the series painted for Mr. Ruskin, to be presented to Schools
of Art.

in *al fresco* freedom. In the next space close by us, but shut out from our view by the rocky wall of our dining-room, the servants could have their relays of plates and eatables, and could carry on all needful preparations; while on the other side of us is a famous ball-room, in front of which the sea is even now advancing and retreating, and challenging us to come unto its yellow sands, and nimbly foot it " in dances and delight."

However, we are on a ramble now, and are not prepared for a picnic. Let us walk on nearer to Glenacardoch Point, towards those fires upon the beach, from whence are rising tall columns of smoke, like so many cloudy pillars, — and see what the people are doing there. There is a horse and cart, men attending to fires, and women wading in the sea.

The scene is in one of the little bays immediately in front of Glencreggan, looking across to Islay, and over the Atlantic in the direction of America. The cliffs rise on our left, sweep round to an acute angle in Glenacardoch Point, and then recede towards Barr. Below the cliffs is a strip of greenest grass, strewn with the richly-flowered boulders; then the buff line of sand and shingle; then a dark and confused mass of half-sunken rocks, thickly bestrewn with sea-wrack. It is low water, and they lift up their heads from the waves like sea-giantesses, their hair hanging over their heads

KELP-GATHERING ON THE WESTERN COAST OF CANTIRE.

wet and dank with salt water. These long tresses, rippling and glistening as the waves, are being plucked from the rocks by veritable bare-legged women, dressed in their oldest clothes tucked up to the knees; who,

KELP GATHERERS.

when they have gathered a lapful, carry it to the shore, or lay it in heaps upon the rocks, from whence it will be transferred to the cart. The kelp-cart is made to perform many journeys backwards and forwards from the half-sunken rocks to the shore; and the horse plunges through the breakers and up the loose shingle, scattering the bright wave-drops from him at every plunge, while his driver freely uses the whip and screams at him in Gaelic horse talk.   Two other men attend to the fires, turning over the heaps of smouldering kelp, and keeping them in a blaze within their circles of stones, or in shallow pits, while the columns of smoke go up like beacon-fires and are answered by hundreds of others along the coast, until one might imagine that the Highlands were up in arms once more and the signal for the gathering of the clans had been given.

Although the manufacture of kelp has somewhat declined in Cantire, yet it is still of considerable importance, and forms the chief part of the livelihood of many families.   Kelp is an article manufactured from the ashes of sea-weed, — or rather, I should say, from the sea-wrack, or *wraic,* or sea-ware (also called " tangles " in Cantire) which, I believe, is not classed among that vegetation of the sea, called *sea-weeds.*   Every visitor to the coast knows its long shiny leaves like tangles of crumpled ribbons, with its little bladders of iodine, which, when well rubbed on to the skin, afford so much benefit in strengthening weak limbs.   Of this *wraic* the *Fucus saccharinus* and *digitatus* is chiefly used for manure; the *Fucus vesiculosus,* or "cut-weed" was considered the best for soda, though now rarely used for this purpose, as soda is chiefly manufactured from sea-salt; and the *Laminaria, Nodosus* (out of which the Highland lads make whistles), and *Serratus,* or "drift-weed," was reserved for the iodine. Thus medicine and art (photography) derive one of their most valuable chemicals from this sea-weed; for, whether strictly and algologically correct or no, yet sea-*weed* we may still call it; and, in Gaelic, kelp is *Luath feamnach,* "the ashes of sea-weed." What the word *kelp* means etymologists don't seem to know.

The kelp harvest lasts from June to September. The value of a kelp shore is so variable and uncertain, that it can scarcely be stated with any approximate correctness. It is regulated by its extent, by the interval between high and low water mark, and by the nature of the rocks. The market price of the article fluctuates; it has ranged from 2*l.* per ton, early in the last century up to as much as 20*l.* per ton, the price it fetched for a short time early in the present century, when the importation of foreign Barilla * was checked. The Kelp of the Orkneys was superior to that of the Hebrides, and greatly used in the manufacture of plate-glass, and it would fetch 10*l.* per ton, while that of the Western Islands (used in the preparation of soap) would only fetch five. But again, the kelp of Colan-

---

* Barilla is a Spanish name given to the ashes of several species of the genera *Salicornia, Salsola, Suæda, Chenopodina,* and their allies.

say and Oransay — partly from the intrinsic excellence
of the weed, and partly from the superior method of
preparing it — could compete with the best *glass* kelp
of the Orkneys. During the season of 1859 the average price for kelp near to Glencreggan was 6*l.* the
ton. About a sixth of the sum is paid as a royalty to
the Lord of the Manor, for permission to cut and
gather the sea-weed. It takes an average of twenty-
four tons of weed to every ton of kelp; and as the
production of kelp for the whole of the Highlands was
last year estimated at about twelve thousand tons (ex-
clusive of the Orkneys, and other portions of Scotland),
some idea may be gained of the magnitude of the traffic
and the importance of this weed. Glass, soap, soda,
carbonate of soda, muriate of potass, but more especially iodine, are the chief articles in whose manufacture the sea-wraic is used: and it is anything but the
alga inutilis of Horace.

In France it is called *varech,* and in the Channel
Islands, *vraic,* where it is largely used for fuel and
manure. So important is it for the latter purpose, that
there is a Guernsey proverb *Point de vraic, point de
hautgard.* " No sea-weed, no corn-stacks." The times
of the *vraic* harvest are regulated by the local authorities, and the sea-weed can only be gathered under
municipal restrictions. " So violent is the scramble
between the contending parties," says Sir George Head,

"that peace officers are summoned at the harvest, or gathering. A day twice in each year is set apart for this ceremony, when neighbour against neighbour, in brute strength and rivalry, contend fiercely for this tribute of the ocean. Persons of all ages, of different denominations and sexes, wives, maids, and widows, married men and bachelors, leave and licence by the proper authorities being given, may be seen striving together indiscriminately in the fury of competition, and each anxious to possess him or herself of more varech than the other, if not absolutely quarrelling and fighting, at least tousling and tumbling one another up to their middles in water." * As in the Highlands, there is a difference in the kinds of vraic ; that which is cut or scraped from the rock, and called *vraic scie*, being considered much superior to that washed ashore by the tide, and called *vraic venant*. In Guernsey alone, the value of the yearly yield of *vraic* is upwards of three thousand pounds.

Macculloch, in speaking of the value of the kelp-shores on the western coast of Scotland, says, " that an island was pointed out to him, which was then worth to the lessee two thousand pounds a year, but had been let on a long lease to his ancestors at forty pounds —

* Home Tour in the United Kingdom, p. 172. For further particulars, see Barbet's "Guernsey Guide," Inglis's "Channel Islands," and Plees's "Account of Jersey."

the value of the kelp having made the difference." The kelp at Glencreggan found its chief market at Glasgow. When it is considered that twenty-four tons of sea-weed have to be gathered, and burnt, and conveyed to market, before the value of one ton of kelp can be obtained; and that the sea-wrack can only be obtained in certain places, under certain conditions, and at a certain time of day and period of the year,—we may easily conceive that the money is hardly earned. As kelp-gathering necessitates the keeping of at least one horse and cart, it is usual for the farmers to rent the kelp-shores, and employ certain of their labourers in the work. The expense of cutting, gathering, drying, burning, &c., is estimated at from three to four pounds per ton.

I am permitted to make use of the following interesting note, received from a Government official in the Falkland Isles. "Kelp is as near of kin to Rams-gate sea-weed as a Canadian forest is to the widow Mac Cormack's cabbages. Imprimis — Kelp cannot grow between 'wind and water;' it is always planted below low tide. It grows to the height of 30 or 40 feet, with a clear stem or trunk of 3 to 4 feet in girth, the leaves 7 feet long and a foot broad, and lying on the surface for miles along the coast, and at times for half a mile through, presenting the most complete and unconquerable breakwater that the world contains. The

largest and most ruffled waves of the wild seas where it
grows become tame and smooth as they traverse this
barrier, and leave their surge and curls behind it, while
the water beneath is always glassy and oily, no matter
what wind. I have seen porpoises for hours playing
through these sea-groves, and the seals and sea-lions
are at home in them, like deer in a forest. But to
men, the kelp is a true Siren. Nothing but a long
acquaintance with the various colours that the kelp
presents, as the wind, and air, and sun, and water, and
underlying rocks and sands affect it, can give a sense of
its beauty! But a man cannot get away from it — its
long arms encumber him, and drag him down. I have
in my mind at this moment, two men who threw away
their lives while trying to struggle through only a few
yards of kelp; the one, a captain of a fine Flemish
barque, who, his ship breaking up on the rocks, tried,
with a lead line in his mouth, to wear through the few
yards of kelp and water that lay between his ship and
the shore and could not; and he was seen to go down
by the only man of twenty-three who escaped that
morning." The " kelp " here referred to (though properly speaking the kelp is not the weed, but the manufactured article) is evidently different from that
gathered on the Scotch coasts. This South American
" kelp " may perhaps have been the *Sargassum bacci-
ferum*, or gulf-weed, whose matted cords of old stopped

the Spanish ships, and drifting masses of which form into floating islands, dreaded by sailors. This beautiful species is to be found on the West Highland coasts, whither it has been borne by the gulf stream. Or, this South American "kelp" may be of the *Laminaria* or *Chorda* species, which grow to a height of 40 and 50 feet, and will stop the course of a ship's boat, and drown hapless swimmers by twining round their legs.

In many cases, the manufacture of kelp in the Western Highlands was voluntarily abandoned, as it was supposed to drive away the herring from that part of the coast where it was carried on. This, however, was a mere vulgar error, invented in order to account for the erratic propensities of the fish. The women whom I sketched assured me that kelp-gathering was a very sorry subsistence; and that they often got back home too tired to change their wet and dripping clothes. Emigration has already been very largely carried on from the Western Highlands and Islands, chiefly to America and Australia. Dr. Livingstone's brother, writing from Central Africa, advocates a new field. "I wish," he says, "we had a few hundred good industrious Scotch families on these fertile Highlands. Instead of, as at home, toiling for a bare subsistence, here they could cultivate largely sugar, cotton, &c., benefit the natives by their example, and furnish materials for our manufactures at home."

Assuredly some of the " common objects on the sea-shore " at Glencreggan, who work so laboriously and live so poorly, might do a good service in Dr. Living-stone's mission-field; though if the fisheries off the Cantire coast were better attended to than they are, there would be the less need for emigration.

And this leads me to consider some few common objects both on, and off, the sea-shore at Glencreggan, which I will class in a chapter by themselves.

CHAP. XXVI.

COMMON OBJECTS ON AND OFF THE SEA-SHORE.

Otters. — Their Dens. — Otter-hunting. — Dogs. — The Master-otter, or King of the Otters. — The Note of an Otter. — Seals and Seal-shooting. — Fish varieties. — The Scotch Minister interrupted. — Lobsters and Crabs. — Imprisoned Voyagers. — The Gulf-stream. — The Voyage of the Seed. — Tropical Plants on Highland Shores. — Hugh Miller. — Dr. Neill. — Rev. C. Kingsley. — Mr. Campbell. — Westerly Currents and Gales. — Unsafe Anchorage. — Luminous Appearance of the Sea. — Medusæ. — Poetical Extracts.

THE *débris* of rocks on the Atlantic shore at the Glencreggan Undercliff was a favourite resort of the otter, one of the few wild animals now remaining to us that were found in the British Isles at the time of the Roman invasion. The otters frequent those parts of the coast where mountain-streams run into the sea, and where caves and fissures in the rocks, or large stones loosely scattered upon the shore, afford them secure hiding places. Into these rocky recesses and caves, which the Cantire people call their *dens* (*geos* is the Gaelic word), the otters carry their booty. They

are great enemies to sport in those streams where the
salmon and trout are preserved, not so much from the
amount of fish that they actually destroy,—though this
is by no means inconsiderable, as an otter has been
known to kill ten salmon in one day, — as from the fact
that they scare the fish from their spawning place, and
cause them to desert the stream. The otter, too,
appears to slay fish from the mere love of sport, as he
frequently leaves them on the shore almost untouched,
or only devoured in their choicest parts. It is not
surprising, therefore, that an active gamekeeper should
regard this amphibious creature as a mortal foe.

During the winter of 1859–60, the Glencreggan
keeper killed five otters in the short space between
Beallachaghaochan Port, and Glenacardoch Point. I
had no opportunity of witnessing the sport, but it was
thus described to me by those who were annually accustomed to take part in it.

The rocks by the shore are searched for the otter's
spraint. When this is found, it is easy to find the *den*,
whither he has carried his fish, but by no means easy
to drag him from his retreat. The otter is evidently
aware that he has but a small chance for his life if he
ventures forth; and he accordingly keeps as close as
a badger, and is as difficult to be " drawn." Terriers,
and not the weird-looking otter-hounds, are the dogs
chiefly used for this purpose; and, where circumstances

permit, they are aided by the men dislodging the stones under which the otter is secreted. Sometimes the dogs and the otter grapple with each other underneath the stones, and roll out together. But, generally (and this is what is desired), the otter watches his opportunity, and makes a rush from his den over the narrow belt of shingle, and among the rocks into the sea. This is the exciting moment for the sportsman, who is lying in wait, gun in hand, and finger on trigger, watching for this *bolt;* and, as a matter of course, unless he is very dexterous and is a good shot, the otter preserves his life. Occasionally the sport is pursued at night by torchlight; dogs are not then needed. The shooter lies in wait until the otter leaves his den in quest of food.*

Mr. Colquhoun, in his "Rocks and Rivers," devotes to the otter a chapter, in which he says, "In the West Highlands, especially, many of the resident proprietors pique themselves on the excellence of their otter-terriers. Some few keep hounds for the purpose, but the terrier is a very good substitute in these wild districts, and, of course, far more easily procured. . . . Terriers are best in rocky cavernous places, and seldom fail to make the otter bolt if they can get near him. From the abundance of prey, these sea-hunting otters

* Otter hunting in the Hebrides is described and very well illustrated in the "Penny Magazine," vol. iii. pp. 496, 503.

grow to a great size. . . . Many a fine fish have I seen lying on the shingle, with only a few bites out of its neck, and it was seldom honoured by a second visit from its captor."

The fabulous *master-otter* — so invulnerable, and whose skin possesses such charms, that, where a portion of it is, the house cannot be burned, or the ship cast away, and nor steel nor bullet can harm the man who owns but one inch of it — is fully believed in by the Cantire people.* It is thus mentioned by Daniel, in his "Rural Sports : — "In Scotland, the vulgar have an opinion that there is a king or leader among the otters, spotted with white and larger. They believe that it is never killed without the sudden death of a man or some animal at the same instant ; that its skin is endowed with great virtue, as an antidote against infection, a preservative of the warrior from wounds, and insures the mariner from all disasters upon the sea." This legend may have arisen from the value of the otter's skin, which, despite its American rivals, becomes a valuable perquisite to its captor. I did not hear of its flesh being used as an article of food, though we know that, from its fishy nature, the Church of Rome allowed it to be eaten on *maigre* days.

Mr. Colquhoun says, that the *note* of an otter is

* See a description of it in Maxwell's "Wild Sports of the West," p. 194.

" something between a squeal and a whistle;" it is
" singularly plaintive," and has " something of the mo-
dulated whistle of the buzzard or the kite, but far
more sweet, soft, and musical, rising in a low cadence
from the shore, and then melting into the clear air."
So that if when wandering " by the sad sea waves " on
the Glencreggan shore, we hear this mysterious and
" most musical, most melancholy " song, we need not
ascribe it to any mermaid or siren, but simply to our
friend, the otter, serenading his otteress.

Seals also come to the caves on this coast during
their breeding season ; and at other times may be
seen swimming about very close to the shore. About
five miles below Glenbarr, on the western coast of
Cantire, is a favourite place for them. There are many
rocks there out in the sea, which are the resort of seals,
who may be seen upon them from the shore singly and
in groups, basking in the sun. They are not easy to be
shot ; for their quickness of eye is so great, that at the
first flash they plunge suddenly under water, and are
out of reach before the ball can touch them. They are
even more destructive than the otter in their onslaughts
upon fish, and have this advantage over it, that they
can seize fish with their paws, and also break nets
with them. They give the best sport to the shooter
when they swim about like dogs, with only their heads
exposed above the water. The greatest dexterity is

then required to shoot them, so quick are they in their movements. The common method pursued in Scotland of hunting them in caves by torchlight, and killing them with blows from bludgeons, is well known.*

Besides salmon and trout, the otter, no less than the seal, finds a plentiful variety of fare wherewith to tickle his palate. The sea-fish along this coast are red rock cod of the largest size, ling, tusk, skate, plaice, lythe or white pollock, haddock, whiting, mackerel, seath, coal fish, conger eel, soles, and turbot. The enumeration of this list insensibly reminds me of the anecdote of the Scotch minister, who was preaching about Jonah, and was eking out his scanty ideas by " vain repetitions." "And what, me brethren!" said he, " should ye suppose was the fish that swallowed Jonah! Maybe it was a haddock! Nae, my brethren, but it was not a haddock! Maybe it was a turbot! Nae, my brethren, but it was not a turbot! Maybe it was a saumon! Nae, me brethren, but it was not a saumon! Maybe it was a mackerel! Nae, me brethren, but it was not a mackerel! Maybe, it was a harrin! Nae, me brethren, but it was not a harrin!" Here, a member of the congregation, who either feared that his

---

* Rocks and Rivers, p. 165. See Pennant's "Zoology" and "Scotland;" "Letters from Scotland;" the Rev. G. Low's "Fauna Orcadensis;" also "Penny Magazine," vol. iv. p. 101, where there is a picture of seal-hunting in Scotland.

minister was going through an interminable catalogue
of fish, or else thought that he was in a dubious or
ignorant condition, suddenly piped out, "Maybe it was
a whal!!" "Maybe, ye're an auld fule!" responded
the irascible preacher, "for tackin' the word o' God out
o' the mouth o' his minister!"

Beside the fish already mentioned, herrings also pass
by the coast during July and August, pursued by
aquatic birds, whales, porpoises, and the all-devouring
cod. Lobsters and crabs of the largest size are numerous, and are generally used as bait in cod-fishing.
With the exception of a few large brown mussels ad-
hering to sunken rocks, no bivalved shell-fish of any
description is to be found along this part of the coast;
but in West Loch Tarbert oysters of large size but
good quality are plentiful. In shallow bays a few
prawns and shrimps occur, and great shoals of sprats
and herring fry.

From the Glencreggan coast up to the fishing-village
of Muasdale, we shall find abundant evidence that this
is a crab and lobster-shore; for lobster-pots and lobster-
traps will be scattered upon the shingle, or piled in the
cobles. The "pots" are made of wicker-work; the
"traps" of network, stretched over hoops; and the
former bear a very close similarity to a lady's crinoline.
Rows of these traps and pots, baited with fragments of
fish, are lowered at night in likely places along the

rocks, and raised in the morning, when the negro scavengers of the sea are found to have made their way through the tapering holes in the net-work, and to have climbed up the pots "hand over hand," and then gone down after their bait into the tunnel-like well, never to return. Lobsters form a chief portion of the income of the Muasdale fishermen, who catch them in large quantities, and send them off to Tarbert or Camp-belton, from whence the steamers will convey them —

THE FASHIONABLE LOBSTER-POT.

who knows where? A shilling was the standard price for a lobster at Muasdale—size making no difference.

In a storm that happened while we were at Glen-creggan, when

"The western wind was wild, and dank wi' foam;"

one of the Muasdale fishing-boats was dashed upon the rocks, and so damaged that she could not be made sea-worthy under six weeks' labour—no small loss to the owners. They are accustomed to place their crabs and lobsters in well-boxes (pierced with holes) and sunk in the sea, if it should not be convenient to send them to market immediately upon their capture; and occasionally these well-boxes are torn from their moorings by one of those fierce storms that will suddenly arise on this coast during the prevalence of the equinoctial gales,—

> " When western winds the vast Atlantic urge
>   To thunder on thy coast;"

and the poor lobsters and crabs are floated out to sea in their wooden prison, there to perish, unless a giant wave should happily dash the box against a rock, and release them by shivering their prison to pieces.

Not only are the westerly gales of great violence upon this coast, but the great gulf-stream from the Atlantic also sets in with much force, as though, by the gifts that it brought with it from tropical climes, it would seek to recompense the fishermen and others for the losses occasioned through the destructive western gales. Pennant tells us, that a part of the mast of the *Tilbury*, man-of-war, burnt at Jamaica, was taken up on the western coast of Scotland; and that plants, natives of Jamaica, are also found on the western shores of Islay, and other islands of the Hebrides. He supposes the seeds of the plants to fall into the water of the Jamaica rivers, and to be carried down the river to the sea; from thence, by tides and currents, and the predominance of the east wind, to be forced through the

Gulf of Florida, and into the North American ocean.
When arrived in that part of the Atlantic, they fall in
with the westerly winds, which generally blow two-
thirds of the year in that tract; which may help to
convey them to the shores of the Hebrides and Orkneys.* Washed on shore, haply the seed may take
root; and thus, this tropical plant is mysteriously conveyed across the globe, to come to maturity in a
northern clime. Here is a subject for a poet in this
voyage of the seed! Its birth in the Western isles of
the Indies — its travels down the river, and across seas,
and gulfs, and oceans, until it finds a resting-place on
the Western Isles of Scotland. The migrations of
Indus himself could scarcely have been more startling,
than for a seed dropped in Jamaica to find itself growing into a plant in Islay or Jura.

Hugh Miller has an interesting passage on this point,
which I cannot do better than quote at length.† "I
had frequent occasions to remark that much of the
wood used in buildings in the smaller and outer islands
of the Hebrides must have drifted across the Atlantic,
borne eastwards and northwards by the great gulf
stream. Many of the beams and boards, sorely drilled
by the *Teredo navalis*, are of American timber, that
from time to time has been cast upon the shore,—a

* Hebrides, p. 233.
† Cruise of the Betsey, p. 46.

portion of it, apparently, from timber-laden vessels
unfortunate in their voyage; but a portion of it also,
with root and branch still attached, bearing the mark
of having been swept to the sea by transatlantic rivers.
Nuts and seeds of tropical plants are occasionally
picked up on the beach. My friend gave me a bean or
nut of the *Dolichos urens,* or cow-itch shrub of the
West Indies, which an islander had found on the shore
sometime in the previous year, and given to one of the
manse children as a toy; and I attach some little
interest to it, as a curiosity of the same class with the
large canes and the fragments of carved wood found
floating near the shores of Madeira by the brother-in-
law of Columbus, and which, among other similar
pieces of circumstantial evidence, led the great navi-
gator to infer the existence of a western continent.
Curiosities of this kind seem still more common in the
northern than in the western islands of Scotland."

"Large exotic nuts or seeds," says Dr. Patrick Neill,
in his "Tour through Orkney and Shetland," "which in
Orkney are known by the name of Molucca beans, are
occasionally found among the *rejectamenta* of the sea,
especially after westerly winds. There are two kinds
commonly found; the larger (of which the fishermen
very generally make snuff-boxes) seem to be seeds from
the great pod of the *Mimosa scandens* of the West
Indies; the smaller seeds, from the pod of the *Dolichos*

urens, also a native of the same region. It is probable that the currents of the ocean, and particularly that great current which is seen from the Gulf of Florida, and is hence denominated the Gulf-stream, aid very much in transporting across the mighty Atlantic these American products. They are generally quite fresh and entire, and afford an additional proof how impervious to moisture, and how imperishable nuts* and seeds generally are."

Mr. Kingsley, in his prose Idyll of "North Devon," has the following passages on this subject of the Gulf-stream:—"In the very water which laps against our bows, troops of glossy-limbed negro girls may have hunted the purblind shark in West Indian harbours, beneath glaring white-walled towns, with their rows of green jalousies, and cocoa-nuts, and shaddock groves. For on those white sands there to our left, year by year, are washed up foreign canes, cassia beans, and tropic seeds; and sometimes too, the tropic ocean snails, with their fragile shells of amethystine blue, come floating in mysteriously in fleets from the far west out of the passing Gulf-stream, where they have been sailing out their little life, never touching shore or ground, but

* At the drainage of Whittlesea Mere, in 1851, an ancient British boat was discovered. It was hollowed from the trunk of an oak, and was twenty-seven feet in length. Within it were several bushels of nuts.

buoyed each by his cluster of air-bubbles, pumped in at will under the skin of his tiny foot, by some cunning machinery of valves, — small creatures truly, but very wonderful to men who have learned to reverence not merely the size of things, but the wisdom of their idea, raising strange longings and dreams about that submarine ocean-world which stretches, teeming with richer life than this terrestrial one, away, away there westward, down the path of the sun toward the future centre of the world's destiny."

And again, where he meets with the fragment of a wreck : — " In what tropic tornado, or on what coral key of the Bahamas, months ago, to judge by those barnacles, did that tall ship go down ? How long has this scrap of wreck gone wandering down the Gulfstream, from Newfoundland to the Azores, from the Azores to Biscay, from Biscay hitherward on its homeless voyage past the Norwegian shore ? "

And yet again : — " The Atlantic gales are sending in their *avant-couriers* of ground-swell * ; six hours more, and the storm which has been sweeping over 'the still-vexed Bermoöthes,' and, bending the tall palms of West Indian Isles, will be roaring" over the moors of Glencreggan.

* In speaking of Gaelic as a highly descriptive language, Mr. Campbell says: "The thundering sound of the waves beating on the shore is well expressed by *Tonn*, a wave; *Lunn*, a heavy Atlantic swell." — *West Highland Tales*, vol. i. p. 130.

Mr. Campbell, in the Introduction to his "West Highland Tales," makes repeated mention of the "fairy-eggs" and drift-logs that are carried by the Gulf-stream to the Scottish coast. I will quote one of many passages :— "That smoked rafter (in the Highland hut) certainly was once a seed in a fir-cone somewhere abroad. It grew to be a pine tree; it must have been white with snow in winter, and glittering with rain-drops and hoar-frost in bright sunshine at various times and seasons. The number of years it stood in the forest can be counted by the rings in the wood. It is certain that it was torn up by the roots, for the roots are there still. It has been to warm seas, and has worn a marine dress of green and brown since it lost its own natural dress of green branches. Birds must have sat on it in the forest, crabs and shells have lived on it at sea, and fish must have swam about it; and yet it is now a rafter, hung with black pendants of peat smoke. A tree that grew beside it may now be in Spitzbergen amongst walrusses. Another may be a snag in the Mississippi amongst alligators, destined to become a fossil tree in a coal field. Part of another may be a Yankee rocking-chair, or it may be part of a ship in any part of the world, or the tram of a cart, or bit of a carriage, or a wheelbarrow, or a gate-post, or anything that can be made any-where."

The westerly currents and gales make the harbourage

and anchorage along the Atlantic shore of Cantire very
unsafe during the winter season and the vernal and
autumnal equinoxes; for no part of the shore is indented by an arm of the sea until we come to West
Loch Tarbert, in the northern portion of Cantire. Such
vessels as venture upon the coast in the spring and
summer seasons to land coals and ship potatoes for the
English and Irish markets, are abruptly obliged to
weigh anchor and sail for the opposite island of
Gigha, where they lie in security until such time as
the wind blows from a more favourable direction. But
the sound between the mainland and the adjacent
islands of Gigha and Cara abounds with sunken rocks
and shelves, which sometimes prove fatal to vessels.
When the cloud-caps are seen on the Paps of Jura,
mariners have a sure prognostication that "varra
coorse" or "saft" weather is to follow, and they take
their measures accordingly.

Off this coast, too, may be occasionally observed that
wonderful luminous appearance of the sea, occasioned
by myriads of microscopic animals of the Medusa tribe.
Macculloch has devoted an entire chapter to this subject, to which I would beg to refer the curious reader.
"The whole water (he says) from Shetland to the Mull
of Cantire was rendered a body of light by these minute
creatures."   And again he says : — " This spiral creature
extended from the Mull of Cantire to Shetland, rendering

all the sea muddy for miles in breadth and fathoms in depth ; and so numerous, that a pint of water contained five thousand, or ten thousand, — it is the same thing. The computation must be left to Zedekiah Buxton ; but if all the men, women, and children that have been born since the creation were shaved, and all their separate hairs were lives, these would not amount to one generation of this spiral people born on Monday morning to die on Wednesday night, and so on for ever and ever. Oceans in breadth and miles in depth, all active, all bustling and busy; every atom of water a life; a universe of self-will, and desire, and gratification, and disappointment; and the occupation of the whole being to destroy and be destroyed, to eat and be eaten. Thus it has been from the creation, and thus it will be ; — truly, we feel woefully insignificant in the middle of this crowd. I really cannot think, with Cato, that the world was made for Cæsar. If the majority is to have it, the ocean is something more than the highway of nations ; and we of the earth and the air,—men, mites, midges, and all, — would scarcely be missed, though the tail of a comet should once more sweep the ocean to the top of Ararat and Cotopaxi."*

* Highlands and Western Isles, vol. iv. chap. i. See also Kingsley's "Miscellanies," vol. ii. p. 305 ; and Macculloch's "Western Islands," vol. ii. pp. 189—202.

Macculloch, on this subject, has quoted the lines from
Cowley : —

> " The fish around her crowded, as they do
>   To the false light that treacherous fishers show :"

and a recent writer * brings forward the evidence of
Captain Scoresby, Darwin, Gosse, and Professor Forbes
on the phosphorescent light of the marine animalcule.
Scott thus speaks of the luminous appearance : —

> " Awaked before the rushing prow
>   The mimic ocean-fires glow,
>   Those lightnings of the wave ;
>   Wild sparkles crest the breaking tides,
>   And flashing round the vessel's sides
>   With elfish lustre lave.
>   While far behind their livid light
>   To the dark billows of the night
>   A gloomy splendour gave."

And Coleridge thus : —

> " Beyond the shadow of the ship
>   I watched the water-snakes ;
>   They moved in tracks of shining light,
>   And, when they reared, the elfish white
>   Fell off in hoary flakes.
>   Within the shadow of the ship,
>   I watched their rich attire ;

---

* " On the Luminous Appearance of the Sea, caused by Noctiluca
Miliaris," by J. W. Lawrance, Esq., of Peterborough, 1859.

Blue, glossy green, and velvet black,
They coiled, and swam, and every track
Was flash of golden fire."

Such were some of the common objects on and off the sea-shore at Glencreggan.

CHAP. XXVII.

MUASDALE ; A WATERING-PLACE — IN CLOUDLAND.

The bending Line of Shore. — An ideal Watering-place.— The Highland
Aberystwith. — Muasdale's Superiorities. — Lions of the Neighbour-
hood. — Climate and Longevity. — Necessities and Attractions. — A
Prophecy. — Killean Manse. — The minor Prophets. — Muasdale
Village. —A Farina Mill. — Legend of the fourteen Farmers of Muas-
dale. — Clachaig Glen. — Legend of Beith and the Arch-fiend. — The
two Bridges. — The dry Bones of a Sketch. — How to manufacture a
Picture. — Plenty of Smoke. — Half-price Distinction.

RETURNING to Beallachaghaochan Port and Bay, let us
wander northward up the beach to Muasdale. The
varying hues upon the sun-lit sea remind us of Southey's
lines :—

> " How beautiful beneath the bright blue sky
>   The billows heave ! one glowing green expanse,
>   Save where along the bending line of shore
>   Such hue is thrown, as when the peacock's neck
>   Assumes its proudest tint of amethyst,
>   Embathed in emerald glory."

   " The bending line of shore," for the next mile and
a quarter, is marked by two crescents ; the middle horn

being occupied by the Manse of Killean, and the further
horn by the Church — both Church and Manse standing
on the very verge of the Atlantic. Muasdale Village
lies between the two, in the second crescent. The high
road from Campbelton to Tarbert, which has wound
round the spur of the Cliff in whose base is Beallachaghaochan Cave, runs along the level by the sea-shore,
being divided from the sands by a narrow strip of cultivated land. On the other side of the road is another,
but wider strip of flat land, now covered with golden
corn ; and from this rises an amphitheatre of hills,
following the crescent shape of Beallachaghaochan Bay,
and in character, much the same as the Isle of Wight
Undercliff. Close by us, where are the fishing-boats
and the children at play, the sea is studded by a crowd
of half sunken rocks, a valuable field for the kelp
gatherers, and where, after a storm, we saw so much
sea-weed, that the spot bore a similitude to a tan-
yard. From here to the further point of the crescent,
where the Manse is, the beach is smooth and sandy,
and well adapted for sea-bathing throughout its greater
extent ; though here and there, it is rough with large
boulders of red sandstone, trap, or whin.

The double crescent curve of the shore reminds us
of Aberystwith, with its first sweep from the Castle
Hill to the Marine Baths, and its second from the
Baths to Constitution Hill. Here, the Manse occupies

that central position, which, at Aberystwith, is mono-
polised by the Baths.　Now, what a delightful situation
for a fashionable watering-place, this Muasdale would
be, if one could only get the fashion to it — if one
could only see the way to reach it and to leave it with

VIEW FROM BEALLACHAGHAOCAN TO MUASDALE AND KILLEAN.

any degree of comfort.　And yet it is scarcely more
inaccessible than Aberystwith is even at this present
hour; and as Aberystwith is a creation of the last half-
century, perhaps the next fifty years may do as much for
Muasdale; and, in the absence of railroads, four-horse
coaches may run in the summer season, from Camp-

belton to Tarbert, and thence to Ardrishaig and the
Crinan Canal, and round by Inverary to Tarbert, or
Loch Lomond — thus conveying travellers who might
object to the sea voyage from Greenock to Campbelton,
through a magnificent range of country, surpassing
even the Wye and Severn scenery on the two routes to
Aberystwith.

But Muasdale would be greatly superior to Aberystwith in its sea-view, as well as in its position. In our
imaginary Highland watering-place, the moors and
glens would be a great element of attraction, and would
afford an endless variety of lovely walks close at hand;
whereas at Aberystwith, you can only vary your walk
from the Castle Hill to Constitution Hill, by going
from Constitution Hill to the Castle Hill. Here too,
along this crescent of hills might arise the Muasdale
Marine Parade, which would leave that at Aberystwith
in the shade; for here, instead of being on a dead level,
the houses might be built up the face of the hill, as
they are at Ventnor, high above the sea, and with the
hills sharply rising like a rampart of rock behind them;
and above them might spring up even a higher crescent, that might rival the York Crescent at Clifton in
position and beauty, and yet should have this one
among many other advantages over the Southern
Queen, that the Argyle crescent of our Muasdale
watering-place, though perched so high, should have

hills behind it, upon which you could step out of your back door (as at Malvern Wells); but they would be Highland hills, crowded and tumbled together, empurpled with heather, gashed with glens, and musical with rills and torrents.

Here is one of these rills; it makes its way towards that part of the crescent, in the direction of the Manse, and there dashes over the face of the rocky rampart, in a cascade, thin but tall, and finds its way through the sweep of greensward, and down to the beach. This might be made a pretty feature in our new watering-place, and at this extremity of the Crescent, there is Beallachaghaochan Cave, with the Port and Bay. As for other "lions," there is, on the one side, within the compass of an easy walk, Glenbarr Abbey, with its lovely glen, and the walk home by Glenacardoch Point, and the sea-shore where we saw the kelp gatherers, and those detached rocks; and on the other side, is Muasdale Village, and Killean, with certain beautiful attractions, of which I will presently endeavour to give you an idea. On the important subject of climate, I have already spoken. It is mild and salubrious, despite the " varra coorse " and " saft " weather ; in proof of which, you may notice those fuchsias in front of the fishermen's cottages down on the beach at Muasdale ; they are barely a stone's throw from the sea, and are frequently (literally) watered by its spray — they face

the Atlantic, and the strong westerly gales — and yet
they are growing up to the top of the cottage, with
trunks like little trees, and are covered with a profusion of bloom, as we saw them in the Glen
Garden, at Glenbarr Abbey, and as the reader may
have seen them at Bonchurch. The grim testimony
of the grave-yards may also be brought forward to
show the advanced age attained by the generality of the
natives. I have already mentioned the death, in April
last (hastened by the unusual severity of the previous
winter), of an old woman, aged one hundred years; and
when Mr. Macdonald was preparing his Statistical
Account of the parish of Killean, he mentioned the
recent death of a woman aged one hundred and three,
and that the united ages of five men in the parish,
who were then alive, amounted to four hundred and
thirty-five. We may be sure then, that even at the
worst seasons of the year, our Muasdale watering-place
would be a healthy resort.* In fact, it may be attri-

* This part of the world must indeed be considered a healthy one,
if we may credit all the records of the longevity of its inhabitants.
Provost Brown, of Inverary, headed one of the contending parties in a
shinty match, and carried the town's colours in procession among the
victors, when he was a hundred years old; and he lived for sixteen
years after. But Gilrour MacCrain, of the Isle of Jura, was a patriarch
whose age far outtopped that of Provost Brown, and even exceeded
that of Parr or Jenkins; for it is said that he died in the reign of
Charles I., after having kept one hundred and eighty Christmasses in
his own house. *Credat Judæus!*

butable to the healthiness of the district, that no medical man is to be met with between Campbelton and Tarbert, so that at present, if any one at Muasdale should need surgical aid, he must send fifteen or twenty-four miles for his doctor. But we know that eagles will flock to the carcass; and we may feel sure that if our ideal watering-place should ever take the semblance of reality, the M.R.C.S.'s, and L.A.C.'s, to say nothing of the M.D.'s, will fully recognise their duties to society and to themselves.

Then, for other necessities or attractions, there is a capital road, equal to any turnpike road in England, with the immense superiority that it has no turnpike throughout its whole length and breadth. There is a daily delivery of letters, brought by a dashing mail-cart, which traverses the road twice a day, and has its relays of horses all the way from Campbelton to Loch-gilp-head. There are communications with the outer world even now, by means of carriers, who will bring to you what cannot be supplied by the wonderful village-shops that deal in every thing — though, of course, our watering-place *in nubibus* (which answers to the Romanists' *in partibus infidelium*) would arise in all the completeness of fashionable shops with plate-glass fronts. If you are of the Presbyterian persuasion, there are two Churches (the Established and Free) within five minutes' walk; and there are some excellent sites for Church of England Churches, if you are inclined to build, and support them.

Then there is fishing and shooting in abundance; ranging from salmon to seals, from grouse to sea-gulls, and from hares to otters. There is also the little excitement of a sea-port in the crab and lobster-fisheries of the Muasdale men, and the consequent supply of those dainties, with prawns and shrimps, Loch Fyne herrings, and Loch Tarbert oysters, fresh to your table. There is also the neighbourhood, which, though it may not exactly permit you (unless you boat over to Jura) to " follow the stag on the slippery crag," yet will enable you " to chase the bounding roe, with a yoho, yoho," like the gentleman in the song—provided that you go to the right place, and obtain the laird's permission. And as for the scenery in general, what more could you require? Before you, is the broad Atlantic, studded with half a dozen of the Hebrides, and a view ranging from the Giant's Causeway up to the misty mountains of Mull — a century of miles visible in one unbroken range. From your front door, you face the glorious sunsets; from your back door you can step out on to the hills, and (if you have imbibed enough mountain air to constitute yourself a parishioner, and make you feel national) you can cry with Macgregor, " My foot is on its native heath!" for you will be knee-deep in heather; and if you continue your hill-

climb for about a quarter of an hour, you will find
yourself some fifteen hundred feet above the level of
the sea, and looking over the lovely Isle of Arran, and
up to distant Ben Lomond. Facing round, you will
see the Atlantic waves on the farther side of the southern group of the Highland Archipelago; and if you
want a pleasant excursion on a calm day, you can boat
over to Gigha, and Cara, and on to Islay or Jura or
Colonsay; or you might even go over to the Irish coast,
and visit the Giant's Causeway.

What more could be required by the fastidious
visitor or daring speculator; if only this "very eligible
spot" was not quite so far distant? But if the day
should ever come, when tourists, having exhausted all
other spots in Great Britain, should turn towards
Cantire, I think that it would not require much of the
prophetic power of Scotch second sight to foresee the
realisation of my Highland watering-place—at present
situated in cloud-land—and to predict that Muasdale
would make itself a name, and be found a fashionable
quarter.

But let us now leave this ideal Muasdale, with its
aëry, sunset-facing crescents, rising like tiers in an
amphitheatre on the sharp hill-sides, and let us pass on
to the real Muasdale. First in position, as well as importance, is the Manse of Killean, a large well-built
house, erected in 1803, on a low projecting headland at

the crescent's verge, and standing so close to the sea, that the waves, in rough weather, fling their spray against its white face. A cluster of trees behind it assist in screening extensive outbuildings; there is a paddock in which are some sheep and poultry, flanked by the carriage-drive, up and down which a peacock is proudly strutting. On the other side of the paddock is a walled enclosure,—the Manse garden, — where (as Wordsworth says)—

> " The good priest, who, faithful through all hours
>   To his high charge, and truly serving God,
> Has yet a heart and hand for trees and flowers,
>   Enjoys the walks his predecessors trod,
> Nor covets lineal rights in lands and towers." *

Such is the Manse of Killean, — a type of the better class of residences provided for the Clergy of the Church of Scotland, and to be distinguished from that class of Manse mentioned in Dean Ramsay's *Reminiscences*, where a Scotch pastor, who has been introduced to a little closet, asks if it is meant for his bed-room; " 'Deed ay, Sir," is the answer, " this is the prophet's chammer." Whereupon says the pastor, " It maun be for the *minor* prophets then."

The present Minister of Killean is the Rev. Duncan Macfarlane, who is much respected for his worth and attainments, and to whom I (and my readers) are

* Memorials of a Tour in Scotland, 1831, vol. iv.

indebted for valuable information most kindly communicated, and here gratefully acknowledged.*

Following the high-road along the sea-shore, and passing the Manse, and commencing with the second of the two Muasdale crescents, we come upon a great heather-tufted grey boulder, standing upon the roadside to our left, whose shelter and support have been picturesquely adapted to the requirements of a fisherman's cottage. Then we come to Muasdale itself, a fishing village, down by the shore, on the level between the sea and the cliffs, and like Barr and all other Cantire villages, in having one street of outwardly-whitewashed and inwardly-dirty cottages, one storey high, and thatched with heather—with two superior houses for the inn and the shop; and yet with an exception to prove the rule, for that tall chimney which has already caught your eye, and those lines of sheds (now shut up and deserted) pertain to a manufactory. It was a Farina Mill, erected for the manufacture of starch from potatoes; a process, which, as it would appear, proved as successful as the extraction of sunbeams from cucumbers. It proved a total failure —

* The Rev. D. Macdonald, in the "Statistical Account" of the parish, mentions as a portion of the minister's stipend, " 7 chalders, 2 firlots, 2 lippies bear; 14 bolls, 1 firlot, 3 pecks, 2 lippies meal, Kintyre measure ;" which statement will, I trust, be more intelligible to the reader than it is to the author. The stipend is elsewhere given as 178*l.* 9*s.*, besides the house and glebe.

unfortunately for the people of the district, to many of whom it would have afforded a livelihood.

Not so, with the inn; it still flourishes, as it did in the days when it was supported by the fourteen farmers of Muasdale. These gentlemen (says the local legend) were boon companions fond of each other and fonder still of whiskey; and their mutual affection and likings induced them to be frequently in each others company, tasting " the barley bree " until " the cock did craw, and the day did daw." Now, Campbelton Fair was an annual festival to them. They went to it in a body, transacted their business and pleasures, and then rode back together to Muasdale with fourteen horse power. Once when they had set out from Campbelton on their homeward journey, the fourteen farmers of Muasdale drew themselves up in a staggering row outside the town, while one of their number endeavoured to count the party, to see if they had their full complement. He counted thirteen ; and then, having " just a drappie in his ee'," could not see that he himself was the fourteenth. He tried again, with the like ill success; he could only make out thirteen. When the negro had to count the pigs, he was able to do so with all " 'cept one little pig; and he frisk about so, massa himself could'nt count him." And, perhaps, the fourteenth farmer staggered about too much, to permit himself to be counted. So another of the fourteen tried ; and he, likewise, was only able to count thirteen. Then, the fourteen farmers turned back to Campbelton to look for their missing friend. A man met them on their way, and asked them what they were coming back for. They told him that they had not their full number of fourteen. "Stand in a row," said the man, " and I will count you." He did so, and found their number correct. So the fourteen farmers turned their horses' heads towards Muasdale, and jogged home with great delight.*

* Compare this tale with an incident in "The Tale of Sgire mo chealag," in Mr. Campbell's "West Highland Tales" (vol. ii.), where the young lad "saw a boat going to fish, and there were twelve men counted going into the boat, and when she came to land there was within her but eleven men, and there was no knowing which one was lost, for the one who was counting was not counting himself at all. And he was beholding this. 'What reward would you give me if I should find you the man that is lost by you?' 'Thou shalt get any reward if thou wilt find the man,' said they. 'Sit there,' said he, 'beside each other.' And he seized a sharp rung of a stick, and he struck the first one a sharp stroke. 'Mind thou that thou wert in her' (the boat). He kept on striking them, till he had roused twelve men, and made them bleed on the grass. And though they were pounded and wounded it was no matter, they were pleased because the man who was lost was found; and after the payment they made a feast for the one who had found the man who was lost" (p. 376). Mr. Campbell also gives an Islay version of the story, in which the foregoing incident is converted into some labourers sheltering from a storm under a dyke. When the storm is over, they give as a reason for not getting up that their legs are so mingled together that they cannot recognise their own legs. The young lad is offered half a hundred marks if he can make them recognise

Conducted to the rear of the "wauking-mill" at
Muasdale, are a number of open wooden troughs,
placed on upright supports, at various heights from the
ground, which serve as the artificial conduits for the
water that flows down Clachaig glen. This beautiful
glen runs from west to east behind Muasdale village,
with many

"Runlets babbling down the glen,"

and falling into its chief stream, which rises in the
lochs of Dirigadale and Dubhlochan high up among
the hills, and passing by Crubasdale, discharges its
waters into the Atlantic at the back of the "wauking-
mill" and the further end of Muasdale Village. It is
a mountain stream that almost approaches in dignity
to a river, and possesses the same characteristics as
Barr river.

There is a legend told of this river and Clachaig
glen, which runs thus: — About a century ago, there
lived in this glen a man named Beith. He was a pious
and intelligent man, but was frequently troubled by
the arch-fiend, who appeared before him in terrible
shapes. One night when Beith was returning home,
he was going up the glen by the side of the river, with
the intent to cross it at a safe and narrow place high

their own legs. He cuts a long and strong bramble, and gave them "a
good tight raking about their legs, and it was not long till every one
knew his own legs" (p. 387).

o 3

up towards Dubhlochan; and had come to a place where it was wide and dangerous, with steep and rugged rocks on either side, when to his surprise, he perceived that an elegant bridge had been thrown over the river. He was about joyfully to set foot upon it, when the thought that it was an invention of his dire enemy the Evil-one to entice him to his destruction, fortunately arrested his progress. Beith dropped upon his knees and uttered a fervent prayer; when, immediately, the bridge disappeared with a tremendous noise, as if ten thousand iron chains had rattled down the glen; and Beith, preserved from death, went thankfully on his way home, feeling more than ever convinced that the devil's power must be resisted by faith and prayer.

When we have passed through Muasdale village, the Clachaig river makes its appearance from a narrow tortuous glen, whose rocks on either side rise precipitously to a height of some two hundred feet, and then fall back only to seek higher elevations. Out of the eternal shade of this picturesque defile dashes the silvery torrent, broken into multitudinous sparkles by the rough boulders of its mountain-bed, and hurrying onwards to the sea by leaps down a succession of rocky shelves and stairs. It is crossed — as soon as you have passed through the village, and not twenty yards from the sea — by two bridges, placed side by side, and not

CLACHAIG GLEN, MUASDALE, CANTIRE.

more than two or three yards apart. The further one is the old and disused bridge, built with very low parapets and rising to an acute angle over the centre arch, — just such a bridge as we see in Wales. The new bridge, which has also very low parapets, takes the road at the level; and against it on either side of the stream towards the sea, are two large masses of rock so fashioned that they would appear to have been placed there by design. Not so, however, for they are the natural ramparts of the bridge, and are only noteworthy from their position; there are rocks that, in themselves, are more worthy of observation, a few yards further on the road. These are their _avant-couriers_.

An idea of the outlines of this scene, — these rocks, the dashing river, the two bridges, the glen and its precipitous walls, the troughs for the " wauking-mill," the strips of greensward on each side the stream where the Muasdale women bleach their linen,—all this may be gathered from my sketch, but an idea of the outlines of the scene only. The real beauty of the scene, and all its varied colouring of rock and herbage, must be left to the imagination. In cases such as this, where by any imaginative art dry bones have to be dressed into a goodly shape, the reader has a task to perform not unlike to that which is often required from the artist of an illustrated newspaper. A great battle, a dreadful shipwreck, or some equally important event, has happened at some spot where there is no special artist of the paper to depict the troops as they appeared in the moment of victory, or the hapless ship at that precise point of time when it sank with every soul on board; but some one who has certain safe data to go upon, bethinks himself of the picture-paper; and, with intentions that rise superior to his performance, strives to make his amateur pencil depict the scene—of battle, let us say. He achieves this something in the following way : He puts down a few scratches, and writes underneath, "150th Regt. advancing:" then a few more hurried scratches in another direction with the legend, "natives in retreat." A large blot does duty for "Begum on an elephant," a series of dots for "village in flames," and a horizontal zigzag for "the Brandicherri Hills."

From these rude helps an ingenious artist, accustomed to the work, will contrive to manufacture a very effective and dashing picture, which, if only the costumes be tolerably correct, and there be plenty of smoke, will be as efficient a representation of a battle as any reasonable person could look for.

That "plenty of smoke," indeed, may be accepted as a leading formula in depicting any of the battles of life. Behind its friendly screen those actions that possibly might not bear the blaze of broad sunshine, can, by imagination's aid, be transfigured to deeds of daring heroism. If our actions can only be enveloped in "plenty of smoke," they will loom twice as big, and distinction may be achieved at half-price. The painter of tea-trays could not have afforded to supply the Battle of Waterloo at one shilling each, thirteen to the dozen, if he had not stencilled his figures through punctured forms, and then, with a liberal brush, thrown in plenty of smoke. Those misty wreaths afforded evidence of the hotness of the conflict, and testified to the courage of the brave General whose cocked hat surged above the sea of gunpowder.

As I began this chapter in the clouds, it may be here appropriately terminated in smoke.

CHAP. XXVIII.

KILLEAN — A SCOTCH KIRK AND SABBATH.

A romantic and unexpected Road. — Fisherman's Wife. — Detached Rocks. — Their Beauty and Geology. — Legends anent them. — Vitrified Fort. — A botanical Witness to Man. — Nature's Testimony to human Vices. — Weeds follow the Steps of Man. — The Shore. — Killean Free Church. — The Village. — Killean Church. — A faithful Minister. — St. Killian. — The Presbyterian Service. — Liberty of Conscience. — Hymnology and Singing — Objections to Organs. — Sir Walter Scott's Opinion. — Presbyterian "Simplicity." — Reality and acting. — Scotch Liturgy. — Standing in Prayer. — Ancient Customs. — The revival Movement in Cantire. — A Gaelic open-air Service. — Its Characteristics. — The Covenanters.

FROM Muasdale and the bridges over the outlet of Clachaig Glen, the high road winds among some detached rocks to Killean, about half a mile distant. Macculloch, as I have before said, scarcely makes mention of the country between Machrihanish Bay and Loch Tarbert, although he speaks of the "very amusing road, conducted nearly the whole way on the margin of the water, which affords in itself some pleasing scenes, besides the fine maritime views which it presents of the channel of Jura, and of that of Gigha, terminated by the long outline of Jura and Islay, in which the Paps form a predominant and beautiful feature. In a summer evening, and with a calm sea, a more engaging ride for ten or fifteen miles cannot well be imagined." He then adds, "About Ballochanty, and near Killean, where the road winds among some detached rocks, this road is particularly romantic as well as unexpected." *

"In the centre of the parish," says the Rev. D. Macdonald, "and in the immediate neighbourhood of the sea, an aggregate of pyramidical rocks occurs, from which the ocean has evidently receded. In the fissures of these rocks, several acres beyond the sea-mark, quarriers have frequently dug out fossil bivalved shell-fish, of a species not now to be found along the coast of the parish, but abundant in Loch Tarbert, and the eastern shores of the peninsula." (Query, Oysters ?)

This portion of the road well bears out Macculloch's praise : it is "particularly romantic, as well as unexpected;" we come upon it suddenly after passing through Muasdale Village, where the road winds round the spur of the cliff at the entrance of Clachaig Glen. Midway between this spot and Killean is a fisherman's cottage, between the road and the sea-shore. Here is the fisherman's wife, in her white cap and blue dress,

* Highlands and Western Isles, vol. ii. pp. 83, 84.

plodding along barefoot with her baby at her back, and
another bairn at her heels. There is a strip of potato-
ground between the high-road and the beach, and a
level wheat-field between the road and the cliffs.   The

BETWEEN MUASDALE AND KILLEAN.

detached rocks are scattered on either side of the road,
between this woman's cottage and Killean; and they
form a most remarkable as well as beautiful feature.   I
have denoted them in this, and in other sketches; but

it would be useless to do more, without bringing in the aid of colour,—and even then, very large dimensions would be required to give anything like an adequate idea of their beauty. They are similar in their character and the richness of their floral charms to those Titanic nine-pins that we saw on the shore below Glencreggan, and of which we have since met with isolated specimens. But here, there are forty or fifty (or it may be more — for I did not count them,) congregated on a more open plain, but still in a limited area; and the greater portion of them of much greater size than those on the Glencreggan shore. Some of them must have been fifty or sixty feet high, and of about the same diameter at their base. Mere black and white could not convey to the reader's mind an idea of their glorious medley of colours. They are of most picturesque forms; and like the Glencreggan rocks are covered with lichens, and wild-flowers, and heather. In my ideal Muasdale, they would form a chief attraction to the visitors, and would be within five minutes' walk from their aëry crescents.

I have already quoted from Hugh Miller on the geological character of these detached rocks found in more than one place along the coast of Scotland. Elsewhere*, he speaks of their picturesqueness, thus :—" It is formed

* Rambles of a Geologist, pp. 362 363. See Appendix, " Geology of Cantire."

exactly of such cliffs as the landscape gardener would make if he could,—cliffs with their rude prominent pebbles breaking the light over every square foot of surface, and furnishing footing by their innumerable projections to many a green tuft of moss and many a sweet little flower. Some of the masses too, that have rolled down from the precipices and stand up like the ruins of cottages, are of singular beauty—worth all the imitation-ruins ever erected, and obnoxious to none of the disparaging associations which the mere show and make-believe of the artificial are sure to awaken."

The Cantire Highlanders regard these detached rocks as so many erections by the hands of man; and have various hypothetical legends to account for their frequency. Some think them to have been rude Druidical altars, on which human sacrifices were offered; but the prevailing opinion (as in the case of this large group of rocks between Muasdale and Killean) is, that a great battle was once fought upon the spot, and that the rocks are the rude monuments erected to commemorate the conflict and the heroes who are buried beneath them. This belief may have been strengthened by the frequency of the vitrified forts on the Cantire coast, some of which are in this neighbourhood.

"An ancient chapel," says Macculloch (speaking of the old Church of Killean) "with coupled circular-

headed windows, will here attract the antiquary's notice. But as I cannot afford to detail all these
particulars, I shall only notice that there is a vitrified
fort here," — which is one of thirty-three, of which he
gives a list. It is marked out, not only by its luxuriance of vegetation — which is accounted for, by the
hill-forts also having been hill-folds, — but also by the
rankness of the weeds, and thistles, and nettles — a
botanical witness that man had once a dwelling on this
spot. A most trustworthy and delightful author has
made the following interesting observations on this
subject, which may be here quoted with advantage.
He has been speaking of that lovely dingle, called
" Nightingale's Bower," at Old Storridge *, on the
Herefordshire confines of Worcestershire, which was
the scene of a disastrous flood in the autumn of 1852,
that swept away " the Bower " cottage, and its inmates.
" On the heap of stones that formerly helped to sustain
the cottage-roof, a monstrous rank growth of weeds
now malignantly flourish; for singularly enough, as if
to symbolise the crimes or woes attached to human
nature, none but the vilest plants take up their residence, where man has once dwelt or been located :

---

* The name is supposed to be ancient British, from the Chaldaic
Tar, or *Tor*, a fire-tower. The summit of Old Storridge Hill is pointed
out as the scene of St. Augustine's conference. For various opinions
and testimonies on this point, see Allies's " Antiquities and Folk-lore
of Worcestershire," p. 205.

" ' The old grey abbey lies in ruins now:
    Where once the altar rose, rank nettles grow.'

" So here, amid the ruins of an uptorn hearth, were congregated great nauseous burdocks, dense masses of prickly thistles, thick clusters of stinging nettles, made still more hideous by being hung with heaps of black spinous caterpillars, and enormous plants of poisonous hemlock, that rose above eight feet in height.   One of these, large as a hazel-bush, was truly a botanical curiosity; for it had more than eighteen branching stems radiating from the same root.   Who could forbear moralising upon such a spectacle?   For still, as of old, thorns and thistles soon cover the ruins of man's habitations; and, however much Nature may adorn solitary spots of her own selection, she refuses to throw any but the rankest and most lurid plants where the ground has been contaminated by human vices.   So prophesied Isaiah of the structures of Idumæa—'Thorns shall come up in her palaces, nettles and brambles in the fortresses thereof;' and how often are we reminded in the present day, of where some dwelling or garden has formerly been, by the nettles, thistles, or wormwood that almost choke the spot. This appears to be the case generally in the world; for either weeds delight to dog the footsteps of man, go wherever he will; or the turning up of the soil, and the manure left there, unfits it for the old flowers of the country, but makes a pabulum for rank strangers, which they quickly take advantage of. Thus, North America has become a garden for English weeds; and Professor Buckman told me that he saw them among the back-woods of Ohio, wherever the ground was up-turned. Schleiden says, that Russian steppes are peculiarly fertile in weeds called " Burian " wherever cultivation has loosened the soil. They rise, he says, to an incredible height; and " these thistles, as in the Pampas of Buenos Ayres, distinguish themselves by acquiring a size, a development, and ramification, which is truly marvellous."*

Leaving that remarkable and highly picturesque group of rocks, let us go down to the beach, and follow the crescent shore towards that low projecting headland on which stands Killean Church, similarly situated to the Manse, its dark stone walls washed by the spray of the Atlantic. Let us rest awhile here, on this great shiny stone, while I sketch the view. There is a natural cup of water in the sand at my feet, within easy reach of the brush by a Rob Roy arm; and though the water is very brackish, yet, as it leaves some of its shiny salt particles upon the paper, it is of use in imparting to the pictured representation of the beach, that glistening effect produced by the sun-rays on wet

---

* "Pictures of Nature around Malvern," by Edwin Lees, F.L.S., pp. 210, 211. See also " Rambles of a Geologist," pp. 364, 365.

sand. The beach is rough, with great boulders of trap and red-sandstone; the breakers come in with "thunderous fullness" on our left; to our right are Tennysonian "thymy promontories." There are the purple Paps of Jura rising ruggedly from above the low line of Gigha; and still further in the dim distance, the shadowy shoulders of Ben More. The blue hills stretch grandly to the right, growing stronger in colour, as they sweep round the bay in the middle distance, and are then lost behind the hill near to us, on whose verge, and not two hundred yards distant from the Established Church (which is upon the sea-shore) stands the " Free Church" of Killean. It is a building of some pretensions—red brick with stone dressings, with a turreted tower and a lean-to on either side. Interiorly it is a large parallelogram, lighted from either side, with the pulpit and precentor's desk in the centre of the further wall. The body of the church (which is without galleries) is filled up with four ranges of seats, on a flooring that rises slightly towards the entrance end,—an arrangement which permits the congregation who sit furthest from their minister, not only to have a good view of him, but of their fellow-worshippers also. This Church was built at the time of the secession, by subscriptions and collections in the district and throughout the country. The Minister's Manse — facing to the west, and commanding a most glorious view — stands to

KILLEAN. CANTIRE.

the right of the Church; to the left are spacious schools.
Like the Church, the schools are built of red brick;
and in this respect differ from the Manse and all the
other houses and cottages in the district, which are invariably white—though they do not, like the Welsh,
whitewash the outside of the roofs.

We come down from this Church by the side of a
tumbling torrent, where we shall probably find some
bare-legged lassies washing linen. By the road-side is
a row of miserable cottages, which is indeed the Village
of Killean—though the united parish of Killean and
Kilchenzie is very extensive, containing an area of 81
square miles (or 51,840 acres *, of which not more than
a ninth part are arable) and several hamlets, among
which are Barr, Glenereggan, and Muasdale. Passing
these and going on towards the shore, the dark stone
walls of Killean Church rise before us. It was once
called Liananmore. The remains of its predecessor
still exist, and may be seen a little further on the road,
towards Tayinloan.† Its round-headed windows have
been already mentioned by Macculloch. They are not
so rude as in other ancient examples in Cantire, and a
double-light in the eastern wall has mouldings with
the tooth ornament. The walls, with the exception of

---

* So says the "Statistical Survey." Fullerton's "Gazetteer" makes
the area to be "26,250 Scots acres."

† See Appendix, "Ecclesiology of Cantire."

the west, are still standing; and a small chapel or
vestry remains on the north side of the chancel. The
Church is said to have been thatched with heather.
Divine service was performed in it about a century ago,
when a Mr. M'Lean was the minister; of whom it is
said that he was a man of excellent character, pious
and faithful, and was instrumental in bringing about a
great reform in the parish with regard to church dis-
cipline. Macdonald, the laird of Largie, being found
guilty of some delinquency, was obliged to suffer a
public rebuke before the congregation on the Sabbath-
day. After the service, the laird said to Mr. M'Lean,
"You have been very severe on me to-day." The
minister answered, "Not more severe than you deserved."

Many of the Macdonalds of Largie are buried in
the churchyard, which is very crowded, for this was the
parish church of Killean. The burial ground is surrounded by a small stream, which (according to one
etymologist) gave the name to the parish, *Cil*, a church,
and *Abhainn*, a river. But Killean more probably derives its name from St. Killian, who, in the latter end
of the seventh century, travelled from Scotland, the
place of his nativity, and preached the gospel with such
success among the Eastern Franks, that he converted
vast numbers of them from Paganism to Christianity.
The modern church (the one down upon the sea-shore,

shown in my sketch) was built in the year 1788, and is
in the style of architecture that might be expected
from that unecclesiological era. It contains galleries.
There is a tablet commemorative of Colonel Macalister,
uncle to the present owner of Glenbarr Abbey, who
served in India, and was drowned on his way home in
the ship *Ocean*. He left 1000*l.* to the poor of the
parish of Killean, and is buried in the burial-ground
of Paiten, which we passed on our road from Kilchenzie to Glenbarr. The minister of Killean has to do
alternate duty at Killean and Kilchenzie.

To one who has been brought up in the Church of
England, and accustomed to the privilege of her established liturgy, the Presbyterian form of worship must
surely seem altogether deficient in a congregational
tone.* Everything in that system of worship is left to
the minister, who, apparently, has full licence to offer
up any forms of prayer that he may think fit, and the
congregation can be no more said to join in his prayers,
than they do in his sermon. If they have the ability,
the wakefulness, or the desire to follow him with tolerable readiness and attention, they can give their silent
assent to the prayers he offers up before them — if he
can express himself coherently, and in a manner

* Perhaps this opinion will be assigned to that "Swing of the Pen-
dulum" described in "The Recreations of a Country Parson," second
series, pp. 255. 276.

adapted to their comprehension; but that is all that can be done on either side. The congregation are no fellow-worshippers *with* their minister, but are as completely under his control and guidance as if they were a congregation of Romanists, and he their priest. It is singular how extremes meet, but it is so here. That " liberty of conscience," of which the Presbyterians make such boast, is no more liberty than is the spiritual bondage of the Romanist. In both cases, the minister does everything, and the layman nothing; for the only part that the Scotch Presbyterian can take in the service of his church, is to join in hymns of terribly human composition, that are not even up to our Tate and Brady standard. They are not fellow-worshippers with their minister, or rather with the rest of the congregation (for the minister will most probably sit down during the hymn, and take no part in it) until the hymn is given out and the precentor leads off with a prolonged nasal howl, or if it be a fashionable city church, until the verses of the hymn are rendered with operatic care by some twelve to twenty men and women ranged on a railed platform in front of the pulpit. Then the tongues of the congregation are loosed, and they endeavour to atone for their enforced silence, by singing which is truly earnest and thoroughly congregational. The singing is unaccompanied even by Nebuchadnezzar instruments, and the notes of the organ are unknown *, the Scotch Presbyterians having a very remarkable objection to any musical instrument in a place of worship. The English church at Glasgow is derisively called "The Whistling Kirk," from its possession of an organ; and a Presbyterian minister in Arran, was compelled by his parishioners to part with his piano-forte; a "whistling manse" being, it must be presumed, next akin to a "whistling kirk." †

Sir Walter Scott makes Frank Osbaldistone say, with regard to this subject, " I had heard the service of high mass in France, celebrated with all the *éclat* which the choicest music, the richest dresses, the most imposing ceremonies, could confer on it, yet it fell short in effect of the simplicity of the Presbyterian worship. The devotion in which everyone took a share, seemed so superior to that which was recited by musicians, as a lesson which they had learned by rote, that it gave the Scottish worship all the advantage of reality over acting." ‡ This however seems to me to be a most unfair way of putting the case. That "devotion" should be "recited by musicians as a lesson," is, to begin with, rather a puzzling statement. But what essential difference can there possibly be in congregational psalmody

* Pennant says: "There is no music either in this or any other of the Scotch churches, for *Peg* still faints at the sound of an organ." — *Scotland*, p. 49.

† Lord Teignmouth's "Scotland," vol. ii. p. 398.

‡ Rob Roy, vol. ii. p. 31.

being led by paid assistants, whether they be nasal-droning precentors, or smart young women (in the best dresses, smartest bonnets, and newest fashions that their means will command) perched with an equal number of the male sex, in the most conspicuous part of the kirk,— or by choristers in " the richest dresses ?" In any case, the real " devotion " has nothing whatever to do with the singers or their dresses, and Presbyterian " simplicity," if it means anything at all, means a pre-posterous and persistent objection to the human voice being accompanied by an instrument. Out here in the Highland wilds, the " simplicity " is truly great, from the force of circumstances, but in Glasgow or Edinburgh the " simplicity " vanishes in the engagement of the best singers that the means of the congregation will afford.

Unaccompanied psalmody, when well sung, is always impressive, more especially when heartily joined in by the congregation, as our Cathedral special services can testify. Fourteen years ago this was tried on a larger scale, and with the greatest success, in Durham Ca-thedral; where on Wednesday afternoon the organ was silent, and the service, and chants, and anthem were unaccompanied. From the skill of the choir the effect was very beautiful, — although they were paid " mu-sicians," and had " learned by rote " what they sang,— and the congregation, *being well led*, were able to join in the singing with as much ease as they would have done if the voices of the singers had been accompanied by the organ, and the service and chants rendered "with all the *éclat* which choicest music could confer upon them." But why unaccompanied singing should necessarily be "reality" and not "acting," I cannot see. Outward "simplicity"—where it is not of that stupidly ignorant class which (for example) would object to an organ in a place of worship—is very often but a quaker assumption, and the cloak for a much lower form of pretension than mere acting. As the Scotch Presbyterians have already taken one leaf out of the Romanists' book in the passive manner in which they surrender their service to their minister, they would greatly improve that service by borrowing from the Romanists a slight infusion of that *éclat* of choicest music, "learned by rote," which their great novelist has condemned as "acting." The unaccompanied psalmody of a kirk in the Highland wilds gains simplicity at the expense of melody, and is only flattered by being called singing.

The non-reading of the Scriptures was another point in the kirk service which struck me as being "conspicuous by its absence." The only portion of the Bible read to the congregation was the minister's text. Here, again, the inferiority of the service to that of the English Church is manifestly apparent; and this, together with its lack of a liturgy, are important points, in which the modern Presbyterians have sadly degenerated : for the custom appears to be but a modern one, as the early Scotch reformers *had* a liturgy, which (like our own) included the public reading of the Word of God.*

One of their customs may seem to us to be curious: they stand at prayer, and sit during the singing of hymns. In the early Latin Church, the preacher (after the custom of the Jewish synagogue) used to sit, while the congregation stood, but then the sermon was only about ten minutes long. The Presbyterian peculiarity of standing in prayer has, however, the sanction of antiquity, and may even be traced to apostolic times. For in the early Church from the time of the Apostles, while kneeling was considered the proper posture for prayer during the six days of the week, it was considered most fitting for the congregation to *stand* in prayer on the Lord's days, and also on the fifty days between Easter and Whitsunday. This was in memory of our Saviour's resurrection; " for," says Justin Martyr, " the kneeling in prayer being symbolical of our fall in sin, the standing is a significant symbol of our rising again from

---

* I here speak from my own experience, which was not confined to Cantire, but extended farther afield. But I am told by one of their ministers, that a chapter in the Bible *ought* to be read in the kirk services, and that he always does so in the Gaelic service, and usually reads a *portion* of a chapter in the English service. At any rate, so far as my personal experience went, and so far as I have been able to ascertain from others, the *rule* is as I have stated it.

that fall." Other early writers make the kneeling as symbolical of repentance and mourning, but all unite in ascribing the standing posture during prayer as a token of joy in the resurrection of Christ. And this practice was sanctioned and decreed by the Council of Nice, and can be traced up to the seventh century; so that the Scotch Presbyterian form, strange as it may seem to a member of the Church of England, has at any rate the sanction of Apostolic custom and the first six centuries of the Church. Perhaps the ultra High-Churchmen who dwell so strongly on the precedent of those early times, will abrogate the Prayer-book rubrics in favour of this custom of the early Fathers and Apostolic days. But no sanction can be derived from those times for the Scotch custom of sitting while the praises of God are sung.

When the service has come to an end, a great proportion of the men will be seen to at once cover their heads as they rise to leave the building; and, if the long-handled box has not already been brought round, there will be found in the porch of the church a dish for the reception of alms. This is done every Sunday, and is another apostolic custom followed by the Presbyterian Church,—a custom which the Church of England has here and there restored with great benefit to herself and members, — the small contributions to the weekly offertory swelling into a goodly aggregate, that

suffices for the educational and other needs of the
parish. As soon as the one congregation has poured
out of the church, another pours in, — for there are two
services, in Gaelic and in English,—and as the minister
has not ten minutes rest between them, he must be
well nigh exhausted when the second service is over.
This, however, does not terminate his labours for the
day; and he frequently, in the summer season, walks
some miles to give a third service, either out of doors
or at a school-house. In this way services had been
given by the Rev. D. Macfarlane in the school-room at
Barr.

Here also (in the Barr school-room), many special
services were held during the week, commencing just
after our departure from the neighbourhood, in connection with the Revival movement, that course of religious reaction which (as has been observed) " follows
the direction of the gulf-stream, setting from the New
World towards the western and northern coasts of the
British Isles." This connection between the gulf-stream
and religious reaction was exemplified in Cantire. The
scenes and phenomena that attended the meetings at
Barr were as extraordinary as in other places.* The

---

* Lord Teignmouth, in speaking of the religious habits of the Arran
people, tells us that they considered some external bodily sign or con-
vulsive emotion as a necessary token of true repentance. When a
woman had fallen into convulsions while listening to one of their

people flocked from a distance to the spot in greater numbers than the room would hold, and the windows were broken by those standing on the outside, in their anxiety to hear the preaching and prayers. Many of the congregation came from so great a distance, that by the time they had got back home, after the conclusion of the night's service, it was the hour for them to commence their day's work. Yet the physical difficulties under which they must thus have struggled did not prevent them from again and again attending the meetings; and this (as I was told) without neglecting their occupations, although "they went about their work as though they were scared." The weekly meetings in the Barr school-room were continued all through the winter, and till late in the spring, and were then abandoned for Sunday-night meetings, which were well attended. During the summer the minister of the parish, who took an important part in the Revival movement, informed me (with regard to Killean parish) that "it has produced saving, and I believe permanent, good to and in many. There is a thirst for religious knowledge, and an attendance on ordinances, greater and better than was formerly the case." But when the harvest was past and the summer ended, the majority

preachers, he "is said to have coolly observed, after they had ceased, 'Poor thing! what a struggle she had with the devil.'" — *Scotland*, p. 398.

had returned to their old ways; and in a letter that I received, it is written : " You will be sorry to hear that the good of last year's revival has nearly disappeared, and that whiskey-drinking is as bad as ever."

The " Revival " was general throughout Cantire. At Campbelton it created an extraordinary sensation during the whole of the winter, accounts of which appeared from time to time in the English newspapers, and need not be further referred to here ; nor was I witness to any of the scenes, as I had left Cantire before the movement had well begun.

I was, however, an accidental witness to a novel and very impressive open-air service at Barr, given by the minister of the free-church at Killean, on a Sunday evening, chiefly for the benefit of those who were unable to attend his (or any other) church. His preaching was in Gaelic, and therefore was altogether a dead letter to me. It was given *ore rotundo*, with great energy and action, and engaged the devout attention of his hearers. The spot in which they were assembled, was a field to the rear of the village, where the ground sloped towards the sea and river. They sat before the preacher upon the green grass, rising in so many tiers with the rise of the hill side, and picturesquely grouped. In front was a row of old crones muffled in plaids, with their white mutches tied down by a black ribbon, and their parchment faces wrinkled and seamed by age and exposure. Among the women, the long blue cloaks like bathing gowns, with thick woollen petticoats of dark blue, or red and black stripes, predominated. A few of the lassies wore

OPEN-AIR PREACHING IN CANTIRE.

their pretty loose jackets of light pink, but had no other covering for their heads than their own vails of hair. Their elders had nothing more than a cap, or a plaid wrapped nun-like round their heads to protect

them from the sharp evening air. The only bonnet
wearers were the men who wore "the blue bonnets"
of Scotland. Here and there was a plaid; and, though
tartans were sadly deficient, yet, altogether, there was
more of the Scotch element in the dresses than I had
seen on any other occasion : —

> " The preacher rose, and every voice grew still,
> Save echoing breezes round the lonely hill;
> With solemn awe he opes the blessed Book,
> Earnest in voice, and heavenly in his look ;
> While from his lips the soothing accents flow,
> To cheer his flock, and mitigate their woe." *

The minister sheltered by a few trees stood before
his congregation with an open Bible in his hand. The
sun was setting over the Atlantic, and flooding the
scene with a heavenly halo of golden light. The sea
was close at hand within sight and hearing, its
breakers rolling up on the shore with monotonous re-
gularity; and the only sounds to be heard beside the
preacher's voice, were the occasional plaintive cries of
the gulls, and the crow of the moor-fowl, mingled with
the deep diapason of the waves. The scene insensibly
carried back the thoughts to those days of the Covenanters, when

> " In solitudes like these,
> Thy persecuted children, Scotia, foil'd
> A tyrant's and a bigot's bloody laws."

---

* Weir's "Covenanter's Sabbath."

" Then rose the song, the loud
Acclaim of praise. The wheeling plover ceased
Her plaint ; the solitary place was glad ;
And on the distant cairn the watcher's ear
Caught doubtfully at times the breeze-borne note." *

" Those who have been in the brae country of Scotland (says Mr. Logan in his ' History of the Highlanders ') cannot forget the picturesque effect of the congregation of a kirk on Sunday, loitering in the churchyard till the commencement of worship, or moving along the mountain paths, the men in their varied tartans, and smartly cocked bonnets, the married women in their gaudy plaids and snow-white mutches or caps, the girls with their auburn hair neatly bound up in the snood." †

The next morning I made a coloured sketch of the scene from memory. When it was exhibited to some who had been among the congregation, they acknowledged its accuracy by believing it to have been an impossibility that the drawing should have been produced by an effort of memory; and they therefore remained under the impression that I must have had

* Grahame's " Sabbath."
† See also Pennant to the same effect. (" Tour in Scotland in 1771," p. 83.) From what he adds, and from what we learn from other sources, it would seem that the sarcastic reproofs in Burns' " Holy Fair " were richly deserved.

recourse to my pencil to "take them off," while their minister was preaching to them. So I fear that I left behind me a reputation for not keeping a Scotch Sabbath with Scotch strictness.

CHAP. XXIX.

LARGIE.

Bradge House. — Tayinloan Village. — The Pig of Cantire. — Largie
Castle. — The Macdonalds. — Proposal to shoot Largie with a Piece
of Silver. — Popular Tales and the Tellers of *Sgeulachdan*. — The
Fairies of Largie. — The Laird of Largie and the '45. — Another
Version. — Macdonald's Pipers. — A Highland Improvisatore. —
The learned Gentleman and MacMurchy. — The Story of the Laird
of Largie and the beggar Captain. — The Macdonald's Grants of
Property. — Model legal Documents. — The Hangman's Rock.

LEAVING Killean and its churches, we pass the farms
and groups of cottages, called respectively Beach-
menach and Tigha-chroman, and then come to the
ruined kirk and kirkyard of Killean, which we have
already noticed. To the right is Bradge House, a
modern mansion, the residence of Colonel Hall. We
are now abreast of the islands Cara and Gigha, which
are only separated from us by less than three miles of
waves. The geological character of the coast from here
to Tarbert has been thus given by the Rev. D. Macdonald—"Sandy bays and low rocky headlands, the
latter of which are frequently composed of red sand-

stone, alternating with pudding-stone, mica imbedded with veins of quartz, veins of basalt, and a few detached blocks of the same scattered along the shore,—whinstone, alternating with basalt, sandstone, and red shiver."

Nearly two miles beyond the ruined kirk of Killean, and seven from Glencreggan, is Tayinloan, from whence there is a ferry, and a post to Gigha. Tayinloan is a pretty village, imbedded in trees, like many a village in the heart of England. Its whitewashed village inn and post-office, backed by a mass of foliage, and the trout-stream overhung with trees, made a pretty sketch; but the most remarkable (though the least picturesque) object in the view (when I first looked upon it) was a pig! a veritable porker, who, stretched at full length on a couch of mud, *sub tegmine fagi*, was reposing in Sybarite fashion, and dreaming, doubtless, of grains and " histie-stibble." He is worthy of special mention, as being the only pig that I saw in the country; and to me, therefore, he was "*the* Pig of Cantire." He was in good condition " pinguem et nitidum," despite his muddy couch, and evidently

" Epicuri de grege porcum."

To the right of this village is Largie Castle *, the

* Not marked in Johnstone's large map. " Ballochayarran " is given in its place; but this was the ancient Gaelic name for the place

Cuthbert Bede, delt.

seat of the Hon. Augustus H. Macdonald Moreton.* The old castle of Largie was merely a fortified house, strong but plain in character, and of small size; and the little that remains of it forms a portion of a farm-house. The modern Largie Castle is of recent erection, and is a fair specimen of the nineteenth century repro-ductions of those baronial edifices erected in Scotland in the early part of the seventeenth century, wherein the characteristics of a French style predominated. Within, the Castle is arranged and fitted up in accord-ance with the comforts and luxuries of modern life. It is well situated in a finely-wooded park, containing timber of large growth. Since the commencement of the present century, the Largie plantations have been considerably increased, and are in a very flourishing state. The chief stream flows down to Tayinloan, through a lovely glen from Loch Ulagadale, and Loch nan Each. The poor upon the estate are well-cared for; and the charities of the various members of the

now known as Largie, in the same way that Ceann-an-loch was the ancient Gaelic name for the modern Campbelton. The word was spelt thus for me by a native of the place, Bealach-a-ghearran. The way Mr. Johnstone has spelt it gives the pronunciation.

* Second son of the first Earl Ducie; married Mary Jane, daughter of the late Sir C. Macdonald Lockhart, Bart., whose name he has assumed. (She died, 1851.) Educated at Merton College, Oxford. B. A., 1826. Is a member for county of Gloucester, and a M. and D. L. for county Argyle. Was M. P. for West, and afterwards for East Glouces-tershire, 1835–1841. See Walford's "County Families" for 1860.

family,—more especially of the late Mrs. Macdonald
Moreton, and of her mother, Lady Macdonald Lockhart,
have been considerable, and productive of much good.
The improvements upon the estate are advancing with
the spirit of the times, and its agricultural condition
has been greatly improved.

Mention has more than once been made in these
pages of the Macdonalds of Largie, who have always
been one of the first families of Cantire—so much so,
indeed, that it is said that Cantire proper was at one
time reckoned within the boundaries of their estate,
from Alt-nau-scunnach to Alt-a-bhile.   They were the
Macdonalds of Clan Ronald Bane ("the light or white-
haired"), and reigned despotically in Cantire, until their
power was crushed in 1591, by James the Sixth of Scotland, who banished Angus the reigning laird, and made
over all his possessions and authority to the family of
Argyle.   James Macdonald, Largie's heir — the then
rightful laird—escaped with difficulty.   The story that
is told of his escape is this: He was taken prisoner by
a troop of horse, and conveyed to Campbelton.   On the
road, one of the officers proposed to the captain that
they should halt and shoot "Largie" with a piece of
silver.   The captain would not accede to this; and
afterwards whispered to Largie that he would be invited
to dine with the officers at Campbelton, and would be
asked to sit near the head of the table; that he must

avoid doing so, and must take his seat as near to the
door as was possible; that he must watch his opportunity, and, when the officers had had pretty well of
wine, he must slip out of the room; and that at the
door he would find a bay mare with a knot in her
bridle. Largie took the Captain's advice, and all came
to pass in due order; he escaped from the room, found
the bay mare at the door, and galloped off, hotly pursued. He led his pursuers northwards, along the eastern
coast of Cantire, and by the time he had reached
Carradale they were distanced. Largie then left his
horse, and got on foot to the Largie Moors, where he
lay concealed for a fortnight, and then escaped to the
Western Islands; while Campbell of Inverawe took
possession of Largie. At the end of eleven years, when
the Duke of Argyle was beheaded, Largie was restored
to its former laird.*

At Saddell, at Dunaverty, and at Campbelton, we
have seen that the chief traditions and historical records were connected with the powerful clan of Macdonald; and I have already, in previous chapters,
related some of the popular tales connected with the
Macdonalds of Largie. But more remain to be told,

---

* Supposing this tradition to be correct, it would appear that the
other possessions of the Macdonalds at Cean-loch, Dunaverty, &c., were
not restored to them. See chap. viii.; see also Appendix, "The Macdonalds."

a circumstance not to be wondered at when the importance of the family is borne in mind, and when, in a country like that of Cantire and other old-world parts of the Western Highlands, a teller of stories, who is " good at sgeulachdan," is invested with a local interest and popularity, which cannot adequately be conceived by the civilised Englishman who reads his daily " Times " and subscribes to Mudie's. These narrators of popular legends and tellers of old stories, have orally handed down from generation to generation much that is valuable and interesting, and which cannot be obtained in any other way than from the lips of the reciters. They belong to a race now well-nigh extinct, and only to be found in such Western Highland districts as Cantire, where railroads and tourists are unknown and Gaelic has not succumbed to English.* Mr. J. F. Campbell has done a good work,

---

* They are capitally described in the introduction to Mr. Campbell's " Popular Tales," but at too great length to be quoted here. But his remarks on another branch of the subject must be made room for. " Surely Gaelic books containing sound information would be a vast boon to such a people. The young would read them, and the old would understand them. All would take a warmer interest in Canada and Australia, where strong arms and bold spirits are wanted, if they knew what these countries really are. If they heard more of European battles, and knew what a ship of war is now, there would be more soldiers and sailors from the Isles in the service of their country. At all events, the old spirit of popular romance is surely not an evil spirit to be exorcised, but rather a good genius to be controlled and directed. Surely

in rescuing from almost certain oblivion a goodly number of " Popular Tales of the West Highlands;" and although his published volumes contain but very slight references to Cantire, yet, as both he and his collectors are still at work, we may hope to be favoured with another instalment of these curious and interesting stories, in which the Cantire legends and "sgeulachdan" can have fuller justice done them than in the present work.

In the notes to his Islay tale of " The Smith and the Fairies," Mr. Campbell says, " Mr. John MacLean, Kilchamaig, Tarbert, Argyle, has sent me a version. The scene is laid on the Largie side of Cantire. The farmer's wife was idle, and called for the fairies, who wove a web for her and shouted for more work. She first set them to put each other out, and at last got rid of them by shouting 'Dunbhulaig on fire!' (This was the name of a farm, where the faries had a favourite haunt.) Their song when at work was, —

> ' Work, work, for a single hand
> Can but little work command,

---

stories in which a mother's blessing, well earned, leads to success, — in which the poor rise to be princes, and the weak and courageous overcome giants, in which wisdom excels brute force, — surely even such frivolities are better pastime than a solitary whiskey-bottle, or sleep, or grim silence ; for that seems the choice of amusements if tales are forbidden and Gaelic books are not provided for men who know no other language, and who, as men, must be amused now and then " (pp. 27, 28).

> Some to tease, and card, and spin ;
> Some to oil and weave begin ;
> Some the water for waulking heat,
> That we may her web complete.
> Work, work, for a single hand
> Can but little work command.'

And, when they departed in hot haste, their lament was,—

> 'My mould of cheese, my hammer, and anvil,
> My wife and child, and my butter crock ;
> My cow and my goat, and my little meal kist ;
> Och, och, ohone ! how wretched am I.' " *

So much for the Fairies of Largie. Turn we now to other popular tales and storied traditions connected with Largie and the Macdonalds.

In the " Forty-five," the then Laird of Largie was for going out. He was to join with other lairds in taking ship at Tarbert. The minister of Kilcalmonell invited him to spend the night at the manse, on his way to Tarbert, and by the over exercise of hospitality, contrived that Largie should be late in getting up the next morning. And so it happened, that when Largie arrived at Tarbert with his contingent, the fleet had sailed. Thus was the property of Largie saved in '45. Afterwards, Largie went to Paris, and gave grand entertainments to the Prince, whereby he got so much into debt, as to be obliged to sell a portion of his estates.

* Vol. ii. pp. 53, 54.

The foregoing was told to me by the present Laird of Largie, who also kindly put me in possession of the family legend touching that Largie, whom it was proposed to shoot with a piece of silver; but from another source I have the following version of the story :—

In the "Forty-five," the proprietors of Cantire raised their men against Prince Charles, but Macdonald of Largie declared for the Prince. Upon this, the Laird of Tarbert sent him word, that if he intended to join the Prince, he would meet him on his way in passing, and that they would have a hot day of it, and that few Macdonalds should remain to join any party. On this, the Laird of Largie thought fit to change his mind, so he sent his men with the rest of the men of Cantire. Macdonald had two pipers, MacMurchy and MacLeolan, who played alternately. When they reached Inverary, MacMurchy played "the Campbells are coming," in order to announce their approach. The Duke of Argyll was in company with other gentlemen at the time, and did not take any notice of the tune, but when Mac Murchy had finished, and MacLeolan struck up the air called "Fir Chinntyre," or "the Men of Cantire," the Duke immediately recognised it, and turning to those near him, said, "Come, gentlemen, we must go out and welcome the Cantire men." The Duke gave a grand ball to the Cantire men at Inverary, at which

Macdonald's pipers were present. The Duke himself danced "a high dance," to which MacLeolan was the piper. When the dance was ended, the Duke said to MacLeolan, "You are the sweetest player I ever heard, and you are the most ill-looking man I ever saw." MacLeolan replied, with a shrewd smile, "I think it was the same tailor that shaped us both." The Cantire men marched to Falkirk, but the battle was over before they reached it. They took refuge in a church, which was presently surrounded by some of the victorious Highlanders of Prince Charles's party. With their clothes crimsoned with blood, they burst into the church, with a cry that the Cantire men should be massacred; but their purpose was prevented by one of the Cantire men coming forward and saying, that it was against their inclination to fight against Prince Charles, but that they had been forced to do so by their lairds, and they begged to be leniently dealt with. Their request was granted, and after being detained as prisoners for some time, they were set at liberty, and returned to Cantire.

This MacMurchy, the piper of Largie, who had been sorely grieved at the Duke of Argyll passing over his playing, was accounted a very excellent poet. But that it did not require any very high powers of reflection, taste, or imagination, to constitute the poet of a clan, we may judge from the following Cantire legend of him. A learned gentleman, who was a poet, one day visited Largie in disguise, in order that he might test MacMurchy's powers. The piper received him kindly, and entertained him with some tunes, the while some scones of bread were being toasted at the fire. The learned gentleman and poet either did not consider this as an entertainment, or thought it a fit subject for his manufactured verse. So he jumped up, and making for the door, exclaimed, (or rather *declaimed*,)

> "Piobaireachd is aran tur,
> 'S miosa lem na guin a bhais,
> Fhir a bhodhair mo dha chluais,
> Na biodh agad duais gu brach."

which meant, "Piping and raw bread are worse to me than the pangs of death. O man, who hast dived both my ears, may you never get a reward!" MacMurchy, instead of losing his temper, and answering the stranger in prose that was more hearty than complimentary, dropped the pipe from his mouth, and immediately replied to him in this impromptu verse:—

> "Slad a dhuine fan ricial,
> 'S olc an sgial nach boin ri bun,
> Tha mo bhean a t-eachd on Chill,
> Is ultach d'on im uira muin."

which meant, "Stop, man, and give ear to reason! bad is the story that has no foundation. My wife is coming back from Chill, with a load of butter on her back."

The learned gentleman and poet found that MacMurchy was quite his match as an improvisatore, so he accepted the invitation, and waited till the gude wife came home. Then he eat of the buttered bannochs, and passed a very agreeable evening with the piper of Largie.

In a previous chapter * I had occasion to speak of the numerous vagrants who used to wander through the now depopulated Mull of Cantire, and, by the aid of their fiddles and tale-telling powers, maintained a sufficiently comfortable and prosperous existence. I have met with a popular story of a Cantire vagrant, which has a peculiarity and romance of its own, and which, from its connection with Largie, may be here told. It is the story of the Laird of Largie and the Beggar Captain.

A long time ago there was an Irish gentleman, tall, handsome, and strong, who traversed Cantire for years, sleeping chiefly in caves, and begging his way from house to house. He was insane, but quiet and peaceable. The tale told of the loss of his reason is a romantic one. He was an officer of high rank in the army, and had distinguished himself in battle. The war over, he returned to his native country, to the girl he had left behind him. They had been engaged for some time, and had sworn to be true to each other till death. Her father refused to give him her hand, so they eloped,

* Vol. i. chap. v.

but were overtaken in a deep glen by her relatives and
a body of armed men. The officer made a desperate
defence, protecting his bride with uncommon bravery;
but he was soon overpowered by numbers, and, in the
melée that ensued, an unfortunate stroke from his sword
pierced his bride's breast, and she fell dead. He no
longer attempted to defend himself, and was hurried
off to prison, where he was condemned to death. He
contrived, however, to make his escape, and fled across
the waters to Cantire; but his reason had sunk under
the shock, and for the remainder of his life he wandered
about these hills and dales a harmless fugitive, talking
to himself in those continental languages in which he
could pour forth the tale of his sufferings, with none to
understand his words, though with all to pity him.
His connection with Cantire is said to have been se-
vered thus: he had wandered to Largie, and, in search
of food, had approached Macdonald's house. The
illustrious chieftain, who was the then Laird of Largie,
was wont to devote his nights to whiskey, and, even
when he was alone, would have his importance denoted
by twelve lighted candles placed before him on the
table. The poor demented officer, attracted by the
genial light streaming out upon the darkness, made his
way to the window, and saw Macdonald seated before
a plentiful table. Clammed with hunger he made his
way into the room, and asked for food. Macdonald

seized his sword and ordered him away. The poor man replied that he did not come for any harm, but that he wanted some food ; and, as there was plenty on the table, Macdonald should feed the hungry. Macdonald's reply was a flourish with the sword. The poor gentleman parried the thrusts with his staff, and, being an expert swordsman, wrested the weapon out of Macdonald's hand. The chieftain, finding himself outmastered, invited his opponent to the table, plied him with whiskey, and, when the few poor senses that were left to him were overcome by the strong drink, Macdonald ordered his men to carry him away, and put him in a boat, and leave him at Kilberry. This was done, and the poor man was never afterwards seen in Cantire. What became of him is not known.

This Laird of Largie was a character as exceptional as unpleasant; for, in a general way, the Macdonalds were much celebrated for their hospitality and generosity. A night's lodging or a simple meal was often rewarded with the grant of a farm; that of Coul, in Islay, was presented to one who had given a flounder to a Macdonald when much exhausted. The grants of property from these Lords of the Isles were sufficiently laconic and unique; and, though divested of all legal jargon and circumlocution, were not on that account the less strong and expressive. The following are specimens, and are model legal documents for perspicuity and brevity, although in a great measure divested, by translation, of the spirit of the original : "I, Donald, chief of the Macdonalds, give here in my Castle to Mackay, a right to Kilmahumay, from this day till to-morrow, and so on for ever." "I, Macdonald, sitting upon Dundonald, give you a right to your farm, from this day till to-morrow, and every day thereafter, so long as you have food for the great Macdonald of the Isles." The saving clause in the latter charter is worthy of all imitation. Dundonald was a castle of the Macdonalds, a few miles north of Campbelton, on the western coast, annually visited by "the great Macdonald" when he collected his rents. Near to the castle was a cliff, still called *stac-a chrochaire*, "the Hangman's Rock," from which, doubtless, those who were behind-hand with rent or civility, were suspended with very little ceremony.

CHAP. XXX.

A CANTER THROUGH CANTIRE.

A wet Prospect. — The Glass low; Spirits ditto. — Proverbial Phila-
begs. — Fortune's Favourites. — On the Road. — Rhunahourine
Point. — Kilcalmonell Parish. — Clachan. — Dunskeig Hill. — Vitri-
fied Fort. — West Tarbert Loch. — Its Scenery. — And Patrick. —
The Land of the Campbells. — The King of Trees for the Painter. —
Ruskin and Turner. — Whitehouse. — Laggavoulin. — The Hill of
Love. — Tarbert. — An End at the Beginning.

TEWART'S open car from Tarbert has come to
Shedden's Inn, at Barr, the over night, in
readiness to carry us away from Glencreggan to Tarbert. The morning is wild
and stormy; there have been torrents of rain all through
the night; and the Atlantic, as far as can be seen, is a
troubled sea of waves crested with snowy breakers. At
breakfast time, everything looks as unpropitious as
possible for a twenty-six mile drive in an open car. An
umbrella would be torn to shreds in such a gale of wind;
and, though my wife can envelope herself in a water-
proof cloak, yet this protection does not ensure that
" perfect comfort in a storm " of which the advertise-

ments boast, when that storm is blowing off the Atlantic and must be braved for at least five hours. But
our car must return on that day to Tarbert, and the
inexorable programme of our engagements demands
that we should reach Glasgow by the next evening.
Rooms have been taken for us at Tarbert, and there is
nothing left for us but to prepare for the worst and to
resist all the temptations that are so kindly held out to
us to extend our stay at Glencreggan.

Old Rudd is consulted about the weather, so are the
Paps of Jura, so is the barometer, so are the peacocks'
screams. They one and all pronounce the weather to
be "varra coorse," but old Rudd's meteorological ex-
periences throw a gleam of hope over the prospect. His
prophetic eye can discover a glint o' the sun aboon;
though, for all that we can see, there is no prospect
that we shall discern those proverbial philabegs in the
sky to-day. The glass and our spirits are in harmony,
for both are very low; but pleasant visits must come
to an end, and portmanteaus must be packed, and we
must start on our way, although

> " It rains, and the wind is never weary."

But travellers in the Highlands must look for a little
"coorseness" in the weather, as a foil to the many
pleasures conferred by the natural beauties of the
scenery.

Twelve o'clock comes; Old Rudd is right! He has (probably) never studied Longfellow, so he does not come up to us about mid-day, and exclaim —

> " Be still sad heart! and cease repining;
> Behind the clouds is the sun still shining;"

but he expressively says, "Wha's richt noo?" and points to a break in the cloud, where there is sufficient blue sky wherewith to construct the proverbial philabegs. The rain has ceased; the wind gradually drops, and only delays until it has helped the hot sun to dry the roads; and, in an hour's time, by one of those sudden changes that occur in the West Highland weather, we have a glorious autumn day. Again do we find ourselves fortune's favourites.

It is half-past two; the last adieus have been made; the old Scotch toast " Happy to meet, sorry to part, but blithe to meet again," rises to our lips; and, as we trot down the hill by Ballachagbaochan Cave, Glencreggan is lost to sight. We pass our ideal watering-place at Muasdale — the Manse — the fishing village — the bridges over the river at the mouth of Clachaig glen — the winding road through the detached rocks — Killean and its two churches — Tayinloan Village and Largie Castle, where we reach the point beyond which I had not conducted the reader. I will therefore beg his (imaginary) company in the car, while I point out to him the most noticeable places between here and Tarbert, in this our " Canter through Cantire." It is a warm and sunny afternoon; the distant landscape is unusually sharp and clear after the storms of the morning; and it is the very day of all others for a long drive through a lovely and romantic country; for the scenery between Glencreggan and Tarbert is more varied and picturesque than that between Glencreggan and the Mull of Cantire; and, whatever differences of opinion there may be, as to the peculiar charm of the scenery of the Mull, there is an agreeable unanimity of sentiment regarding the enchanting shores of West Loch Tarbert.

Passing on from Largie and Tayinloan, we come to Killean mill, and then to the little village of Rhunahourine *, where a narrow neck of mossy land, about a mile in length, projects into the sea. Rhunahourine Point is the northern boundary of the parish of Killean and Kilchenzie; and we now enter upon the parish of Kilcalmonell, which extends from here sixteen miles to Tarbert, and which is united to the parish of Kilberry on the opposite shore of Loch Tarbert. " Kilcalmonell," says the Rev. J. M'Arthur, " rises sometimes with a gentle acclivity, at other times with greater abruptness, from the sea to its highest elevation.

* Thus spelt to me; elsewhere called Runahaorine, and (in Johnstone's large map) Runahuran.

The general altitude of the range of the hills in which it terminates on the south-east, does not exceed 1500 feet," a loftier range than the Malvern hills, "whilst the few valleys by which the uniformity of the acclivity is disturbed, rise not more than 100 or 150 feet above the level of the sea." Kilcalmonell, — in Gaelic *Cil-culman-culla* — signifies the burial-place of Malcolm O'Neill.

Next we pass over a pretty stream through the hamlet of Ballure and then by Beallachroy mill, standing beside a stream that flows from Loch Garasdale. Then, seven miles beyond Tayinloan, we come to Ronachan House, beautifully situated by the sea-side, and the residence of Allan Pollock, Esq., a wealthy and extensive proprietor in Scotland and Ireland. We now descend to Clachan, a large and pretty village in a valley, with a church and manse, inn, post-office, shop, grain-mill, and smithy. *Clachan* means "a village;" * but this is *the* village, *par excellence;* and is also called " The Kirktoun of Kilcalmonell." Here is Balnakill House, the residence of Alexander Morrison, Esq., Dean of the Faculty, Glasgow. It lies in a thickly-wooded

---

* Mr. Campbell says, " The Gaelic language is essentially descriptive, rich in words, which, by their sound alone, express ideas ;" and instances "the hard, sharp knocking of stones in *clach*, a stone; and thence all manner of compound ideas follow, as *clachan*, a village; *clachair*, a mason; *clacharan*, a stone chat."—*West Highland Tales*, vol. i. p. 131.

glen, surrounded by well-kept grounds and gardens; at which we had a peep, and which we found luxuriant with flowers. Here, again, we were struck with the great size and beauty of the fuchsias. Clachan glen is watered by streams flowing from Loch-nan-gad, Loch-an-Cuilan, Loch Ciaran, and Loch-na-Crine; they unite near to the church, and passing under the high road, fall into the sea at the foot of Dunskeig hill. Bealachruadh glen is also close by; and the fishing and shooting is very good. "A good many inhabitants resided in this glen fifty years back," writes a local authority; " but, at present, it is almost depopulated, in order to leave space enough for the sheep and heather fowl. Can the bleating of the sheep, the dogs' bark, and the chatter of the moor-hen, delight the ear of the philanthropist more than the joyful sound of the children amusing themselves with their innocent play in this glen ?" The writer leaves the question unanswered, but evidently anticipates a " No," not thinking it possible for philanthropists to be found among sheep-farmers and sportsmen.

Clachan inn offers rather superior accommodation; and, as it is midway between Barr and Tarbert, here is the baiting place for man and beast. The high road leaves Clachan by a very formidable ascent over the side of the hill of Dunskeig *, on whose lofty summit

* Also written *Dunsguey*, and *Dunscaith*.

are the remains of a vitrified fort. It is one of those ward hills, where beacon fires blazed, that are common on the western coast; and, besides its vitrified fort, there are the remains of walls and entrenchments. It commands the entrance to Loch Tarbert, and is admirably adapted by nature for a place of defence. Having told our driver to pick us up a mile or so along the road, we cross the bridge and toil up the hill. After a while, leaving the high road, we thread our devious course over peat bogs, marked by their rough shag of dark green, and are presently rewarded by a magnificent prospect, rendered the more beautiful by the excessive clearness of the atmosphere and the full splendour of sunshine. The coast of Cantire stretched in long perspective to our left, bounded by its monarch of mountains, Beinn-an-Tuirc. Rathlin Island, and the coast of Ireland, lay like a blue cloud on the distant sea. Before us studding the Atlantic waves, were the half dozen of the Hebrides, — their chiefs, Islay and Jura, overlapping each other, and appearing as one long island, that occupied no small share of the horizon of our view. At our feet was the entrance to West Tarbert Loch.

This loch is about eleven miles in length, and of an average width of three quarters of a mile. It more resembles an inland lake than an arm of the sea, and indeed has very much the character of many of the

English lakes. Macculloch's description of this loch is a very true one, if we bear in mind that he reserves the epithet of the picturesque in scenery to those places where the combinations of wood, water, and hills are on a larger and grander scale than at West Loch Tarbert. "The navigation of Loch Tarbert is exceedingly beautiful, without being strictly picturesque. The ground is neither high nor bold ; but the shores are varied in form and character, often beautifully wooded, and in many places highly cultivated ; while a considerable rural population, and some houses of more show and note, give it that dressed and civilised air which is by no means an usual feature on the shores of the Highlands. It is a great addition to the beauty of this inlet that, owing to the fall of the tide being exceedingly trifling, it is never subject to that display of mud at low water which renders the Wye, among many other rivers, so often an object of deformity rather than of beauty. I know not what Loch Tarbert may be at other times, but when I made its circuit, it was with sunrise on one of the loveliest mornings of June. The water was like a mirror; and as the sun reached the dewy birch woods, the air was perfumed by their fragrance, while the warbling of ten thousand thrushes on all sides, with the tinkling sound of the little waves that curled on the shore and the gentle whispering of the morning air among the trees, rendered it a perfect

scene of enchantment." * Another writer, who soars
into bolder and more auctioneering flights, says : "Over
all its extent it has the calm and smiling aspect of a
fresh-water lake, and is picturesque and lovely. Three
islets stud it in its progress ; soft and moderately high
hills recede in gentle and waving ascents from its
margins; woods and inclosures, and cultivation fling
their images upon its waters; and a profusion of cottages, farm-houses, villas, and mansions, with the villages of Laggavoulin and Kilcalmonell, sit joyously upon
its banks."

Over against Dunskeig, on the opposite side of the
loch, with the little island of Trien lying between, is
the headland of Ard Patrick, where tradition affirms
Saint Patrick to have landed on his way from Ireland
to Icolmkill. On the further side of Ard Patrick Point
is Storoway Bay. Magnificently situated on the high
ground about a mile from the very extremity of the
Point, is Ardpatrick House, the residence of Captain
Campbell, R. N. This is the land of the Campbells, as
is but fitting in Argyleshire. At Kilberry is the residence of John Campbell, Esq., and farther on is Drim-
namucklach, the property of another John Campbell.
A little way up the loch, on its western side, is Estcairt
House, and the beautiful house and estate of Dunmore,
the residence of W. Campbell, Esq., which is opposite

* Highlands and Western Isles, vol. ii. p. 85.

to Stonefield House on the eastern side of the loch, the
property of John Campbell, Esq., " of Stonefield," the
laird of Tarbert, who lives at Barmore castle, about two
miles north of Tarbert, leaving Stonefield for the residence of his factor, D. Sinclair, Esq. Along the eastern
shore of the loch are also the pretty villa residences
called Kilhammaig, Grassfield, Kintarbert, and Dippen,
with Gartnagrenach House, the residence of General
Cunningham. Woodside House and other villas are on
the western shore; so that the number of the better
class of residences seems to prove that the attractions
offered by the pleasing scenery of West Loch Tarbert
have been appreciated.

By and by, when we have descended Dunskeig
Hill (where we have vainly endeavoured to make a
scrambling sketch), and our carriage has picked us up,
we shall see all these houses as we advance to Tarbert;
they assist in forming leading points in those varied
pictures that pass before our eyes as the beautiful
panorama of West Loch Tarbert is unrolled to our view.
It is an excellent road all the way, though some of the
pitches and zigzags remind us of the descent to Bonchurch, and of that to Ventnor from the Carisbrooke
road. Our driver takes us down them at a sharp trot,
and we are thankful when the horse has quickened his
pace into a gallop on the level. Every now and then
the loch is shut out from our view by woods of birch,

firs, oaks, ash, and beech; or by towering masses of rock, its sternness softened by heather and wild flowers. Corn-fields and their reapers and gleaners stud the landscape on every side. At one point we pass some deer in a little park, where there is a very strong and neat fencing composed of stone in the lower part, and thick wire in the upper. At another point we canter along by the side of a wood fringed with re- markably fine beeches; and the road winds down under shady boughs to a bridge crossing a mountain stream, where a bevy of bare-legged children are paddling in the water, and leaping from boulder to boulder. At another point we come upon grand masses of Scotch firs, their trunks blazing out a fiery orange in the light of the setting sun, and their dark crowns appearing almost black against the calm September sky, save where the twisted stems seem to leap out of the dark- ness with limbs of fire. No wonder that our greatest landscape painter so loved to introduce this tree as a leading feature in the foreground of so many of his pictures! for picturesque purposes it is a very king of trees,—*the* king, Ruskin used to say; but in the last volume of his "Modern Painters," with that bold in- consistency and dogmatism that distinguish " Professor Dusky's opinions on Art," he has dethroned his former arboreal monarch, the stone-pine, and has proclaimed the aspen king in its place; and has had his head so turned by the unapproachable glories of his new sovereign, that he has brought himself to the conclusion that not even Turner could paint an aspen-tree, and that it could only be described by Keats. As Keats was stung to death some years ago, it therefore follows that the aspen tree is not only more easily to be imagined than described, but is one of those things that must be seen to be believed.

Sir Walter Scott's praise of "the ever-green pine" will be remembered by all readers of "The Lady of the Lake," * but his description of the tree in an essay in the "Quarterly Review" (No. 82), may not be so well known.

" A noble tree growing with huge contorted arms, not altogether unlike the oak, and forming therein a strong contrast to the formality of the common fir. The appearance of the Highland fir, when planted in its appropriate situation amongst rocks and crags, is dignified and even magnificent; the dusky red of its massive trunk, and dark hue of its leaves, forming a happy accompaniment to scenes of this description."

Sir Thomas Dick Lauder thus defends the picturesqueness of " the ever-green pine."

" When its foot is among its own Highland heather, and when it stands freely on its native knoll of dry gravel or thinly covered rock, over which its roots

* " The Boat Song," canto ii. xix.

wander in the wildest reticulation, while its tall, furrowed, often gracefully sweeping red and grey trunk of enormous circumference raises aloft its high umbrageous canopy, then would the greatest sceptic on this point be compelled to prostrate his mind before it with a veneration which perhaps was never before excited by any other tree."

About midway between Dunskeig and Tarbert, we pass through the village of Whitehouse, which boasts an inn. Close by, are the two burial-places of Kilchamaig and Claogh Mhichail. In the latter lie the remains of the Rev. Donald M'Keich, of Campbelton, and Miss Lucy Campbell, of Campbelton, a lady of great wealth and charity, who built and endowed two schools at Campbelton and extended her kindly deeds to Glasgow. Now we have a pleasing view of the little village of Lagga-voulin, or "the Mill in the Valley," whose name characterises its situation, and is as grateful to the ear and tongue, as is the reality to the eye. Now we sight, on the opposite shore, the lofty hill of Sliobh-ghoil, "the Hill of Love," the scene of the death of Diarmid, Fingalian Achilles, and ancestor of all the Campbells, of whose prowess with the wild boar we had an account in our eighteenth chapter. It is fitting that the burial-place of the *Camshuil*, or "one-eyed" hero, should be in the midst of the land of the Campbells, though our previous legend would have it that Beinn-an-tuirc was not only the scene of Diarmid's exploit, but of his death also. But these Fingalian heroes, like Homer, were not only born in ever so many places, but terminated their legendary existence at various times and places, and in divers ways, a circum · stance which in no way detracts from the poetic mystery in which they are shrouded.

The road at one time bears us at some distance from the loch, and soon after, turning sharply to the left, brings us close upon its waters. From this point, the view up the placid loch, and out to the open sea and the Hebrides, was exquisitely beautiful. Then we lose sight of the loch again, and pass by a fir plantation, and up a steep hill, the pheasants running and flying at our approach, and the rabbits swarming everywhere, as indeed had been the case for the last twenty miles. The rocks appeared to be alive with them, while the hill-sides were dotted everywhere with flocks of sheep and herds of the shaggy Highland kyloes.

At length the loch narrows amid the encircling hills, and we approach East Tarbert, and the end of our canter through Cantire, ending at the beginning, for at Tarbert is the commencement of the peninsula of the Land's-end of Scotland. As we descend the hill that leads down into the town and come upon an angle of the quay that forms three sides of a square, the lofty Castle Rock, crowned with ruins, makes a fine background to the scene ; herring-busses and various vessels crowd the harbour, boats pass across, the three lines of white houses are reflected in the water ; and with the last rays of sunset to gild the scene, the town of East Tarbert presents a picturesque appearance, and fitly closes that picturesque drive of twenty-six miles, which has formed our canter through Cantire.

CHAP. XXXI.

EAST TARBERT AND LOCH-FYNE HERRINGS.

Tarbert; meaning of the Word. — Scott's Account. — The Legend of
Tarbert. — A Blackleg Transaction. — Fables and Facts. — Shak-
speare's Donalbain. — The Norwegian Dynasty. — Sodor and Man. —
The Bishop of Cantire. — The Tarbert Canal Company, Limited. —
A Chain of Forts. — Paul Jones the Pirate. — Tarbert Castle. — The
Key of Cantire. — The Eastern Loch ; its wild Character. — Tarbert
Town. — The Capital of Herringdom. — Statistics of the Fishery. —
Phosphorescence of the Herring. — Superstitions of the Fishermen. —
Old Form of Prayer on putting to Sea. — The King of the Herrings.
— Folk-lore of the Herring. — Things not generally known anent the
Herring. — A cleanly Lodging. — The Merry Dancers.

TARBERT is a common name in Scotland. It denotes
an isthmus ; the word being framed (according to late
etymologists) from the Gaelic *Tár*, " to drag or carry,"
and *beart*, "goods of all kinds;" but Pennant says,
that the name Tarbert, or Tarbat as it is often written,
is from *Tarruing*, " to draw," and *Bata*, "a boat."
" Boat-carrying," indeed, seems the meaning of the
word ; because over these narrow necks of land between
two sea or fresh-water lochs, the inhabitants were
accustomed to drag their boats. These Scotch Tarberts

therefore, are similar to the "carrying-places" of North America, the "portages" of Canada, and the Diolkoi of the Greeks; and even at the present day, especially during the herring-season, the fishermen of this Tarbert on Loch Fyne frequently haul their boats across the isthmus, which is barely a mile in width at its narrowest point. Sir Walter Scott's reference to this overland transit of vessels, will be familiar to the readers of *the Lord of the Isles* :—

> " Ever the breeze blows merrily,
> But the galley ploughs no more the sea,
> Lest, rounding wild Cantire, they meet
> The southern foeman's watchful fleet,
>   They held unwonted way;
> Up Tarbat's western lake they bore,
> Then dragg'd their bark the isthmus o'er,
> As far as Kilmaconnel's shore,
>   Upon the eastern bay.
> It was a wondrous sight to see
> Topmast and pennon glitter free,
> High raised above the greenwood tree,
> As on dry land the galley moves
> By cliff, and copse, and alder groves.
> Deep import from that selcouth sign,
> Did many a mountain-seer divine;
> For ancient legends told the Gael,
> That when a royal bark should sail
>   O'er Kilmaconnel moss,
> Old Albyn should in fight prevail,
> And every foe should faint and quail
>   Before her silver Cross."

Scott's " Kilmaconnel " is the Kilcalmonell of Cantire, separated by a small stream from the parish of South Knapdale, which lies north of the isthmus. " It is not very long since," says Pennant, "that vessels of nine or ten tons were drawn by horses out of the West loch into that of the East, to avoid the dangers of the Mull of Cantire, so dreaded and so little known was the navigation round that promontory. It is the opinion of many that these little isthmuses so frequently styled *Tarbat* in North Britain, took their name from the above circumstance; *Tarruing* signifying to draw, and *Bata*, a boat. This too might be called, by way of pre-eminence *the Tarbat*, from a very singular circumstance related by Torsœus."[*]

This legend has been well told by Macculloch, and as he puts it in a new light, I shall do best by quoting his description. "There has been a tale so currently told respecting Loch Tarbet, or rather about the Tarbet itself, that it has been not only generally believed, but reprinted so often, as almost to have taken its rank among historical facts. Pennant, first of the tourists, borrowed it from Scottish history (or fable) and the rest, as usual, have followed him. The story is, that Donald Bane, who had taken refuge in the Western Islands after the death of Duncan, ceded these isles to Magnus the Barefoot [†], on consideration of his receiving the aid

[*] Voyage to the Hebrides, p. 167.

[†] *Berfætta*, or " Bareleg." For which, if the story had been true,

of Norway against the family of Malcolm. Magnus, by this contract, was to have all the islands; and the definition of island (according to the law of the wolf versus the lamb, it would appear) being whatever could be circumnavigated, the cunning Norwegian caused his boat to be drawn across the Tarbet, thus including Cantire within his contract, by a trick worthy of Dido and her counsellors. Now, the whole of this must be an egregious fable. Even the Scottish portion of Donald Bane's history is very obscure; but nothing except the greatest ignorance of the state and history of Scotland at that period, could have given admission to this fiction; when the islands actually belonged to Magnus and to Norway, and neither to Scotland nor to Donald Bane. There is a puerility about the story, independently of this, which should have been sufficient to condemn it; a gross fraud practised against him, who, if he had the power to grant, must have also pos-

---

"blackleg" might have been substituted. As says Miss Sinclair, who briefly refers to this legend, "What would the Jockey Club have said to this rather black-leg transaction?" — *Scotland and the Scotch*, chap. ii. Mr. J. J. A. Worsae, in his "Account of the Danes and Norwegians in England and Ireland," says, that Magnus, after acquiring the sovereignty of the Isles, adopted the dress of the people. "They went about the streets in Norway with bare legs, and wore short coats and cloaks, whence Magnus was called by his men, Barfod, or Barbeen (barefoot or barelegs), says the Icelandic historian, Snorro Sturleson, who, as is well known, lived in the first half of the thirteenth century."

sessed that of withholding, and who could not have suffered himself to be thus cheated. It cannot now be discovered at what period the Norwegian chiefs became
proprietors or kings on the mainland ; whether before
Somerlid or how long ; but assuredly Cantire could not
have been obtained in any manner from him who had
it not to give ; who was apparently a banished man as
well as a rebel, and who, if ever he did bring forces
from the Isles against the family of Malcolm, must
have done so as a suitor and a beggar, by influencing
those powers, whose equal or superior interest it was to
fall on Scotland when in an enfeebled state. This
piece of history must in future be ranked with King
Athirco and with the embassy which Ptolemy Philadel-
phus sent to King Reutha." *

The Donald Bane here is Shakspeare's Donalbain,
one of the sons of Duncan, who was Thane of the Isles
and Western Highlands, and who was murdered at
Inverness, by his cousin-german Macbeth, somewhere
about the year 1045. On the usurpation of Macbeth,
Donald Bane fled " to Ireland," says Shakspeare †, and
he is said to have invaded Scotland, with the aid of
the Norwegian power, at the death of his brother Malcolm ; thus usurping a government of which the legal

* Highlands and Western Isles, vol. ii. pp. 84, 85 ; also vol. iii.
pp. 37, 38.
† Macbeth, Act ii. scene 3.

line of heirs were minors. The subjugation of Cantire by Magnus, is supposed to have been in the year 1098; but the chronology, like the history of this period, is very confused and uncertain. Magnus resided at the English court for a twelvemonth, and was highly esteemed by King Henry the First. He was a pattern king in every way; "and there is abundant reason," says Macculloch, "for supposing that the condition of the Western Isles was far superior, as a nation, during the Norwegian dynasty, to what it ever was afterwards. . . . It was under the Scottish government, and in the hands of the chiefs who followed the Norwegian secession, that they became that barbarous people which we afterwards know them during the contests of the clans. It need scarcely be remarked that the Celts of the Isles and Cantire had thus been long a conquered people under a foreign yoke; amalgamating, however, with their conquerors, if we can indeed grant them this; but, as being the majority in numbers, communicating to them their own language, as the French in Normandy, and the Saxons in England, under similar circumstances, did successively to their Norman brethren."*

In the days of Magnus, and down to the time of Alexander III., the history of the Western Isles was that of the Isle of Mann, where, indeed, was the seat of

---

* Highlands and Western Isles, vol. iii. p. 39.

government. Without dwelling upon the boat-carrying legend of Magnus the Barefoot, we have previously in . these pages seen that Cantire was long reckoned as an island. The peninsula was classed with Bute, Arran, and Islay and Jura and their satellites; and they were called by the general name of " the Southern Isles." Their old connection with the Isle of Mann is denoted to us, up to this very day, in the title of the Bishop of Sodor and Mann, for the word *Sodorenses* means " the Southern Isles." But the Bishop of Sodor and Man ceased to be the Bishop of Cantire in the reign of Edward I., when the peninsula was transferred to the episcopal jurisdiction of the Bishop of Argyle and the Isles.*

* Professor Munch, of Christiana (whose work, "Chronica Regum Manniæ et Insularum," has been already referred to in the first chapter of this book, as noticed in the "Saturday Review"), has invented the new term of *Sudreys*, for the Western Islands. He derives the word from the Norwegian *Sudreyjar*, which was Latinised into *Sodorenses*. He thinks "Sodor" is a "ridiculous addition" to the style of the modern Bishop of Man. Upon which the "Saturday Review" observes, "We do not know that there is any harm in the retention of a title which connects the see with its ancient dignity. It is rather curious that the very same islands figure to this day in the name of another diocese, that of Argyle and ' the Isles.' We do not know whether the transfer was made at the time when the jurisdiction of the Bishop of Man ceased over the Sodors." (Vol. x. p. 564.) In Dasent's "Story of Burnt Njal," the Hebrides are frequently spoken of as "the Southern Isles." "He was a South Islander by stock; that is, he came from what we call the Western Isles, or Hebrides. The old appellation still lingers in 'Sodor (*i. e.* the South Isles) and Man.'" (Vol. i. p. 30.)

It has long been in contemplation to cut a canal across the isthmus which should connect the two lochs, and open up an easy and rapid communication with Glasgow and other places, and save vessels the long and dangerous passage round the Mull of Cantire.

And elsewhere it is said, "Kari gave his word to do that, and then they fared with him a-sea-roving. They harried south about Anglesea, and all the southern isles. Thence they held on to Cantire, and landed there, and fought with the landsmen, and got thence much goods, and so fared to their ships." (Vol. ii. p. 39.) The author of the "Statistical Account of Iona," gives the history of the title, and the date of its limitation to the Isle of Mann. "While the Hebrides were under the Norwegian domination, they divided these islands into two districts, called Nordureys and Sudereys; the first embracing all the islands to the north, and the other all those which lie to the south of the promontory of Ardnamurchan. But the whole two divisions of islands belonged to the diocese of the Bishop of Ebude, and his cathedral and residence being in the island of Man, one of the Suderays, he was from thence styled *Episcopus Sodorensis;* hence the origin of the title of Sodor: and when the Isle of Man was, in the reign of Edward I. of England, reduced under the English government, the bishopric of Sodor was preserved, but its limits being circumscribed to that single island, its bishops assumed and bore the united title of Sodor and Man. All the other Western Islands remaining under the government of Scotland were then erected into a separate diocese, called the Bishoprick of the Isles. The bishops usually resided at Iona, and the great church belonging to the abbey served as the cathedral of the diocese. There has been great diversity of opinion concerning the ancient Sodor from which the bishops of the Isle of Man still derived their title, some supposing that it was the name of a town there, so late as the fifteenth century, and others that the town in Iona was the ancient Sodor. It is now generally conceded that the foregoing account is correct, according to Torffœus, the Danish historian, and explained by Dr. Macpherson" (pp. 325, 326).

Such a canal would considerably diminish the voyage of the Glasgow steamers to Islay, Oban, and Skye, and would be the means of connecting the Atlantic Ocean with the inland seas of Scotland at an important point; while it would be an improvement on the Crinan Canal, for, although the route is shorter by that way, yet it is made virtually longer in point of time by the fifteen locks, which hinder a vessel's progress in its nine mile passage. There are, however, difficulties in the way of the Tarbert Canal, and it has been thought that the ground is too high for the construction of a canal, except at an expense that would not be justified by the results. Others think that its objects are superseded by the Crinan Canal, which conveys the navigation of the Clyde in a direct line to the Hebrides. Others, again, would prefer a railroad across the Tarbert Isthmus, and are of opinion that it would be better and more remunerative than a canal. In the meantime, nothing is done; and those who wish to avoid " rounding wild Cantire," are compelled to realise the full signification of Tarbert, and carry their goods across the isthmus.

It was once well protected. The vitrified fort that we saw on the summit of Dunskeig hill, at the entrance of West Loch Tarbert, was but one of a chain of forts that defended Cantire, and which were continued up to the head of the western loch, and thence across the isthmus to Tarbert Castle on the eastern loch, and from thence to Skipness. There was a fort half-way across the isthmus, where there is a large cairn and a hamlet, named from it Cairnban. Near to here is the road to Inverary. At the head of the western loch is a pier, built for the accommodation of a steamer which maintains a weekly communication between Tarbert and Islay. In 1778, Paul Jones, the pirate, attacked the Tarbert packet and plundered it. Major Campbell of Islay was on board of her, with a large fortune of gold and valuables acquired in India, from whence he was returning to end his days in Islay; and he had safely reached the Sound of Islay, and was close to home, when the pirate attacked the vessel and robbed Major Campbell of all his property.

Of Tarbert Castle, there are the remains of a square tower and some crumbling walls. They stand in a strong position on the summit of a lofty and precipitous rock, that commands the entrance of the eastern loch, and also the approach to Cantire by way of the isthmus. Its position made it the key of Cantire, and made it one of the most important strongholds on the coast; and its strength was in accordance with its position. Some think that it was built by Robert Bruce; though, according to others, he only strengthened and increased it. At any rate, it was here that he held his court in 1326; and here that the Lords of the Isles held many

EAST LOCH TARBERT, ON LOCH FYNE, CANTIRE.

a revel. James II. stayed here; and, in 1685, it was
the rendezvous of the luckless Argyle and the Duke of
Monmouth. It is said to have been supplied with
water from the other side of the loch, conveyed under
the harbour by pipes, laid down in a submarine
passage.

The eastern loch, on which the castle looks down,
is but a small one, barely a mile long; but it is very
remarkable, both in itself and in the contrast that it
presents to the western loch. The soft outlines and
wooded shores of the western loch contrast very forcibly
with the stern wildness and ruggedness of the eastern
loch; and Lord Teignmouth has very happily compared the two Tarbert lochs to paintings by Claude and
Salvator Rosa.* " It is a curious and singularly safe
landlocked natural harbour," says one describer, " and
is entered by so narrow and circling a passage between
low ridges of naked rock, that a steamer in sailing
through it, appears to a stranger to be irretrievably
launched against the crag." " On the northern side of
the entrance of the harbour," says Pennant, " the rocks
are of a most grotesque form; vast fragments piled on
each other; the faces contorted and undulated in such
figures as if created by fusion of matter after some in-
tense heat; yet did not appear to me a *lava,* or any
suspicion of having been the recrement of a volcano." †

* Scotland, vol. i. p. 26.　　　　† Hebrides, p. 165.

" The rude outworks of its rocks," says Lord Teignmouth, " apparently barring access ; the overhanging
keep of its ruined castle ; the village, and the innumerable fishing-boats choking up every nook and
crevice, form a scene singularly picturesque, the effect
of which is heightened by the method in which the
fishermen hang their nets."

Tarbert, however, is something more than a " village." It is a town, containing two churches (established and free) a bank, two inns, several whisky shops,
and a few tolerable shops. The town is built on the
three sides of a square, containing the harbour, the
fourth side of the square being occupied by the narrow
approach to the harbour from Loch Fyne. The quay,
therefore, is the chief street, and the three rows of
white houses are mirrored in the waters of the harbour,
and are looked down upon by the old Castle ruins on
the summit of the steep rock. The ground rises on
either side of the harbour, so that the street leading
into Tarbert from Cantire, is down a steep descent. A
great stone block is built in the centre of the harbour,
having steps at its side, and poles on which nets are
hung to dry, while boats are moored alongside. There
are other poles on the southern side of the harbour,
and a profuse array of black and rusty-looking nets.
Over against them, under the Castle Rock, is the steam-
boat pier, with the offices for the harbour-master, and

a refreshment room for passengers. Altogether, as
Macculloch says, " The village and bay of Loch Tarbert form a very singular spot, wild alike and unexpected."

But Tarbert (East Tarbert, as it is more correctly
called) is chiefly noticeable, as being the chief seat of

EAST TARBERT, CANTIRE.

the Loch Fyne herring-fishery, and as Loch Fyne herrings (or " Glasgow bailies," as Sam Slick calls them)
take precedence over all other herrings, Tarbert may
fairly be called the capital of Herringdom.   It is impossible to pass an hour in the town during the months
of August and September, without being keenly alive

to the fact that it is the herring season. The fish is to be met with everywhere, fresh or dried, in boxes and out of boxes; and down at the chief quay, where the steam-packets receive their burdens, we see large blocks and piles of herring-boxes reaching much higher than the Tarbert houses. These boxes are branded in various ways, to denote their several proprietors; and as vermilion is the colour in the greatest esteem, the pictorial effect of the aggregate of boxes and barrels, is something that is quite Owen-Jonesish. It is a curious sight, and one that makes itself very perceptible to the sense of smell. The modern Highland herring-woman is greatly addicted to drams of whisky, and doubtless it was so in Hogarth's time; but the English vendor of herrings he has represented as a beer drinker. We see her in the "Beer Street" picture, with a pot of beer in her hand, perusing "A new ballad on the herring-fishery."

Loch Fyne is the favourite rendezvous of the herring family, and its shores, during the season, swarm with shoals to a much greater extent than any other portion of the Scottish coast. As many as twenty thousand barrels of Loch Fyne herrings have been cured within a year. In each barrel there are from five hundred to eight hundred herrings, according to their size; and the price of a barrel is twenty-five shillings. The Loch Fyne fishermen denote the vastness of the herring

shoals, by saying that the component parts of the loch
are, one part water and two parts fish. It would
scarcely be possible to tell with accuracy the number
of boats employed in the fishery, for in one single bay
of Loch Fyne as many as five or six hundred boats
will be employed during the season, and eighty barrels
of fish have been taken in one night by the boats of
a single vessel. Despite these large statistics, however,
the numbers now are less than they were a few years
ago. It is feared that the shoals are decreasing, but
sanguine fishermen ascribe the decrease of numbers to
accidental occurrences, and pin their faith on the pro-
lific powers of the fish. Gulls and gannets skimming
over the water and darting at the fish, signify their
arrival, and denote the whereabouts of the shoals;
which are also followed by cod-fish, dog-fish, haddocks,
and other fishy cannibals. As shoals of shrimps have
been observed to float in a glittering coral mass, so the
herring shoals, when near the surface, exhibit the most
brilliant colours, and by night, present a phosphorescent
appearance. "The darkness of the night," says Maxwell, "increased the scaly brilliancy which the phosphoric properties of these beautiful fish produce. They
glowed with a living light, which the imagination could
not create, and the pencil never imitate"—not even
the pencil of Mr. Hunt, who, in last year's Old Water
Colour Exhibition, showed us the herring that he had

so wonderfully painted for Mr. Ruskin. " The shades of gold and silvery gems were rich beyond description, and much as I had heard of phosphoric splendour before, every idea I had formed fell infinitely short of its reality." *

It is by night that the herrings are chiefly caught, dark, breezy nights being the best for this purpose, and from the end of August to Christmas being the best season. " The nets are cast at sun-set, and always on the right side of the boat, in conformity to the supposed injunction of our Saviour to St. Peter. The time of sailing is also governed by many superstitious notions, but a cloudy evening is the best omen. Immediately afterwards, if the weather permit, the fishermen light their fire and cook their supper, consisting of fish, potatoes, oat-cake, molasses, or porridge. But, on stormy nights they fast, being unable to cook their provisions, relieving their fatigue by whisky; and on their return in the morning, invariably receive two drams each from the purchaser of their fish. Cold and hungry, they are often affected by the spirits, and sustain the habitual excitement by repairing to the public-house, thus acquiring habits of intoxication. There are no less than twenty public-houses in Tarbert, which must be partly attributed to its being a great thoroughfare. The superintendent of the distillery of West

* Wild Sports of the West, Letter xxxviii.

Tarbert informed me that the fishermen carried out whisky to sea, observing emphatically, " Sir, the Tarbert man must have his dram, let the world sink or swim." *

Whisky and piety go together in Scotland, therefore it may not surprise us when we are told that these dram-drinking fishermen " after supper, not unfrequently kneel down to prayer, and sing a hymn, and when at home, adopt the same rule." It is to be hoped that their devotions are sincere, and that the domestic worship which they are said to conduct on board their boats in such a praiseworthy manner, is not marred by the infusion of any other spirit than the right one. Martin, in his " Western Islands," gives the " Form of Prayer used by many of the islanders at sea after their sails are hoisted," taken from the Irish Liturgy, " composed by Mr. John Kerswell, afterwards Bishop of Argyle, printed in the year 1566, and dedicated to the Earl of Argyle." He first gives the Gaelic form, and then the English translation, which is as follows :—

" *The Manner of blessing the Ship when they put to Sea.*

" *The Steersman says :* Let us bless our ship.

" *The Answer by all the Crew.* God the Father bless her.

" *Steersman.* Let us bless our ship.

* Lord Teignmouth's " Scotland," vol. ii. p. 371.

"*Answer.* Jesus Christ bless her.

"*Steersman.* Let us bless our ship.

"*Answer.* The Holy Ghost bless her.

"*Steersman.* What do you fear, since God the Father is with you?

"*Answer.* We do not fear anything.

"*Steersman.* What do you fear, since God the Son is with you?

"*Answer.* We do not fear anything.

"*Steersman.* What are you afraid of, since God the Holy Ghost is with you?

"*Answer.* We do not fear anything.

"*Steersman.* God the Father Almighty, for the love of Jesus Christ His Son, by the comfort of the Holy Ghost the one God, who miraculously brought the children of Israel through the Red Sea, and brought Jonas to land out of the belly of the whale, and the Apostle Paul and his ship to safety from the troubled raging sea, and from the violence of a tempestuous storm; deliver, sanctify, bless and conduct us peaceably, calmly, and comfortably through the sea to our harbour, according to His divine will; which we beg, saying, *Our Father,* &c."

This same Martin, who collected many of the western Highland traditions of a century and a half ago, has somewhat to tell of the folk-lore of the herring. He says that the fishermen believed the herring-shoals to be led by "a big herring almost double the size of any of its kind," who was called the king of the herrings, and who was followed by the shoal whithersoever he went. Mr. Campbell refers to this Gaelic story in his "Popular Tales of the West Highlands," and says it has its "counterpart in Grimm. I heard it from my landlady at Port Erin, and I met two Manksmen afterwards who knew it. The fish all gathered once to choose a king; and the fluke, him that has the red spots on him, stayed at home to make himself pretty, putting on his red spots to see if he would be king; and he was too late, for when he came the herring was king of the sea. So the fluke curled his mouth on one side, and said: 'A simple fish like the herring king of the sea!' and his mouth has been to one side ever since." *

Pennant further says: "It is a general observation, all Scotland over, that if a quarrel happen on the coast where herring is caught, and that blood be drawn violently, then the herring go away from the coast without returning during that season. This, they say, has been observed in all past ages as well as at present, but this I relate only as a common tradition, and submit it to the judgment of the learned." On these herring-quarrels I may again quote from Mr. Campbell. "I maintain that there is chronic war in every part of her Majesty's dominions. Not long ago a dispute arose

* Vol. i.; introduction, p. lv.

T 2

about a manner of catching herrings. One set of men caught them with drift nets, another with drag-nets, and one party declared that the other violated the law ; blood got up, and at last a whole fleet of fishing-boats left their ground, and sailed twenty miles down to attack the rival fleet in form. A gun-boat joined the party, and peace was preserved ; but it was more the result of a calm which enabled the light row-boats to escape from the heavier sailing fleet. Both parties spoke the same language, and, on any subject but herrings, they would have backed each other through the world."* Let me here also quote, from another recent author, an anecdote à propos to the subject : — One of the most eccentric clergymen of the latter part of the last century was the Rev. Peter Glas, minister of Crail. His pulpit language was broad Scotch, and his expressions, even in devotion, were particularly simple. Many of his parishioners being fishermen, he usually prayed specially for their welfare. One day, using the expression, " May the boats be filled wi' herring up to the very tow-holes" (spaces for the oars), a fisherman lustily called out, " Na, no' that far, sir, or we wad a' be sunk."†

Although Pennant has been shown, by Yarrell and modern zoologists, to be wrong in his opinion that the

* Vol. i. p. cxxviii.
† Dr. Roger's " Familiar Illustrations of Scottish Character."

herrings annually migrate from the Arctic regions, yet his account of the Loch Fyne herring fishery is very interesting and worthy of notice; and, after the lapse of a century, most of his remarks hold good, and are applicable at the present day.* I do not desire, however, to quote them here, or to detail the past and present history of the herring fishery, yet would I snatch from this history a few remarkable facts, which may be among those "things not generally known" to that otherwise well-informed personage, the constant reader.

More than a thousand years ago, then, the fame of these Loch Fyne herrings had spread far beyond Tarbert and the adjacent coasts, for in the year 836 the Netherlanders came to Loch Fyne to purchase the salted herrings. They were as cannie as the Scots, and they learnt the art and took up the trade of herring-curing. And they must have made the most of their knowledge as years went on, for in 1603 Sir Walter Raleigh speaks of the Dutch selling to other nations, herrings that amounted in value to a million and a half of money; and, from first to last, employing two hundred thousand men in the herring trade, all these men being employed, and all these fish being caught on the coasts of Scotland, and notably in Loch Fyne. And what were the Scotchmen

* See his "Tour in Scotland" (1769), pp. 190, 191; "Voyage to the Hebrides" (1772), pp. 317, 325. See also "Penny Magazine," vol. vi. p. 63.

about, that they should permit this million and a half
of money to be drifted from their own shores to the
Netherlands? It is true that, as Professor Cosmo Innes
shows *, Loch Fyne herrings were appreciated in Scotland in 1590, and that a Loch Fyne tenant of Lord
Breadalbane paid a portion of his rent in herrings; but,
on the whole, the herring-fisheries were neglected for
the whale-fishery, and, in the presence of the monsters
of the deep, they made light of the little herring. It
was a sad lack of Scotch second-sight, and a mistake
that a century of years could not overget. The Dutch
were wiser in their generation, and in Holland the
herring was a mightier fish than the whale. It formed
the foundation of many a fortune and many a house;
so much so, that at length the saying that "Amsterdam
was built on herring bones" passed into a proverb,
much in the same way that it was said in England that
" London Bridge was built on woolsacks." Of such
great importance, too, was the invention of pickled
herrings considered, that a monarch did not consider
it beneath his dignity to pay the last honours to the
inventor; and thus it happened that, in the year 1536,
the Emperor Charles the Fifth erected a magnificent
tomb to the memory of one Beukles, a Dutchman, as a
real benefactor to his country, in that he had invented
the pickled herring. But why the term " pickle her-

* Sketches of Early Scottish History, pp. 255, 376, 386.

ring" should come to signify a merry Andrew, I leave to etymologists and root-hunters to decide.

It is bad policy to harp too long upon one string, however agreeable its notes may be; and men in general find that the most successful executants are those who have more than one string to their bow. For the lack of this knowledge, the Dutch soon awoke to the discovery that their one tune was not always to remain their fortune. They had thrown over the whale for the herring; but had coquetted too long with the delicate little beauty, and now the whale threw *them* over; and when once they had lost their whale fishery, they were unable to regain it. So they did what they could in taking the Scotch herring-fishery out of the hands of the Scotchmen, who were not only whalers, but wailers also, and when too late, bemoaned the loss of what they had carelessly allowed to slip through their fingers. James the Third endeavoured somewhat to benefit the fishery; but his immediate successors did little in the cause; and Hans Heavistern the Dutchman was a cannier man than Sandie MacAlpine, the Loch Fyne Highlander.

Seeing that herrings form the staple commodity of East Tarbert, we are by no means surprised to see a dish-full of them (beautifully cooked) brought up with our tea, in company with the usual Scotch accompaniments of preserves and cakes. After our "canter through Cantire," and our long drive through the appetising Highland air, we are grateful to Mrs. Mac Arthur for her temptingly-spread tea-table; and above all, for the unspeakable comfort of a cleanly lodging, and a night's rest undisturbed by the obtrusive liveliness of industrious fleas. I think it is Christopher North, who speaks of the dangerous power placed in the hands of a chambermaid of a naturally witty and cruel disposition, by committing to her the charge of the blankets; and how, by a wicked selection, she could envelope her victim in vermin, and after a night of one of the plagues of Egypt, cause him to rise in the morning tattooed from head to foot.

But fleas and their final cause, *videlicet* scratching, — considered by many Scotch philosophers to be so salutary in its effect — did not trouble us in Mrs. MacArthur's cleanly lodging on that night — our last night in Cantire; so that from first to last, — from our classical egg even unto our apple, — we had nothing to grumble at, and no tourist grievance over which to snarl. On that night too, at East Tarbert, we saw "the Northern Lights;" and it was the only night during our tour in Scotland on which we observed them. We afterwards learnt from the newspapers that the Aurora was generally visible on that evening, and in less northern localities. It was a beautifully calm and clear night, and the gleams of pale yellow light, here and there tinged with rose, flashed and flickered in the sky with such rapidity, that I could easily understand why these beautiful meteors were locally known as "the Merry Dancers;" and why Sir Walter Scott says of the Monk of Melrose:—

> "The monk gazed long on the lovely moon,
> Then into the night he looked forth;
> And red and bright the streamers light
> Were *dancing* in the glowing north."

CHAP. XXXII.

THE KYLES OF BUTE.

How to leave Tarbert. — The *Iona*. — A Herring-laden Steamer. —
Tarbert Quay. — Street Slaughtering. — Our Caliban. — East Tarbert
Loch. — Loch Fyne. — Aird Lamont. — Last View of Cantire. —
Rough Water. — Entrance to the Kyles. — Calais and the Kyles. —
Scenery and Sea Sickness. — Formation of the Kyles. — A Loch-y
Labyrinth. — Travellers' Opinions as to the Kyles. — Pennant. —
Lord Teignmouth. — Miss Sinclair. — Gushing Raptures. — Maccul-
loch. — A Fairy-like Sea. — Sir George Head. — Passage of the
Kyles. — Rothesay. — The Poet Prince. — The tragical Story of the
first Duke of Rothesay. — My Lord Bute reads my Lady a Lesson. —
Toward Point. — The Firth of Clyde.

THERE are two ways of leaving Tarbert for the Kyles
of Bute — which is the route by which I would conduct my readers away from Cantire, and back to the
spot from whence we first set out on our journey to
the Land's-end of Scotland. The one way is, to catch
the *Iona* — the swiftest steamer on the Clyde, on
her way from Inverary to Glasgow. But to achieve
this — as the *Iona* does not call at Tarbert — it is
necessary to take a boat, and get through the diffi-

culties of East Tarbert Loch, and pull out into Loch
Fyne, far enough to meet the steamer. Then you
must lay-to till she comes; and when she does come,
you must board her, and be hoisted up on to her deck.
Hence there are many drawbacks to this arrangement,
even if the skies be propitious, and the sea as un-
ruffled as a mill-pond; but if the weather be " varry
coorse," and the waves rough and rude, then the arrangement is one which (unlike the teas of adver-
tising grocers) cannot be " highly recommended for
family use."

But there is another way open to us. A steamer,
not quite so expeditious in her movements as the *Iona*,
calls at Tarbert. By all means, let us go by her;
she will obviate that unpleasant boat voyage, by pick-
ing us up at the quay; and though she is somewhat
long over her passage to Greenock (about three hours
and a-half) yet this will allow us the more time to
see the scenery of the Kyles, which is the very thing
we want. And is there no drawback? assuredly; for
there is a skeleton in every house, whether afloat or
on shore, and our steamer's skeleton is one begotten
of Loch Fyne and Tarbert,—-the herring. Her burden
will consist chiefly of herrings. All those great ru-
bric'd boxes which are now ranged on the quay, will be
stowed away upon her after-deck; and if there should
not be room for them there — and there is no knowing

what sort of a load she may bring from Inverary and Ardrishaig—they must be stowed away on the fore-deck, and offend our noses during the voyage.

Let us try the experiment, however, and make ready for our departure. As she will be at the quay for at least ten minutes, or a quarter of an hour, we shall have time to arrive at a final decision when we have seen the actual state of affairs; and if her decks prove to be too odoriferous and herring-crowded, we can then boat out to sea, and waylay the *Iona*. The windows of our lodgings look on to the quay; and a sentinel is posted there, prepared on a given signal to bring forth our *impedimenta*.

The boat is due a little before eleven; and a crowd of herring proprietors steeped in a fishy scent, are ready for her. Various passengers too have walked or driven to the quay; a dog-cart, laden with dogs, guns, game, and everything to betoken that its proprietor has made a successful raid on the Cantire moors, also rattles towards us; and two well-appointed carriages contribute those fair occupants who are to join us in braving the tossings of the waves, and the odours of the herrings.

A quarter of an hour thus passes away while we hang about for our tardy steamer, noting the new arrivals, and watching the boatmen plying to and fro across the harbour, and on its further side, busied at their nets, spread out on high poles, and forming a long line of net-work, like the side of a great poultry-yard. The adventurous gulls are flapping about and darting at their prey, almost heedless of the two boatmen in the centre of the harbour, who are whiling away their time, by firing at the birds, and making the echoes ring from the old castled rock over our heads, where the crumbling ruins have had no tenants, save the birds, for this many a year. Close by the Bank a "Flesher" is slaughtering a sheep in the open street. As we saunter up and down we have a glance at the various stages of the skinning and cutting up; and are thus enabled to fill up our spare moments by meditating on this humanising spectacle, and by speculating on its probable effect upon the minds of the select circle of bare-legged children, to whom the exhibition appears to afford amusement blended with instruction.

At length, after more than half an hour's delay, a puff of steam is observed above the ragged lines of rock that make East Tarbert Loch into a labyrinth; and presently our boat heaves in sight and swings round to the quay. In a few minutes we have decided upon our course; the signal is given to our sentinel at the lodging; and Mrs. MacArthur is desolated of ourselves and our *impedimenta*, which are transferred to the steamer. Our feet for the last time touch the solid ground of Cantire, and then tread the throbbing deck of the steamer. There is a power of herrings on board already; also, a horse and dog-cart, with a few other "inconsidered trifles;" and the Tarbert subscription is quickly added to the general account. But, after all, there is but little luggage on our side of the paddle-boxes, and though the steamer is a very Caliban in respect of its "very ancient and fish-like smell," yet, if we sit well forward, the sea-breeze will waft the perfume away from us, and make things pleasant.

Unless, indeed, it has the contrary effect. For the breeze is rising surely and swiftly; great blue-black clouds have blotted out the sunshine; and, before we are well clear of the quay, a sharp scud of arrowy rain smites us savagely, and the old ruin on the rocky height above us is swept away in a storm mist. It is but an April shower, however, and the sun's rays are drying the deck ere we are half through the labyrinth of East Tarbert Loch; and the crimson moons from the black-cocks in the pile of game close beside us, once more gleam brightly in the sunshine. But ominous clouds, very much of the black-cock hue, are *still* massing "over the hills and far awa';" and, by the time that we have threaded the labyrinthine rocks, and our Caliban has turned his head for his straight run of about ten miles down Loch Fyne, the storm clouds have advanced to meet us, and salute us with a full discharge that drives the ladies into the saloon, and

those who wish to see the scenery into despair. We
are told that we are passing many houses belonging to
the clan Campbell; and, that in one of these houses,
the "Pleasures of Hope" was written; but, our pleasures of hope are all set upon a longing for fair weather,
and, for anything that we can see of houses or shore,
we might be in the middle of the Atlantic, so completely is the landscape on either side obscured from
our view. The storm, however, if it was to come, has
come opportunely; for the scenery of this southern
portion of Loch Fyne, though bold is bald, and (as
Miss Sinclair tells us) is fine only in name.

By the time that the storm has ceased, and sunshine has once more restored the landscape to our view,
and the ladies to the deck, we are nearing Aird Lamont, and our Caliban is churning his way through a
rough sea. The rugged mountains of Arran rise before
us; and, to our right, we have the eastern coast of
Cantire, with the square keep and towers of Skipness
Castle. It is our last sight of Cantire, and we gaze
upon its shores, as do those who are parting regret-
fully from an old friend. It was hereabouts that
Pennant lay, when he wrote thus:— "Weigh anchor
at three o'clock in the morning: are tiezed with calms,
but amused with a fine view of the circum-ambient
land; the peninsula of *Cantyre* here lofty, sloping, and
rocky, divided by dingles, filled with woods, which

reach the water edge, and expand on both sides of the
hollows; *Inch-marnoc* and *Bute* lie to the east; the
mountainous *Arran* to the south; *Loch-fine*, the *Sinus
Lelalonnius* of *Ptolemy*, opened on the north between
the point of *Skipnish* in *Cantyre*, and that of *Lamond*
in *Cowal*, and showed a vast expanse of water wildly
bounded; numbers of herring-busses were now in
motion, to arrive in time at *Campbeltoun*, and animated
the scene." * This quotation describes our field of
view. Inch-marnock is a pretty islet, that once belonged to Saddell monastery in Cantire. Aird Lamont,
or the Promontory of Lamont — so called, because it
forms part of the estate of the family of Lamont of
Lamont — is a notable headland, in rounding which
we leave the waters of Loch Fyne, and enter those of
the Kyles of Bute. The family of Lamont once stood
next to the Duke of Argyle in county importance and
broad acres; and they "are among the very few clans
whose chieftainship remains undisputed, as there is
scarcely another family of the name, besides that of the
present laird." † We see Aird Lamont House, the
modern seat of the family; and then, we enter the
Kyles of Bute, our Caliban fighting his way through
the waves, and staggering and reeling under their
thumps and buffets.

* Voyage to the Hebrides, p. 164.
† Miss Sinclair's "Scotland and the Scotch."

Miss Sinclair tells us, that "Aird Lamont Point is reckoned a perfect Cape of Good Hope for storms;" and, though we have sunshine above us, yet we have the effect of the recent storm below us, and we can readily believe anything bad of this western entrance to the Kyles of Bute. Instead of being "tiezed with calms," like Pennant, we are teased with qualms, like to those which reduced Dr. Johnson to "a state of annihilation."* It is uncommonly rough; we keep our seats and our stomachs with difficulty; there are heavings and tossings from within and without; and some of the ladies who have been enjoying the scenery in a more ghastly manner even than that with which, according to Froissart, the English nation take their pleasures, make a precipitate retreat to their cabin, or calmly resign themselves to their destiny.

"It reminds me of that dreadful passage to Calais," says a lady, who has no sooner spoken, than she becomes "one more unfortunate."

If she had not been too far gone for etymological diversions, I could have told her that these Kyles were reminding me also of Calais, but in a different way. For *Kyle* is but a corruption of the Gaelic word *caol*, which means "a narrow sound;" and

---

* Boswell's "Tour to the Hebrides," Oct. 3.

caolaes signifies the ferry-place across a sound; and hence we get Calais, the ferry-place from France to England.*

But our staggering and rolling, and pitching and tossing does not last long; and when our Caliban has doubled Aird Lamont, and has fairly entered into the still waters of the Kyles, he behaves himself more seemly, and the miseries of sea-sickness have a cessation until we reach Toward Point, at the western end of the Kyles, which becomes an untoward point to many, and renews their woes *da capo*. But this is anticipating evil; let us, while we are in the placid stream of the Kyles, enjoy the lovely landscapes while we may; for as the *Saturday Review* has well said, " Though it is much more important to a traveller that his digestion should be in order than that the landscape around him should be fine, yet descriptions of scenery are more interesting to readers than descriptions of heartburn and rhubarb pills."

All travellers (with the exception perhaps of Pennant and Lord Teignmouth) seem agreed as to the beauty of the scenery of the Kyles. And this can hardly be wondered at; for it is a succession of

---

* Though here again etymologists differ; for Mr. Chambers tells us that " Kyle means a woody region." ("History of Scotland," vol. i. p. 4.) Gaelic scholars would appear to provide five or six varieties of etymology for the English student to pick and choose from.

surprises, and is singularly free from monotony. It appeared to us all the more enchanting, from its pictorial effects being greatly heightened by the brilliant sharpness that was given to the landscape by the sunlight that shone upon us all through the Kyles, the while the dark storm-clouds that had burst upon us in Loch Fyne had rallied their forces and pursued us in dense rolling masses to Toward Point, where for the space of a quarter of an hour they did mighty execution, and then left us to voyage up " the broad and brimming Clyde " under the restored dominion of sunshine. It was a chequered day of shine and shade, of fair and foul ; but all through the Kyles we were happily favoured with the shine and the fair.

The Kyles of Bute form that narrow arm of the Frith of Clyde that flows between the island of Bute and the coast of Cowal in Argyleshire ; and appear upon the map somewhat like a capital M, painfully penned in no very capital style by a village schoolboy. Loch Straven and Loch Ridan form the two points to the upper part of this imaginary capital letter, and the island of Bute is thrust in the first arm. As a necessary consequence of this peculiar formation of the Kyles, the steamer's course is most erratic and bewildering : she is unable to keep her head in the same direction for half a mile together ; the breeze catches her now on the larboard, and now on the starboard, and to the passengers she appears to be vaguely wandering backwards and forwards and in and out of a confused medley of bays and lochs, where we see scores of houses that we covet for a summer residence, but no practicable outlet by which we can make our escape from this loch-ey labyrinth. Both with the beauty of the scenery, no less than with the bewildering character of our route, we may say,

"We're in a maze, as though at Hampton Court!"

Pennant and Lord Teignmouth have been mentioned as two travellers upon whom the Kyles made no favourable impression. Pennant, indeed, never mentions them, although he devotes several pages to a description of Bute, telling us that the land is manured with corals and sea-shells (think of that, O ye poets and syrens!) and that "throstles and other birds of song, fill the groves with their melody; nothing disturbs their harmony; for instinct, stronger than reason, forbids them to quit these delicious shades, and wander like their unhappy master (*i. e.* the then Earl of Bute) into the ungrateful wilds of ambition." Lord Teignmouth does mention the Kyles, but in these words: "The narrow branch of the outlet of the Clyde, called the Kyle of Bute, offers no scenery worthy of notice; but opens nobly on the majestic heights of

Arran." But if all the tots of the *tot homines tot sententiæ* be tottled up, we shall find that there is, in effect, but one opinion on the scenery of the Kyles of Bute.

Miss Sinclair, for example, goes so far as to say that it "has but few equals in the world," and that the Kyles, "in their rugged magnificence, have frequently been compared to the Rhine,"—many travellers, however, assigning the palm to the Scotch beauty. "At every turn," says Miss Sinclair, "the mountains seemed to close round us like those that stopped the Arctic career of Captain Ross. We were imprisoned within a circular barrier of wooded and rocky hills, 'with the blue above and the blue below,' but the narrow sea still found its own way out of the labyrinth, and carried us along with it through a maze of beautiful old castles, villas, and villages, all sprinkled about by the finger of taste (!), and looking their very best under a bright glowing sunshine. I should like to live a hundred summers equally divided among the hundred places we passed during those few hours, while merely catching a momentary glimpse of their velvet lawns, drooping trees, smoking chimneys, which promised internal comfort (!), rustic chairs that seemed spontaneously growing out of the ground (!!) and a noble array of handsome mountains, uniting grandeur to grace, and giving a dash of perfection to the whole.

Never did fifty things at once appear so lovely — never, never."

This authoress would seem to be what is vulgarly termed " a gushing party ; " but rapture and panegyric will be found to enter largely into nearly every description of the scenery of the Kyles of Bute. Take, for example, Dr. Macculloch, who, with a keen appreciation for the beauties of a landscape, yet always described it within the bounds of propriety and truth. He is approaching the Kyles from Rothesay and Loch Straven, and says: " Nor is there anything very interesting in the passage of the Kyles until we begin to approach the ferry.* The long vista of this narrow strait is here striking ; overshadowed, as it were, by the high ranges of hills which rise from the water on each hand, expanding at one extremity into the spacious sound of Rothesay, and on the other losing itself amid rocks and woods, as if all further progress was at an end. Though the passage of the Kyles is everywhere interesting, it is more particularly beautiful between this ferry and the entrance of Loch Ridan, where it is contracted, as well as varied, by four islands. These, and the forms of the land on both sides, render the passage so narrow and intricate, that for a considerable space it seems to be at end, repeatedly,

* Culintraimh. See Appendix : Nelson's Handbook.

in working through it. It is the same, indeed, for
nearly four miles through this intricate and narrow
strait, the land closing in in such a manner as to
appear to meet from the opposite sides. Thus, while
in some places we feel as if passing through the laby-
rinths of an Alpine river, in others we appear to be
enclosed within a lake. It is only by the rise and fall
of the tide, and the appearance of the sea-weed on the
rocks, that we are led to suspect the maritime nature
of this channel, since it is so far removed from the
sea and so involved in all that class of ornament and
scenery which we are accustomed to associate with fresh
water, that it is scarcely possible to divest ourselves of
the idea of being in an inland lake. At the same time
it is no less beautiful than extraordinary; the land
rising suddenly and high from the water, often into
lofty cliffs interspersed and varied with wood, the trees
growing from the fissures of the rocks even at the very
margin of the sea, and aiding, with the narrowness of
the strait and the height of the land, to produce a sober,
green, shadowy tone of forest scenery, which adds much
to the romantic effect of *this fairy-like sea.*" And,
elsewhere, he says, "The Kyles of Bute resemble
nothing on earth."

"The whole way from Rothesay through the Kyles
of Bute," says Sir George Head, "a series of striking
images appeared one after the other." (The usual se-

quence of the parts of a series.) " Sometimes we found ourselves among broken islands, scattered abroad as it were at random in the ocean; at others we steered among abrupt rocks; and again, in a more inland course, as if within the channels of a gallant river, whose mountain-banks are tufted to the water's edge with bright alluvial verdure. The day was made cheerful by incessant changes of scenery, as, passing through a tortuous channel, each moment placed the various objects in a different position, thus embellishing the landscape with ever-varying tints and outlines. Meanwhile we glanced along in our course from point to point, peacefully, as the shadows of clouds on the distant hills."

And so did we; from Lamont Point to Toward Point we peacefully did thread our way through those labyrinthine Kyles (our Caliban's captain holding the clue), touching at Ormadale, and Colintrae, and passing those many note-worthy objects of which a full record will be found in the guide-books, until we come in sight of Rothesay, with its crescent bay and sheltering hills, where the climate is that of Devonshire, and where magnolias and myrtles, cape-heaths and camellias, bloom and thrive in the open air. There is a castle in Rothesay, now " an old ugly thing," says Miss Sinclair, but once the residence of monarchs. Here the lame King Robert III. died of a broken heart on hearing of

the capture of his son by Henry IV. of England; that
son who lived to be James I. of Scotland, and the
husband of the Lady Jane Beaufort, whom,

"With beauty enough to make a world to doat,"

he had seen from his prison window, and to whom he
at once made love and poetry. It was this poet-prince's
elder brother, David, Earl of Carrick, whom his father
made the first Scottish duke, under the title of the
Duke of Rothesay *, a title still borne by our Prince of
Wales.

Does the reader know what a sad fate befell the first
Duke of Rothesay? It happened well nigh five centuries ago, and the tragical tale has been told in Latin
by Hector Boece, and translated into quaint Scotch by
Bellenden. In effect it is as follows, Boece's narrative
being here completed from other accounts. The while
his mother, the Queen Annabella Drummond, was alive,
so long was David, Duke of Rothesay, " holden in virtues and honest occupation;" but, after her death, he
fell into evil courses, and gave himself over to the
worst vices. So, at least, said his uncle, the Duke of
Albany, who for thirty-four years had had the real
power of the state in his hands, and viewed with alarm

---

* In the fourteenth edition of Black's "Picturesque Tourist of Scotland," this and other deeds are ascribed to Robert II., who died 1390,
p. 425.

the growth to manhood of a youth of so much promise, who would be able to defeat his ambitious plans. The lame King Robert was old and imbecile, and was easily persuaded by his brother to believe many foul stories of his son David's enormities, and also to write a letter, in which he begged the Duke of Albany to take charge of his scapegrace son, and " learn him civil and honest manners." Armed with these instructions, the Duke of Albany (who must have been the original Wicked Uncle) carried away his nephew to his castle of Falkland, in Fifeshire, and there threw him into a dungeon with the cruel purpose of starving him to death. But the life of the unfortunate Duke of Rothesay was feebly sustained for some little time; first, by a pitying woman, who (according to Bellenden's version) let meal fall down through the loft of the tower where he was imprisoned; though, according to another narrative, it was the daughter of the governor of the castle who took pity on the hapless prisoner, and, through a small crevice in the wall, pushed thin cakes into his dungeon. But whichever version may be the correct one, both are agreed in saying that the woman was put to death for her merciful action. Yet even this brutal deed did not deter another tender-hearted woman, employed in the family as a wet-nurse, who supplied him with milk from her breasts by means of a long reed, until she also was discovered and slain with great cruelty.

Then was the poor duke destitute of all mortal supply, and was brought to so fearful a condition that he even gnawed his own fingers, "to his great martyrdom," and so died miserably. A Sir John Ramorney is said to have assisted in this cruel deed. The emaciated body of the captive was buried, either in the old church of Kilgour, near Falkland, or in Lindores Abbey, where they still show a stone coffin which is said to have been that of Prince David, the first Duke of Rothesay. Hector Boece tells us that it caused miracles for many years after; but that when the poet-prince James (who was the second Duke of Rothesay) succeeded to the throne, and punished the murderers of his brother, then the miracles ceased.*

So much for an old story and a sad one. By way of relief, take one that is more modern and merrier. It has been told by Miss Sinclair. Ere the Bute family settled at Mount Stewart, they inhabited a house facing Rothesay Castle. When Lord Bute brought home his newly-married countess, a daughter of the Duke of Argyle, he observed during dinner something like discomposure. As soon as the servants withdrew, he ventured to inquire if anything had dis-

---

* I need not remind the reader that the history of this unfortunate Duke of Rothesay forms the groundwork of Sir Walter Scott's "Fair Maid of Perth." Fordun, Boece, and the old Chroniclers are quoted in the *Notes* to the Novel, vol. ii. p. 378.

agreed with her ladyship. She whimpered that she thought when he married *her* he would have had a better place to bring her to. He rose, marched round the table, and, with the formality of the olden time, offered her his arm and led her to the window; then, pointing to Rothesay Castle, he said, "My lady, do you see that building?" "Yes, my lord." "Well, madam, that is the mansion to which I should have had the honour of conducting your ladyship, if your uncles had not burnt it for our family."

But the present hereditary keeper of Rothesay Castle, and descendant of King Robert III., will be able to build ever so many castles if he be so inclined, for, when he attains his majority, he will be one of the wealthiest peers in Great Britain.

Over against Rothesay, on the Cowal shore, are the two Toward Castles; the old ruin is the castle of the Lamonts, the modern edifice is that of Mr. Kirkman Finlay, and its situation is remarkably fine. While we are admiring it the black clouds rise over the Toward Lighthouse, and sweeping over us, suddenly burst upon us with a hurricane of rain and wind, and send us reeling round Toward Point and into the Firth of Clyde. And thus our entrance and exit to and from the Kyles of Bute on that day, were made in far too *brusque* a manner to be agreeable.

But, ere we reach Dunoon, it is all sunshine again,

and the ladies come upon the deck to see the Cloch
Lighthouse shining white on our right hand, and the
Holy Loch and Loch Long before us, with the tumbled
heap of mountains in the distance, crowned by peaked
Ben Lomond. And soon we are between Roseneath
and Gourock, and are steaming up the Clyde, and set
foot on Greenock Quay, the end cf a long journey, and
also of this book —

"Longæ finis chartæque viæque."

APPENDIX

APPENDIX.

.

THE CANTIRE LIFE-BOAT. (Vol. I. p. 93.)

EXTRACT from the Report of the Committee of the Royal National Life-Boat Institution: —

Thursday, 1st November, 1860.   CAPTAIN SIR EDWARD PERROTT, Bart., *V.P.*, in the Chair.

Read and approved the Minutes of the previous Meeting, and those of the Finance, Correspondence, and Wreck and Reward Sub-Committees.

Read letter from LOCKHART THOMSON, Esq., of Edinburgh, stating that Lady Murray had decided to present to the Institution the cost of a life-boat establishment—the same not to exceed in amount 520*l.* Her ladyship wished the boat to be stationed on the Mull of Cantyre, or some other part of the west coast of Scotland, and to be called, after her late husband, Lord Murray.— *To be thanked.*

Also from the DUKE OF ARGYLL, of the 30th October, expressing his admiration of the generous gift of Lady M., and approving of the establishment of the life-boat on the Mull of Cantyre, where he believed one was much needed.— *To be acknowledged.*

Also from Messrs. WATSON, JUN., and Co., agents for Lloyd's

at Campbeltown, of 21st October, stating that Lady M.'s munificence had made much impression on the public mind in that locality, and that every one looked on her generous intentions with feelings of deep gratitude. — *To be acknowledged.*

Also from Captain WARD, R.N., Inspector of Life-boats to the Institution, stating that he had recently visited Cantyre, and that he was of opinion that a life-boat would be of great service on that peninsula ; for sundry reasons he recommended that the boat-house should be built at Campbeltown, whence, being a central position, the boat on her carriage might be transported to various parts of the coast.

Decided : That a life-boat station be formed forthwith on Cantyre.

———————

From a recent statement (June 1861) it appears that the greatest loss of life from shipwreck, of late years, on the British coast, has been in the district from Lambay Island (north of Dublin Bay) to the Mull of Cantire, and the Skerries, where 1456 lives have been lost during the last eleven years.

DERMID*: A POEM. (Vol. II. p. 14.)

THE ARGUMENT.

This poem opens with an address to the valley of Cona, in which its present silence is contrasted with its former busy scenes. Of these the story of Dermid's killing a wild boar of an enormous size, is singled out. After Dermid had killed this boar, he is desired by Connan, who bore him a grudge which the poem accounts for, to measure his length, with his bare soles, against the direction of the bristles on his back. Dermid, it seems, thought it might be a reflection upon his valour to decline the request. He complied; but the consequence proved fatal.

Graina, Dermid's wife, having been alarmed by the story of an old man whom she had met, after parting with Dermid, ran to his assistance with a spear, and arrived just as that which he had was broken in his encounter with the boar: but she herself being wounded by a random shot in the course of the chase, sits down near enough to be witness of the death of her beloved Dermid. Both are interred in the same place, and their elegy sung by the bards.

How peaceful, this night, art thou, O vale of Cona! No voice of thy hounds, no sound of thy harps is heard. The sons of the chase are gone to their rest, and the bed has been made for the bards. The murmur of thy stream, O Cona, is scarce perceived: the breeze shakes not the dew off thy bended grass. The grey thistle hangs over thy bank its sleepy head; its hairs are heavy with the drops of night. The roe sleeps, fearless, in the booth of the hunter; his voice hath ceased to disturb her.

---

* Dermid, the son of Duino, is frequently mentioned in other poems of Ossian, and much celebrated in the tales of later times. These, mixing their marvellous with the original poem, have rendered it in a great measure absurd and extravagant. But they are for the most part of so heterogeneous a nature as to be easily separated.

She sees his tomb, amidst green ferns, before her. Light-leaps over its mound her little kid. He rubs with his horn the moss from its gray stone ; and on the soft heap, when tired of play, he lays himself down to rest.

Vale of Cona*, how art thou changed ! And thou, hill of Golbun, how quiet is now thy heath ! Thou coverest thy head with thy dark veil of mist; and slumberest in the noon of day. No voice of the hunter, no cry of the hound, travels along thy dark-brown side to awake thee. I move forth when all is calm; I lean my gray head on my spear, and listen if I may hear the echo of thy rocks. But thou art silent, O Golbun, in thy bed of clouds : no voice of thine is heard; save when thou repliest to the sportive cry of the deer, when evening has half hid the sun in the wave of the west. Then, thou dost reply ; but thy words are few : thou soon composest thyself again to thy slumber.

Thou wert not thus quiet, O Cona, when the king pursued thy deer, and made thy stream shake between its woody locks; nor was thy silence such, O Golbun, when the son of Duino pursued thy boar, foaming like Lora in his winding course.

Listen, son of Alpin, to the tale ; thou wilt pour its light on the dark stream of future years.

The morning was calm on Cona. Mountains saw in Ocean

---

*
> " Cia tiamhaidh thu nochd a *Ghlean-caothan !*
> Gun ghuth gaothair thu, 's gun cheol, &c."

The *Gleann-caothan*, or *Cona*, of Ossian has been supposed by some to be Glenco in Argyleshire ; and by others, Strathconan in Murray. Both seem to be at too great a distance from the scene of this poem, if we may rely on tradition, which places it in *Sli' gaoil* near Kintyre. What appears most probable is, that Fingal often shifted his habitation for the convenience of hunting, and might give several other places the same name with that of his principal residence,

> " parvam Trojam, simulataque magnis,"
> Pergama."

their gilden heads. The son of the deer beheld his young branches in the stream, when the sound of Fingal's horn is heard. Starting, he asks his mother what it means. She, trembling, bids him fly to the desart.

" This day," said the king, " we pursue the boar, the deadly boar of Golbun." *

* * * * *

We sent the sons of the chase to the hill. Their cries, as they climb, are deep and loud. Golbun with all its woods resounds.

The sound rose on Dermid's ear, as he lay in the cave of his rest. As a mountain-stream in the midst of rain, so leapt his soul with joy at the voice of the chase. " My red spear, where art thou? and where art thou, my dark bow?"

Not so glad was Graina in her cave, to which she had retired with her love from Connan's hate. The dark soul of Connan had loved Graina; but Graina gave her heart to Dermid. " Heed not," she said, " the cry of the hounds; the chase of heroes is not awake on the hill."

" Fair is thy form, my love; and like the bloom of trees in spring is thy beauty; yet this day I must leave thee, with thy child, in the cave. I must mix with heroes on Golbun."

'* Some repeat here a small fragment called *Nòs Seilge,* or " The manner of hunting." As this poem is only a hunting adventure, it is probable these verses ought to have a place in it, if their incorrectness did not forbid it. The most accurate of them are the following, which denote their armour to have been nearly the same as in going down to battle.

> " Gun ar n eide' 's gun ar n airm
> Cha rachamaid a sheilg nan cnoc;
> Bhiodh luireach oirn 's ceann-bheairt chorr,
> 'S da shleagh mhor ann dorn gach fir.
> Bhiodh sgia uain' air a gheibhe' buaidh,
> 'S cloidhe cruaidh gu sgolta cheann,
> Bogha cruadhach agus iughair
> 'S caogad guineach ann am bolg,"

" And wilt thou leave me," said Graina, " loveliest of men ;
wilt thou leave me, thou light of my soul in darkness ? Where is
my joy but in the face of Dermid? where is my safety but in
thy shield of brass? Wilt thou leave me, thou fairer than the
sun when he smiles, after the shower, on the leaf of the birch ;
thou milder than his evening beams, when they play on the
down of the mountain ? Thy son and I will be sad, if thou art
absent, Dermid."

" Graina, dost thou not remember the moans of the crane, as
we wandered early on the hill of our love ?* With pity, thou
didst ask the aged son of the rock, Why so sad was the voice
of the crane ? 'Too long,' he replied, ' he hath stood in the fen ;
and the ice hath bound his lazy foot. Let the idle remember
the crane, lest one day they mourn like him.' Graina, I will
not rest longer here. Fingal might say, with a sigh, 'One of
my heroes is become feeble.' No, king of Morven, the soul of
Dermid is not a stream that will fail; the joyful murmur of its
course shall always attend thy steps. Rest thou in thy cave,
my love; with night I will return with the spoil of roes."

He went, swift as the path of an arrow, when it whistles thro'
the yielding air on its two gray wings. Graina climbs, pensive
and slow, the hill, to view the chase of roes from her rock. The
light of her countenance is mild, but dim; like the moon in
the night of calm, when it moves in silence through the clouds,
and seems the darkened shield of a ghost, hung on high in his
own airy hall !† She meets a son of age in the woods. Bending,
he weeps over a gray stone. " Here," he said, " sleeps the

*   "'S moch a ghoireas a chorr
             Air an lon ata 'n *Slia'gaoil*."

Slia'gaoil, "the hill of love," is still the proper name of a mountain
near Kintyre, said to have been the residence of these lovers, and to have
received from them its name.

† The original word (*Ealachainn taibhse*) signifies properly "the

spouse of my love; here, I reared over her the green turf.
Many were our days on the heath. We have seen one race,
like the leaf of autumn, pass: we have seen another lift in its
place its green head, and grow old. We have turned away our
foot from trees, lest we might crush them in youth; and we
have seen them again decay with years. We have seen streams
changing their course; and nettles growing where feasted
kings. All this while our joy remained; our days were glad.
The winter with all its snow was warm, and the night with all
its clouds was bright. The face of Minalla was a light that
never knew a wane; an undecaying beam around my steps.
But now she shines in other lands; when, my love, shall I be
with thee?

" There too, fair maid, thou beholdest another tomb. Under
it is the cold bed of the son of Colla. It was made by the trembling hand of his father. By the boar of the woods my son was
slain. He fell near the cave of his dwelling. His spouse was
preparing the feast for his return; ' I go,' I said, ' to look for his
coming.' I went; I heard his cry; I ran with the short steps of
age to assist him. Hanging by my robe, his son attends. We
find his father dead. The boar had broke his spear in twain;
and the sword in his cave was left. His child takes him by the
hand, and bids him rise. ' Why,' he said, ' shouldst thou sleep
without?' Alas! he hears thee not; for the tusk of the boar
hath torn him, and his sleep is heavy. This morning sounds
Fingal's horn to pursue the fatal boar. But its voice reaches
not the ear of Tuthal; the morning that shall rouse my son

armoury of a ghost." The whole comparison, which is exceedingly
beautiful, as well as fanciful, is subjoined: —

" Bha a braghad gu seimh a 'soillse,
Mar ghealach ri oidhche shaimhe;
Si gluasad ro na neula balbha,
Mar sgia air *ealachamn* taibhse."

X 4

is distant. O Tuthal, why hadst not thou thy father's spear ? "

" Mournful," said Graina, " is the tale of Colla. My tears in a stream could flow on the tombs of thy spouse and son. My tears could flow ; but I must fly with speed. My Dermid pursues the fatal boar; who knoweth, my love, but thou mayst need a spear? Colla, keep thou this child till I return. I fly to my love with a stronger spear."

Dermid had come to the vale of Cona, like a fair light that grows in darkness. We rejoiced in his presence, as the mariners when the star, that long concealed itself in its cloud, looks again on their dark course, and spreads its beam around. The voice of songs is on the deep ; and seals lift up, through trembling waves, their heads to listen to the music.

We climb Golbun of green hills, where the branchy horns of deer are seen in mist, and where lie thick the mossy beds of roes. From echoing rocks we start the boar, the red deadly boar of Golbun. We pursue him with all our dogs; but he leaves them weltering in blood behind.

Who, said the king, shall kill the boar of Golbun; the boar that is red with the blood of heroes; that hath slain so many of our hounds? His shall be a spear, the gift of a king, a shield with all its studs ; and the herbs of the secret stream, to heal the hero's wounds.

Mine, replied Dermid, shall be the gift of the king ; or I fall by the bristly foe, and lose the fame of the song.

He spoke, and flew over the heath in the gleam of steel. His course was like the red cloud that bears the thunder on its wing when the fields of Fingal are silent and dark. Quaking heroes lift from Morven their eye, and behold in sky the fight of ghosts. It is Trenmor hurling his wrath against Lochlin's sons, when they come to pursue his airy deer.

Already the roar of Dermid is on Benala. From Benala he flies to Benlora. Now the hill of Ledroma shakes under his feet; and now the hill of Elda.

The boar flies before him, but not so fast. His path is marked with wreaths of foam. His noise is like the white tumbling of waves on the isle of storms; like the falling of rocks amidst the groves of the desart.—See! they ascend Drimrnath; the spear of Dermid almost reaches the foe. It falls heavy on its sides; it marks them with red streams. It sounds like the fall of trees, with all their aged branches, on a rock. The vales along their winding banks resound. But see! with fury red-glaring in his eye, he turns, as the stream of flames on a hill when the dark winds have changed. As it were a bulrush or slender reed of Lego, he grinds the hard, tough, spear of Dermid.*

"O that thou wert near me, Graina! that my love would come from her cave, and bring me the spear of battle!"

"Bring it I do, my Dermid. From my cave I saw thy distress. Thither again I return. There look for me, my love, when the strife on the hill is over."

And what though he find thee too, hapless maid! Alas! the days of the years are run. An arrow in its wandering flight had met the fair in the course of the chase. In her breast of snow it is lodged; but she conceals it with her robe from Dermid. Dear hast thou paid, O Dermid, for that weapon in thy hand; who shall tell thee what it cost thee?

With all his terrible might the chief lifts his spear. Like

---

* The original of these two lines is a most remarkable *echo to the sense.* The one line is full of that harsh, grinding sound which it describes, and the other as smooth as the bulrush or reed of Lego of which it speaks. The contrast between them has also a fine effect.

" Chagnadh e a shleaghan readh ruadh'
Mar chuile na Leige, no mar luachair."

a meteor of death, red-issuing from Lano's cloud, a flood of light, it quick descends. The head is lodged in the rough breast of the boar: the shaft flies, over trees, through air. His sword is in the hero's hand; the old companion of his deeds in the hour of danger. Its cold point pierces the heart of the foe :—The boar, with all his blood and foam, is stretched on earth.*

We rejoiced to see Dermid safe; we rejoiced all, but Connan. Measure, said that little soul, the boar which thou hast slain. Measure him with thy foot bare; a larger hath not been seen.

The foot of Dermid flies softly along the grain; no harm hath the hero suffered.

Measure, said Connan, the boar against the grain; and thine, chief of spears, shall be the boon thou wilt ask.

The soul of Dermid was a stranger to fear; he obeyed again the voice of Connan.—But the bristly back of Golbun's boar, sharp as his arrows and strong as his spear, pierces with a thousand wounds his feet. His blood dyes the ground; it flows in wandering rills through the grass. The herbs of the mountain are applied; but their virtue fails.—Dermid falls, like a tall pine, on the heath.†

Ah! how quick the colour forsakes his cheek. It was red

---

* It is from this event that the clan of the Campbells, who derive their pedigree from this Dermid, have assumed the boar's head for the crest of their arms. In the compositions of the later bards they are often called *Sliochd Dhiarmid an Tuirc*, or, "The race of Dermid who slew the boar."

† The death of Dermid, in the manner it is here told, will appear somewhat odd. It is probable he had received some other wound in a more mortal part; and that some of the poem, where his death may have been better accounted for, is lost. The current tradition with regard to this passage is, that Dermid was vulnerable in no part but in the sole of his foot, and that the great art of Connan was to get him

as the fruit that bends the mountain tree *; but now it grows pale as the withered grass. A dark cloud spreads over his countenance, as thick mists that veil the face of the wintry sun, when the evening comes before its time.

" The shades of night gather on my eyes. I feel the decay of my strength. The tide that flowed in my heart hath ebbed away. Behind it I remain a cold, unmoving rock. Thou shalt know it, Graina, and be sad; ah ! the pain of death is to part with my love. But the shades of the night are gathering over my soul. Let Dermid sleep; his eyes are heavy."

Who shall tell it to Graina? — But Graina is nigh. She leans beneath the shade of a tree. She hears the moans of her love: they awake her slumbering soul. Hark ! she pours her faint song on the calm breath of the breeze. See ! her blood and her tears wander on her white breasts, like dark streams on the mountains of snow.

"My love is fallen ! O place me in his bed of earth; at the foot of that rock, which lifts, through aged trees, its ivy head.

wounded there. Whether this account of the matter, though common, be very old or very satisfactory, is a point in which the translator is not concerned.

* In poems chiefly depending on tradition, there must be in different editions a considerable variation. Their comparisons frequently differ; but they are always beautiful, and have the same scope. Thus, for instance, instead of the above simile, many have here another of the same nature, taken from the strawberry:

> " Ged' bu deirge do ghruaidh nan t subh
> Bhiodh air uilin cnuic 's an sheur ;
> Dh' fhas i nois dui'-neulach uaine,
> Mar neul fuar air neart na grein."

Such as may here miss the dialogue concerning *Cuach Fhinn*, or the medicinal cup of Fingal, will remember that it is of so different a complexion from the rest of the poem, that no apology needs be made for rejecting it as the interpolation of some later bard.

The sheeted stream, with murmuring grief, shall throw its waters over our tomb; but oh! let it not wet the dark-brown hair of my love. — The stream still murmurs by; some day its course may wash away the mound. The hunter, as whistling he goes careless by, will perceive the bow of Dermid, and say, 'This is Dermid's grave.' His spouse, perhaps, may be with him. Near the bow, she will observe this arrow in my breast; and say, as she wipes her eye, 'Here was Graina laid beside her love.' — Musing, they move silently along; their thoughts are of the narrow house. They look on each other, through glistening eyes. 'The fondest lovers,' they say, 'must part at last.'

"But stop, hunters of the mountain, and give the mighty his praise. No mean hunter of a little vale was he, whom you have passed so careless by. His fame was great among the heroes of Morven; his arm was strong in their battles. And why should I speak of his beauty; shall his comeliness remain with him in the tomb! — His breast was as the down of the mountain, or the snow on the tree of the vale, when it waves its head in the sun. — Red was the cheek, and blue the eye, of my love. Like the grass of the rock, slow-bending in the breeze, were his brows; and sweeter than the music of harps or the songs of groves, was thy voice to virgins, O Dermid! — But the music of thy voice is ceased, and my spirits can no more be cheered. The burden of my grief is heavy: the songs of Morven's bards cannot remove it. It will not listen to all the larks that soar in the lowly vale, when the dewy plains rejoice in the morning sun of summer. But what hath Graina to do with the sun of the morning; or what hath Dermid to do with summer? When shall the sun rise in the tomb? When shall it be summer in the grave, or morning in the narrow house? Never shall

that morning shine, that shall dispel our slumber, O Dermid?"*

We laid the lovely pair in their bed of earth. The spear of
his strength, with his bow, is beside Dermid; and with
Graina is laid the arrow that was cold in her breast. Fingal

*
> " Cha dealruich a mhaidin gu *La bhrath*
> A dh'fhogras do phramh, a Shuinn !"

The word *la bhrath*, in its literal and primary sense, signifies " the day
of burning," which was the druidical term for the dissolution of the
world *by fire*, as *gu dilinn* was their name for the alternate revolution
which they supposed it should undergo *by water*. In a metaphorical
sense both words came to denote *never*, or "till the end of the world,"
which for many ages back has been their only acceptation. Hence, a
translator is naturally led to render these and the like words by their
present meaning, without adverting to their etymology or ancient signification. This is one reason why more religious ideas do not appear in
the works of Ossian, which, if examined in the original, will be found to
contain many allusions to the Druidical tenets. The word under our
present consideration, though it is now universally understood to signify
never, was used, long after the introduction of Christianity, to denote
the dissolution of the world by fire, as among the Druids from whom it
was borrowed. In that famous prophecy of St. Columba, to which his
monastery owed so much of its repute, it has this meaning, *Scachd la' ro
an bhrath*, &c. " Seven days before the dissolution of the world, a flood
shall cover the other kingdoms, but Iona shall swim above it." Ossian,
who uses the word frequently in his poems, probably affixed to it this
idea, much oftener than that of *never*, as we do at present. In the
original the word is always more emphatical than can easily be expressed
in a translation. An instance or two will make this obvious to such as
understand both languages. One occurs in the battle of Lora, where
Bosmina says to Erragon,

> " 'S nim faicear a d' thalla *gu brath*
> Airm agh'or mo dheagh Ri'."

" *Never* shall they behold in thy halls the victorious arms of the king."

In the first book of Temora, Fingal mourning over the fallen Oscar,
says

> " Gu *la bhrath* chon eirich Oscar !"

" *Never more* shall Oscar rise," is scarce so emphatical.   .

bended on his spear over their grave. A dark stream descended on his cheek. His bards saw his grief. Each assumed his harp, and gave the name of the dead to the song.—Heroes, mournful, stood around. Tears flowed from the eye of hounds, as they rested on dark-brown shields at their feet.

"Peaceful, O Dermid, be thy rest; calm, son of Duino, be thy repose, in thy dark and lowly dwelling! The din of arms is over; the chase of the boar is ceased; the toil of the day is ended; and thou, heedless of the return of the morning, art retired to thy slumbering rest. The clang of the shield, the noise of the chase shall not awake thee. No; Dermid, thy sleep is heavy!

"But who can give thy fame to the song, thou mighty chief! Thy strength was like the strength of streams in their foam: thy speed like the eagle of Atha, darting on the dun trembling fawn of the desart. In battle, thy path was like the rapid fall of a mountain stream *, when it pours its white torrent over the rock, and sends abroad its gray mists upon the wing of winds. The roar of its stream is loud through Mora's rocks. Mountain-trees, with all their moss and earth, are swept along between its arms. But when it reaches the calm sea of the vale, its strength is lost, and the noise of its course is silent. It moves not the withered leaf if the eddying wind doth not aid it. On eddying winds let thy

---

* The following lines, although defective, being only one of the editions from which this passage is made up, are so beautiful as to deserve their room:

> " Bha do neart mar thuilteach uisge,
> Dol asios a chlaoidh do namh ;
> Ann cabhaig mar iolair nan speur,
> No steud eisg a' ruith air sail'.
> A thriath threun a b' aille leadan
> Na aon fhleasgach tha 'san Fheinn,
> Gu ma samhach a raibh t or-chul,
> Ful' chudrom ua foide re!"

spirit be borne, son of Duino, to thy fathers; but light let the turf lie over thy beauteous form, and calm in the grave be thy slumber!

" A vessel rides the surgy deep.* It bounds from ridge to ridge. Its white sails are spread to the wind. It braves the fury of the storm.—'It is the son of Duino's!'—Yes, stranger, it was the son of Duino's; but now the son of Duino is no more. There he hovers, a faint form, above; and the boar is half-viewless beside him.

" The horn sounds on the mountain. The deer start from the moss of rocks; from the banks of their secret streams. The unerring dart of the hunter pursues them on the heath. One of them is arrested in the midst of his course. Panting he tastes the cooling fount. His knees shake, like the reedy grass in the stream of winds. He falls as he climbs the bank. His companions attempt with their head to raise him, but in vain; they are forced to forsake him and fly.—They fly, but the hunter pursues them. 'His speed is like the speed of Dermid!' —Alas! stranger, it is not he. The son of Duino sleeps in his lowly dwelling, and the hunter's horn cannot awake him.

" The foes come on with their gathered host. A mighty stream meets them in their course. Its torrent sweeps them back, and overturns their grove of spears.—'It is,' saith the son of the stranger, 'one of the warriors of Morven; it is the strength of Dermid!'—The strength of Dermid, replies his companion, hath failed. At the foot of that ivy rock I saw, as I passed, his tomb. The green fern had half hid the gray stone at his head. I pulled its rank growth away: Why shouldst thou, vile weed, I said, obscure the name of the hero?

* In this elegy of the bards over Dermid, the various accomplishments of that hero are remarked; and appear the more striking from their being put, for the most part, in the mouth of strangers.

"A youth comes, whistling, across the plain. His arms glitter to the sun as it sets. His beauty is like that sinking beam, that spreads around him its rays; and his strength is like his beauty;—The virgins are on the green hill above; their robes are like the bow of the shower; their hair like the tresses of the sun, when they float on the western wave in the season of calm. They admire the stately beauty of the warrior, as lightly he moves along.—'The youth,' they say with a sigh, 'is like Dermid.'—The memory of the son of Duino rises on their soul, as a beam that breaks on blasted Mora, through the torn edge of a dusky cloud. In sorrow they bend their heads. The tears shine through their spreading locks, like stars through the wandering hair of the moon. They fall like the tears of Ossian when they flow for Oscar of Lego.

"The children of youth are tossing their little spears. They see the hero on the plain. 'There comes Dermid!' Their reedy spears are thrown away, and they forsake the shield of willow. Their steps of joy are quick to meet the maker of their bows. But they see it is not he, and in mid-way they stop. Slow, they return to their play; but the noise of their harmless battle is not heard, for their little souls are sad for Dermid.

"The voice of music and the sound of the harp are heard in Fingal's hall. The benighted traveller is charmed as he approaches. A moment he leans his breast upon his staff, and, sidelong, bends his listening ear.—'It is Dermid!' he says; and hastens to overtake the song.—A beam of light, clear but terrible, comes across his soul. He makes two unequal strides; in the midst of the third he stops. 'Dermid is no more!'— He wipes with the skirt of his robe his eye; and, sighing, slowly walks along. It is the voice of the bards thou dost hear, O stranger; they are pouring the fame of Dermid on future times; clothing his name with the nightly song. The chief

himself, in Selma thou shalt find no more. He sleeps with
Graina in the cold and narrow house. On Golbun's heath
thou wilt find it, at the side of the stream of roes.—A rock,
dark-bending with its ivy mantle above, shelters from storms
the place. A mountain-stream leaps over it, white, and murmuring travels on. A yew spreads its dark-green branches
nigh : the deer rests undisturbed at noon beneath its shade.
The mariner leaning to his mast, as he passes on the darkly-
rolling wave, points out the place, and tells his mates the
woful tale. The tear bedims their eye. They cannot mark
the spot : they heave the deep note of grief, and sail to the
land of strangers. There, they tell the tale to listening crowds
around the flame of night. The virgins weep, and the children
of youth are mournful. All day they remember Dermid and
Graina ; and in the dreams of their rest they are not forgotten."

And often you descend to the dreams of Ossian too, children of beauty. Often you possess his thoughts, when he sits,
alone, at your tomb, and listens if he may hear the song of
ghosts. At times, I hear your faint voice in the sigh of the
breeze, when I rest beneath your green tree, and hang my harp
on its low-bending branch.—But Ossian is a tree that is
withered.* Its branches are blasted and bare ; no green leaf

---

* No image could better represent the forlorn condition of the poet
than this which he has chosen. The words, too, in which he describes
it, are full of that soft and mournful sound which is expressed in the
Gaelic by the diphthong *ao*, and the triphthong *aoi ;* sounds which, so far
as I know, are peculiar to the Gaelic language, and highly congenial to
the more soft and mournful feelings.

> " Tha mise mar gheig na h aonar,
> Si gu mosgain maol gun duileach,
> Gun mhaothan ri taobh, no ogan,
> Ach osna bhroin a' caoi' na mullach.
> 'S fogus an doinion, a sgaoileas
> A crionach aosd' air feadh a ghlinne.
> Mu leabaidh Dhiarmaid s nan laoch lughar
> Aig Caothan nan luban uaine."

covers its boughs. From its trunk no young shoot is seen to spring. The breeze whistles in its gray moss: the blast shakes its head of age.—The storm will soon overturn it, and strew all its dry branches with thee, O Dermid! and with all the rest of the mighty dead, in the green winding vale of Cona.

How peaceful art thou, O Vale of Cona! Thy warriors and thy hunters are all gone to rest. Let the bed be also made for the bard; for the shades of night thicken around him, and his eyes are heavy.

THE MACDONALDS. (Vol. II. p. 231.)

[Condensed from "Sketches of Early Scotch History," by Cosmo Innes, 1861.]

WHEN Angus Macdonald renounced all right, title, property, and possession to Islay, in favour of Sir John Campbell, Thane of Cawdor, the deed of renunciation was witnessed by three persons, one of whom was " Alexander Macdonald, of Lergie." " Soon after the cession of his claims," says Professor Innes, " the old chief of Islay died. His kinsman, Sir Ranald Macdonald, the son of Sorley Buy (afterwards Earl of Antrim), had, in the mean time, obtained a tack of the island, but had not peaceable possession of it. The castle of Dunyveg (in Islay), for a short time garrisoned by the Bishop of the Isles (Andrew Knox) for the government, had been surprised; and the Bishop himself, led into a trap by the sons of the old chief—brother of the captive of Edinburgh Castle—was obliged to leave his son and nephew in the hands of the rebels, as hostages for his performance of some conditions, especially for doing his utmost to obtain grants by the sovereign in their favour." The "captive" was Sir James M'Donald, " who had been ' warded' first in Blackness and then in Edinburgh Castle, since the year 1604; and who was tried and sentenced to death in 1609, but no time fixed for executing the sentence, and was still a prisoner in the Castle of Edinburgh." (p. 536.) Sir James had married Margaret Campbell, of Cawdor, sister of the above-named Sir John. " Early in the year 1615, the Knight of Cawdor, with the help of Sir Oliver Lambard's cannon, had

taken the castles of Dunyveg and Lochgorm, and ruled undisputed sovereign in the island of Isla.   He and the lords of the
council were planning the repression of the bands of M'Donald
and their followers, now mere marauders and pirates on all the
shores and seas of the west, when they were startled by the
intelligence that Sir James M'Donald, so long a prisoner, had
escaped from Edinburgh Castle (24th of May, 1615), and was
hastening to put himself at the head of his clan, to gather
round him the scattered outlaws of the isles, very ready to
follow so daring a leader, and to recover his inheritance.   The
council seemed at first paralysed and helpless; and Sir James,
with a few followers, dashed through Atholl and Rannoch in
safety, and met with no opposition in the isles.   The men of
the north isles flocked to his standard.   Isla was his first object.
He surprised the castle, subdued the island, the natives evidently favouring him rather than the Campbells; and then he
sent out the fiery cross, and overran his hereditary territory of
Kintyre.   But his success was short-lived.   The council, compelled to some exertion in support of law, placed the affair in
the hands of Argyll, though evidently unwillingly; and the
head of the Campbells, with some soldiers hired at the public
expense, an expense sorely complained of by the council,
speedily brought the war to a conclusion.   There was indeed
no open war, no pitched battles.   Equally in Kintyre and in
Isla, M'Donald's undisciplined followers fell from him; and
Sir James himself, almost singly, escaped to Ireland, and from
thence to Spain.   This remarkable person's career was not to
end even there.   After Argyll's apostasy and disgrace, and
when he too had taken refuge in Spain, Sir James M'Donald
returned to England, was restored to royal favour, and died a
pensioner at London (1626).

" We should err if we counted this last chief of the old race of Isla a mere Celtic savage, as those who drew his indictment seem to have held him. He was no doubt unscrupulous, like his time and his country, and human life was not then held in much respect in the isles; but Sir James, with the virtues of a savage, had some tinge also of civilisation, and some qualities perhaps acquired during his long imprisonment. He was a reader, and he writes to his friend Lord Crawford very anxiously about books he left behind him in prison, and some that fell into the hands of his pursuers when he himself narrowly escaped. They were chiefly controversial books of the old religion, all indeed but one, a ' mekle old cornikle in writ.' Though his early exploits show him reckless of blood, in later life he was not cruel, and sometimes spared his enemies when in his power. His letters, many of which are preserved, and have been printed, show a touch of feeling and of self-respect, and of what was due to his ancient race, with a straightness and manliness of expression that contrast favourably with some of the lawyer's letters among which they are found.

" The documents illustrative of his romantic life are to be found in the ' Records of Secret Council,' and among Secretary Binning's letters in the Advocates' Library. Most of them have been printed or used in well-known publications:—Gregory's ' History of the Highlands and Isles,' c. vii. viii.; Pitcairn's ' Criminal Trials ; ' the ' Melros Papers' (Abbotsford Club), &c. pp. 545-6-7."

The history of the Macdonalds is given at some length in the second volume of Skene's " Highlanders of Scotland " (ii. pp. 35—106). They " were anciently included under the general designation of the Siol Cuinn, or race of Conn, a remote ancestor of the tribe." In speaking of the feuds between the Macleans and Macdonalds, Mr. Skene continues thus :—

" At length, towards the close of the sixteenth century, the Macdonalds appear to have united for the purpose of effectually crushing the rising power of the Macleans. At the head of this union was Angus Macdonald of Kintyre, who had married Maclean's sister, and between whom and Maclean disputes had arisen in consequence of both possessing lands in Jura. The Macdonalds of Sleat were involved in the dispute, in consequence of Sleat having landed on Maclean's property in Jura, on his way to visit Macdonald of Kintyre, when the Kintyre Macdonalds carried off some of Maclean's cattle during the night, in order that he might impute the theft to Macdonald of Sleat. In this they were successful, for the Macleans were no sooner aware of their loss than they attacked the Macdonalds of Sleat, and defeated them with so much slaughter that their chief with difficulty escaped." The Macdonalds shortly afterwards sustained a second defeat, and " never again attempted to invade the possessions of the Macleans ; but a bitter enmity existed between the Macleans and the Macdonalds of Isla and Kintyre, who, failing to make any impression upon them by force, resorted to treachery. With this view, Angus Macdonald of Kintyre effected a reconciliation with Lachlan More (chief of the Macleans), and, the better to cover his intended fraud, he visited him at his castle of Dowart, where his purpose was anticipated by Maclean, who took him prisoner, and did not release him until he had given up his right to some of the lands in Isla, and had left his brother and his eldest son at Dowart as hostages. Maclean was then invited to visit Macdonald at Kintyre, which, relying upon the security of the hostages, he agreed to do, and arrived there, having left Macdonald's brother at Dowart, and being accompanied by the other hostage, his uncle, and seventy gentlemen of his clan. They were received with apparent cordiality, but

had no sooner retired for the night than the house was surrounded by the Macdonalds, with Angus at their head, and,
after an obstinate resistance, the Macleans were made prisoners.
Angus now satiated his vengeance by executing two of the
Macleans every day, reserving their chief Lachlan More to
the last; and he had already in this way slain them all except
the chief, when, two of the gentlemen of his clan having been
taken prisoners in Mull, he was obliged to exchange Lachlan
for them. No sooner, therefore, was Lachlan at liberty, than
he applied to the government, and obtained letters of fire and
sword against Macdonald, with an order upon Macleod and
Locheil to assist him. With these means he sailed for Isla,
attacked and defeated the Macdonalds, burnt the whole island,
and drove Angus to seek refuge in his castle, who, seeing that
he could not resist Maclean, bought his forbearance by giving
up to him the half of the island of Isla. On the death of Angus
of Isla, this grant produced some negotiations between Maclean
and James Macdonald, Angus's son; and, in order to settle
their difference, a meeting was agreed upon between them,
but Maclean coming unadvisedly with a small attendance, and
his boats being stranded by the retiring tide, he was surprised
by James Macdonald, and killed after a brave resistance. And
thus fell the greatest chief whom the Macleans ever had,
a victim to the treachery of the Macdonalds of Isla."
(ii. 210, 212.)

For further particulars of the Macdonalds see (in the same
volume) under the heads of " Ross," " Clan Kenneth," " Clan
Leod," &c. See also Major-General Stewart's " Sketches of
the Highlanders," i. 102, &c. " Regiment of the Isles,"
" Macdonald's Highlanders," &c.

THE ECCLESIOLOGY OF CANTIRE.

[After these volumes had gone to press, a valuable work has been published (April, 1861), called the "Old Church Architecture of Scotland," by T. S. Muir, in which the ecclesiology of Cantire has received due attention. As I have been unable to make any use of this book in the body of my work, I have here extracted all such portions as relate to Cantire, and am thus able to give upon good authority a tolerably connected account of the ecclesiology of Cantire.]

" THE Argyleshire churches and chapels form a large portion of the aggregate remains in the mainland of Scotland. They do not possess, however, much architectural interest, being, for the greater part, very rude buildings, with details in most instances even less laboriously fashioned than those in the plainest of the chapels just above spoken of. Regarding their age, it would, in at least many instances, be venturous to speak, except in very general terms. Some specimens are certainly First-Pointed, and others have much of Romanesque expression ; but the greater number have so little of definite character, that it seems nearly impossible to fix the period of their erection, though it is evident that part of them are not older than the fifteenth and sixteenth centuries. The material which has been employed in their construction is the thin slaty stone of the country, interspersed with granite, and other stones of lumpish form ; and of these, without having undergone much preparation, windows and doorways are sometimes made, though, for such parts of the building, dressed sandstone, occasionally of a bright red colour, has much more frequently been chosen. In plan and general appearance, the more definable of the series resemble very closely the First-Pointed chapels in the eastern counties, but with some differences in the adjustment of detail. The doorway—for it is not often that we find more than one—is not, for instance, always in one or other of the side walls; and the windows, which are generally limited to two or three at most, are placed apparently more to meet some local necessity than to harmonise with the conventional rules of church arrangement. The fewness, smallness, and unsettled position of the perforations— which, it may be suggested, were, in all likelihood from the want of glazing material, left quite open—were designed doubtless with a view to shelter in exposed situations, and also perhaps as a means of partial defence against the irruptions of the Northmen and other predatory strangers. . . . The east elevation is not unfrequently blank, and sometimes, in the same instance, the west one also. In a good many cases the vacancy occurs on the north side, but never on the south, at least not on that side in any one of the chapels referred to in the present narration. The west end, when pierced at all, has never more than one short light, placed either in a central part of the wall itself, or in the apex of the gable; and the treatment of the east elevation is seldom more complex,—a single lancet, or narrow round-headed light of moderate length, being a very common allowance in that part of the building, or at most a couplet of long lanciform lights, set sufficiently wide of each other to afford room for the enormous expansion of their splays in the interior wall.

" Such is the general character of churches and chapels of small and medium size still numerously existing, in various stages of dilapidation, in every district of Argyle. It will be scarcely necessary to enter upon any lengthened account of them individually, as they are all much akin to one another, and rarely contain details worthy of much observation. Nevertheless the names of places where remains exist, as well as a passing remark on the remains themselves, may be recited for the benefit of the traveller, who, if happily he hath united to his veneration for antiquity a wakeful love of Nature, will find a tireless delight in tracking their solitary and often very hidden retreats, through a country everywhere abounding in prospects of surpassing beauty and grandeur.

" Commencing with the southern extremity of the long but easily traversed peninsula of Kintyre, which will be found to open conveniently upon the more ramified districts of the country, we find, at Kiels, the ruins of St. Columba, beautifully situated in a burying-ground quite close to the shore. The dimensions are somewhat singular, the length outside being 75 ft. 3 in., the width only 18 ft. 10 in.; but originally the proportions would have been more congruent, for an unbonded junction in the north wall, at about 29 ft. from the east end, shows that the building has been latterly that much elongated. Westward of the junction the masonry is of the usual rude description ; but the stones of the added part are squared, and of the form usually found in Norman work. There is a plain round-headed doorway on the south-west, and two or three small round-headed single-light windows in the north and south walls towards the east end, but no other details of any interest.

" Between Kiels and Campbelton, on the east side of the river, is Kilblaan, remembered only as the site of a chapel and burying-ground; and further on, but lying a mile or two off the road in the direction of Machrihanish, is Kilcoivin, where a considerable portion of the church remains. Kilkieran, prettily situated on the south side of Campbelton Bay, and within quite a short walk of the town, contains some fragments of crosses worth seeing; but nothing of the church, which is said to have been the most important in the south of Kintyre. At a greater distance from the town, and topping a rocky declivity on the opposite side of the bay, is the burying-ground and chapel of Kilchouslan. The chapel, which is rather more than 58 feet in length, is nearly entire, and is curious from having all its apertures square-headed. There is one small, narrow light in the east end, one in the west end, and three, along with a small doorway, in the south wall. The north wall, as is not unfrequently the case, is blank, and seems to have been lengthened about 20 feet, as there is a fissure similar to that at Kiels, at that distance from the east end.

" With the exception of Saddell Abbey, there is nothing of any note on the eastern shore of the peninsula north of Kilchouslan till we come to Skipness. But crossing in a north-westerly direction from Campbelton, and taking the circuitous road to Skipness by the opposite coast, the ruins of two rather interesting chapels are to be met with on the way.

" The first is situated in the road-side hamlet of Kilchenzie, some four miles or so out of the burgh, and about two from the nearly obliterated burial-ground of Kilmichael. In plan and proportions, Kilchenzie resembles very much the chapel at Kiels, the length being 75 feet, the width 22 feet; but the features look a little earlier. There is a south-west doorway, and two or three round-headed windows of small size in the south wall, one window of the same kind being placed in the middle of the east elevation.

" The other chapel is at Killean, about twelve miles onward, and nearly opposite to the low grassy island of Gigha, which is readily visited from Tayinloan in the immediate vicinity. Killean was probably one of the high churches—a mother-church perhaps—of the country, for the details are more elaborated than is customary, and there is the rarity of what seems to be either a sacristy or chantry-chapel on the north-east. There is also, besides the south-west doorway, another one on the south, near the east end; and there are probably other indications of a more than usually distinguished chancel existing in the interior, but of these nothing can be said, as the east end of the building, with the sacristy, is enclosed for burial. All the walls are nearly perfect except the west one, which is down, and contain narrow round-headed lights on both sides, with moulded rear-arches. In the east end is a very long couplet, formerly separated by a buttress; these have a row of the tooth ornament carried round the edge of the external openings, and a moulded label, which after descending in steps to the spring of the gable, and there curving into a quasi-capital to a corner nook-shaft, is returned along the side-walls in a cornice.

"Beyond Killean, to the northern boundary of Kintyre, the only place we meet with of any note is the little wayside clachan or kirk-town of Kilcalmonell; but of the church itself, which presided over a wide province, nothing exists, except perhaps in very partial combination with the modern structure in the adjacent burial-ground. One of its 'pendicles,' however, the chapel of St. Columba, at Skipness, remains nearly entire. Turning off to the right a few miles north of Kilcalmonell, you come to it by a hilly road, from the summit and eastern descent of which a magnificent prospect of Kilbranan Sound and the torn peaks of the Arran mountains is obtained.

"St. Columba—and it is curious to find the name in possession of both extremities of the peninsula—stands prettily, quite close to the shore, and neighbourly with the stalwart ruins of Skipness Castle, which is supposed in part to be coeval with the chapel itself. The external length of the chapel is 82 feet, the width 27 feet,—the largest ecclesiastical structure, therefore, in Kintyre, and probably also in the whole of Argyle, if the cathedral at Iona alone be excepted. The details, though plain as usual, are of very good character, and seem to be of advanced First-Pointed date. There is a plain pointed doorway on the south-west, another on the north-west, and a south-east one to the chancel, which, although sufficiently defined by the disposition of the windows, &c., is not distinguished in the architecture. All the windows have the scoinson-arch, and, with the doorways, are formed of a bright red sandstone, which has rather a pleasing effect, but contrasts oddly with the dark slaty material of the general building. The east window is of two lights simply divided by a monial; those in the side walls are narrow lancets; and of the same kind is one in the middle of the west end, of smaller size, topped by a square aperture in the gable, which is probably quite modern." (pp. 48—52.)

. . . . " The list (of ecclesiastical buildings), particularly of the smaller buildings, with anything like noticeable features, is but a spare one, and is, as will be observed, largely made up of specimens in Argyleshire, where the absence of a crowded population, and the fewer encroachments on the primitive condition of the soil, have tended to preserve the ancient sites and chapels more than in the eastern parts of the country." (p. 56.)

. . . . " Reference has been made to some pillars of memorial in Argyleshire, which from their features were presumed to be of somewhat similar age to those of early Norman date located in the eastern counties. Besides these, Argyle, to which they seem to be entirely confined, contains another and much more numerous class of monolithic pillars, cruciform like them, but quite distinct in expression, and obviously the work of a much later time.

" Here and there a slight variation occurs among the Argyle crosses, but the prevailing type is a thin, flat, greenish pillar, or, more properly speaking, pilaster, of mica or chlorite slate, varying from 6 to 12 or 13 feet in height, from 15 to 20 inches in width at the bottom, and from 3 to 6 inches across the narrower faces. They are generally fixed into a square plinth of one or more steps, taper upwardly, and terminate in a large disk or solid girdle, with short arms projecting from the summit and sides.

" The sculptured ornaments, with which the broader faces are profusely overspread in low relief, are generally elegant, and often of singularly complex character; but there is seldom much diversity of design, the same pattern, or mere varieties of it, being common to all the pillars, as well as being frequently repeated over and over again on both faces of the same stone. These ornaments consist, for the most part, of angels, men, animals, a sort of niche or canopy (sometimes enclosing a figure, but oftener vacant), with a pointed head trefoiled, and a peculiar description of conventional foliage run into garlands of circular and ovate form. Both faces of the disk are occasionally covered with intertwined, radiated, or other sort of purely ornamental work; but more frequently one of the faces—generally the west one—and part of the stem, carry a bold sculpture of the Crucifixion, which, wherever it appears, is of course always the most prominent and characteristic feature of the monument. (These specimens are found in Northern Argyleshire, and the Isles.)

" It does not appear that anything certain is known touching the precise age and origin of these very interesting pillars. Mr. Howson (*Transactions of the Cambridge Camden Society*), like

Dr. Macculloch and others, is disposed to trace them to Scandinavian sources, though, as he observes, many of the sculptured figures indicate a moderate age. A more positive indication of such, he might have added, is to be found in the dates on some of the inscribed specimens, none of which reach further back than the end of the fifteenth century. Most of the finer and more perfect pillars, to be sure, are without inscriptions, and these, in some instances, may belong to a somewhat earlier period; but the unvarying uniformity of style observable in all, and the close resemblance of the ornamentation to that on the sepulchral slabs, on which early dates are not to be found, can scarcely leave a doubt of their altogether being the work of the same age, and that none of them are likely to be older than the first quarter of the fifteenth century.

"There is a current belief in places where these pillars and slabs exist, that they were all brought from the island of Iona. Hence the popular name of *Iona Stones*, that is given to them all over the district. It would not be easy, perhaps, exactly to determine how much of this belief has originated among the inhabitants themselves; but pretty certain it is, that by far the greater proportion of it is the propagation of petty antiquaries and guide-book makers, from whose accounts one might be led to suppose that Iona was one vast burial-ground, and for centuries back had been supplying tombs, crosses, and effigies to all the other places of interment in the country.

"With few exceptions, all the ancient cemeteries in Morven, Lorn, Knapdale, and Kintyre, besides those in Mull, Isla, Jura, Oransay, and most of the smaller islands, contain, individually, specimens, more or less abundant, of the sepulchral slab, and occasionally one or more crosses, or fragments of them, precisely similar to those in Iona. Here and there some of the slabs, it is possible, may be wanderers from that island; but to imagine that all, or even any considerable number, came thence, would be to maintain, not only that stones of the Iona type were not in use anywhere except in Iona itself, but that, until the monumental exodus took place, no memorial of any kind lay over the body of military chief or churchman deposited in less sacred ground than the Relig Orain; for it must be remembered, that, saving the 'Protestant' slab, with its long-winded eulogy, no other description of memorials than those just referred to are anywhere existing in the county.

"What has been said of the sculptured slabs may be applied in like manner to the standard crosses, which it would be quite as absurd to suppose were originally erected solely in Iona. So far, indeed, from this being likely, there is reason to believe that the cross of the Iona type was common to every place of sepulture in Argyle; though the sacred symbol, with its curious traceries, gracefully overshadowing, and marking to the distant eye, the silent city of the dead, is now to be met with only in few places.

"Besides crosses of this kind, Argyle contains others of miscellaneous character, the which will be spoken of hereafter: meantime the following are to be cited as probably all the existing specimens of the more common type: —

"KINTYRE. 1. *Campbelton.*—A very fine and perfect cross, nearly 11 feet in height, mounted on six steps. On the east face there are four figures, in pairs, placed in the disk, and an angel with a cross in the south arm. In the upper part of the stem is a kind of shallow niche with a pointed head trefoiled, containing foliage; next below, another niche, segmental-headed and trefoiled semicircularly, containing a book and chalice; then successively, two square divisions, one filled with an inscription in Lombardic letters, and the other enclosing two animals with their tails running out into mazy foliage. The west face is covered principally with floriated work: but there are some animals at the base and summit, one of which is apparently a mermaid. The edges of the pillar are rounded off in a slender roll, or bead-moulding, and, as is not uncommon, there is a stripe of foliage down the inferior faces.

" 2. *Kilkieran.*—Several interesting fragments in the burying-ground. One has an inscription commencing with the usual *Hæc est crux,* reticulated and floral decorations, and a trefoil-headed niche pictured with the Crucifixion. The person of our Lord is surrounded by four figures, one of which is piercing the body with a spear, and another presents the sponge on the end of a reed.

" 3. *Kilchouslan.*—The lower portion of the stem, rather more than 4 feet in length, lying in the chapel. One of the broader faces has a horseman and a sword; the other one presents a galley, two animals, and ornaments of the intertwined pattern." (pp. 98–101.)

(No woodcut illustrations are given to any of the Kintyre specimens of crosses, slabs, or chapels. A woodcut is given of the Inverary cross, but it merely represents it in outline, and does not attempt any delineation of its intricate ornamentation. The following is the letter-press description) : —

" INVERARY. — A very fair specimen, 8 ft. 4 in. in height, raised on a modern plinth of three low steps. The stem is of the ordinary tapering form, but the disk is an oval semicircularly notched into a floriated cross pattée, covered on both faces with foliage, and a hybrid animal in one of the arms. On one of the broader faces the stem is entirely overspread with floral and interlaced decorations. On the other there is, at the top, an empty panelled compartment or shallow niche, with a pointed head trefoiled, under a segmental arch; following next below is a tissue of foliage; then four animals, combatant,

like swine and tigers ; under these a figure on horseback with
a hawk on his wrist ; and last of all, two lines of an inscription,
the preceding portion of which is carried in two lines along
the whole length of one of the inferior faces of the pillar.
Common report seems to be equally divided between Iona,
and Kiels in Kintyre, as the first standing-place of this cross ;
although Old Inverary, now absorbed in the ducal park, or
the ancient burying-ground of Kilmalew in the immediate
neighbourhood, could be suggested as much more likely than
either.' (pp. 102–3.)

. . . . " Of places besides Iona which may be profitably visited with a view to these pictured memorials (*i. e.*
sepulchral slabs), are particularly to be mentioned the bury-
ing-grounds at . . . . . Kiels, Kilcoivin, Kilchenzie,
Killean, Skipness in Kintyre . . . From repeated shift-
ings carelessly performed, and other easily-imagined causes,
resulting from the too frequently abandoned condition of the
Highland *Kil*, the slabs are many times found in a worn, frac-
tured, and fragmentary state ; but there seems no reason to
believe that any of them have suffered *in situ* from deliberate
misusage, if we except only an occasional instance of a stone
being appropriated to distinguish some Celt of the present day
claiming hereditary relationship with the chieftain in whose
memory the stone was originally fashioned. Of this easy
method of securing *post-mortem* renown, almost every ancient
place of sepulture in the Highlands can show examples. A
stone at Kilchoman, for instance, is coarsely re-dedicated to a
' Colin Campbell, Sunderland, deceased, May 1633.' At Kil-
martin, a modern ' McTavish ' flourishes on the brisket of an
ancient warrior, whose own name is unrecorded ; and, at the
same place, a ' Peter Campbell, Esq.,' mars a beautiful slab
bearing a wheeled cross, and a two-handed sword on the left
side of the stem." (pp. 109–10.)

. . . " The *nail-head*, the *pellet*, and the *cable*, are other figures to be found among the moulded work of these and other churches, and, sometimes with the tooth ornament, on the greater number of the sepulchral slabs in Argyle. The nail-head, particularly, seems to have been a very favourite embellishment all over the mainland and islands of western Scotland. It is sometimes found encircling the capitals and bands of window and vaulting-shafts, but much oftener forming a spotted *limbus* round the pictured slabs and standard crosses." (p. 119.)

. . . . " The small, but much elevated, SANDA — the Avoyn of Dean Monro — lies a short distance out from the Mull of Kintyre, and may be readily visited from Newton village, some nine or ten miles south of Campbelton. The island itself is very picturesque, but besides a greatly ruinated chapel, about 33 feet in length, and two crosses, nearly 7 feet in height, contains nothing that is interesting.

" GIGHA, lying off the west coast of Knapdale, a few miles, and with a ferry to and from Tayinloan, is a pretty island well worth visiting, though the antiquities in it are not of much importance. At Kilchattan, a retired spot up a bit from the landing-place, are the remains of a chapel, externally 38 feet in length ; it is of the ordinary Argyleshire pattern, with the usual lanciform window in the east end. Martin says, ' It has an altar in the east end, and upon it is a font of stone which is very large, and has a small hole in the middle which goes right through it.' The altar has disappeared, but the font — a rather small specimen of octagonal shape, with a circular cavity flat in the bottom—still remains, along with several sculptured slabs of a good character. On a hillock above the burying-ground, there is a plain truncated pillar ; and, at Tarbert, some two miles or so away towards the north end of the island, there

z 2

is, besides the 'Druid's Stone,' a broken cross, 6 feet in height, with traces of carved work on one of its broader faces." (pp. 124–6.)

(A full description of the ecclesiology of Islay, Jura, and others of the Western Isles, is also given in this book; but the foregoing extracts are all that immediately relate to Cantire.)

The following extract, bearing upon this subject, is taken from the Preface to the " Sculptured Stones of Scotland," Spalding Club, 1856. The illustrations to this splendid work are chiefly taken from specimens found in the northern and eastern districts of Scotland; and do not include any examples from Cantire.

" If we compare the Scotch crosses with those in Ireland, we shall find many points of resemblance, and yet very marked differences. It may be said that almost every ornament which occurs on the crosses of the one country may be traced on those of the other, especially in all the varieties of interlaced knot-work and raised bosses. The stem of the cross in both countries is divided into compartments, each surrounded with a moulding, and occasionally with a rich border.* . . . . The Scotch monuments bear most strongly the impress of Irish art, as exhibited on crosses, shrines, and other remains, ranging in point of date from the seventh to the eleventh century. Nor is this otherwise than might have been expected, for 'all the affinities indicated by the later and well-defined relics of native art point to a more intimate intercourse and community of

---

* See a paper by Mr. Westwood in the " Archæological Journal," December, 1853.

customs and arts between the natives of Scotland and Ireland, than between those of the northern and southern parts of the island of Great Britain." * While the genial influences of Christianity were imparted to various districts of Scotland through other and earlier missions, yet to that of St. Columba and his followers we must attribute the widest range and the most abiding impression. We have seen that in Ireland it was the custom of St. Patrick to consecrate the pillar stones of the heathen to Christian uses, and the erection of crosses seems to have followed.

" The purposes intended by their erection probably were various. . . . It may reasonably be supposed that the feelings which found their expression in the erection of crosses in the sweet solitude of Iona, would issue in similar erections by the followers of St. Columba in other parts of the country. It may also be supposed that crosses were erected by the early missionaries in place of the older stones of the native inhabitants, with the view of altering and sanctifying the principles, whatever they were, which had led them to set up their rude pillars. If we should suppose that many of our Scotch monuments are sepulchral, and may mark the last resting-place of the most illustrious of our early missionaries, it is easy to understand how others might wish to be laid near the same spot; how they would come to be fit meeting-places for the converts, or be chosen as sites for the wooden church which succeeded."

* Wilson's " Prehistoric Annals," p. 467.

GEOLOGY OF CANTIRE.

THE following are the chief passages relating to the geology of Cantire, in Macculloch's " Description of the Western Islands of Scotland," 1819.

" The gneiss of Mull and Morven are portions of the same mass of strata, and have originally been covered by a deposit of secondary rocks, consisting of limestone and sandstone, with coal occasionally interspersed. The essential characters of this deposit correspond with those of the northern islands, and no less with the more extensive tracts which occupy the centre of Scotland ; of which a portion, similarly detached, and strongly corresponding in position and present connections with this, is still to be found near the Mull of Cantyre, forming the present coal field of Campbeltown." (ii. 71.)

" It may probably be concluded that the central trap of Jura is the origin of the veins on the neighbouring coast of Cantyre, of which a very remarkable collection occurs at Killean, since no other neighbouring mass can be traced to which they can be referred. Those of the Mull of Cantyre may also possibly originate in the same source, unless Arran should here be supposed the central point from which these diverge. In a general view this fact is important, as it confirms the rule already deduced from former observations made in this country respecting the connection of trap veins with extensive masses of the parent rock. It serves still further to approximate the great trap district of the Western Isles to that of Ireland, by

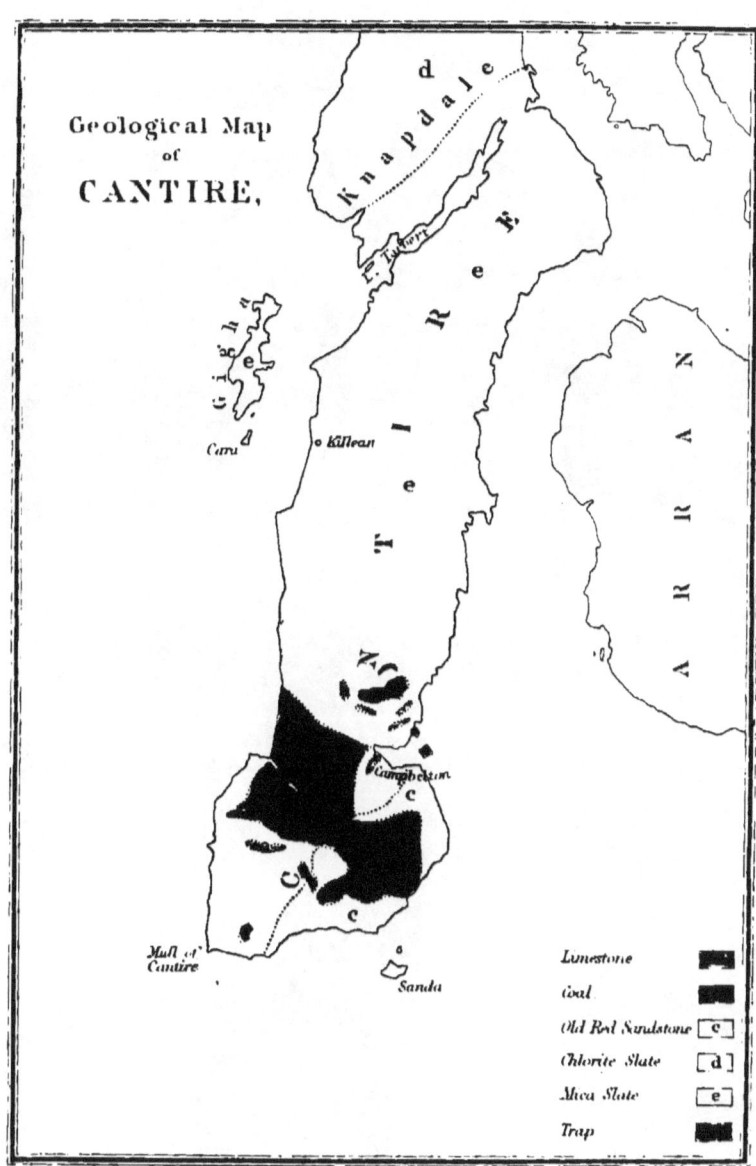

Geological Map
of
CANTIRE.

Knapdale

d

Gigha

c
e

Caru

d

Killean

T e i r e e F.

R e e F.

A R R A N

Campbelton

c

C

c

Mull of Cantire

Sanda

Limestone
Coal
Old Red Sandstone   c
Chlorite Slate   d
Mica Slate   e
Trap

London, Longman & Co

interposing another point which conduces to diminish the apparent distance between two tracts of which the connection may once have been much more intimate than it is at present." (ii. 214.)

" The circumstances under which the veins of trap are found, here and on the adjoining coast, are interesting. After passing Killean, on the coast of Cantyre, they almost entirely disappear in proceeding northwards. . . These examples prove that the prevalent trap veins of the western coast of Scotland are processes diverging from the great masses so conspicuous in this part of the island." (ii. 272.)

" If a line be drawn nearly parallel to the southern shore of the eastern branch of Loch Fine, at a small distance from the sea, and prolonged to the western coast of Cantyre, it will represent the south-eastern boundary of this (chlorite) series; that boundary being coincident with the bearing of the strata. . . . The southern limit, however, is unassignable; a great number of indefinite gradations and irregular alterations taking place before the chlorite series is finally established to the exclusion of the micaceous schist, which forms the southern part of Cantyre, and the districts to the south of Loch Fine. This ambiguous tract, however, rarely exceeds two miles in breadth; in a few places it may extend to four." (ii. 283-4.)

" The beds of micaceous schist, on the eastern shore of Cantyre, have an eastern dip, while those on the opposite side dip to the westward." (ii. 288.)

" In Gigha, the direction of the shores is oblique to that of the rocks, and the same disposition will be found to pervade the southern part of the peninsula of Cantyre." (ii. 299.)

" On many parts of this peninsula, portions of red sandstone are to be seen detached from those immediately adjoining, occasionally insulated at a great distance from any similar rock, and occupying very minute spaces. Independently of these fragments of sandstone strata, alluvial deposits of a red colour are also found in the same tract, being most numerous in the neighbourhood of Campbeltown, whence they extend interruptedly to the north of the alluvial plain which lies near that town, and along the western shore as far as Tyanloan. These alluvia all consist of red clay and sand, with occasional fragments of red sandstone interspersed, and they are disposed in the form of detached banks or low hillocks, insulated from the surrounding land, and easily distinguished by their outlines. They vary in depth, from four or five feet to sixty or seventy; opportunities for examining their sections occurring in many places where they are cut through by the streams from the hills. Where these sections are sufficiently deep, it is evident that they lie on masses of red sandstone; and, in searching for the common line of separation, it is also perceptible that there is a gradual transition from the solid rock to the loose clay; the fragments of the former diminishing in size and number till they vanish in the mass of rubbish and red earth. Where the sandstone strata are more solid, and reach the surface, they also present the same tendency to gradual decomposition, being covered with thinner and more partial deposits of the same alluvial matter. It is easy, therefore, to perceive in Cantyre that which is less obvious in Arran — that the alluvia in question are untransported materials formed in their present places by the destruction of subjacent beds of sandstone." (ii. 337–8.)

" In the account of the chlorite series of Argyllshire, it was shown that a tract of micaceous schist succeeded it towards the south, being continued in that direction as far as the Mull of Cantyre. At that place it is immediately followed by the red sandstone, without any interposed substance; a fact easily

explained by considering the unconformable relation of this
rock to the primary strata, and the irregularity of its margin
consequent on the peculiar situation which it occupies with
respect to these. The same schist may be traced from this
peninsula, as far at least as to the mountains of Mar."
(ii. 454.)

" There can be no reason to doubt the identity of the whole
deposit of red sandstone, from the east coast of Scotland even
to the western side of Cantyre, as it possesses everywhere a
set of common features, together with a common relation to the
strata which it follows and to those which succeed it. But,
throughout the whole of this tract, it presents a great variety
both of dip and of direction ; the angles of elevation varying
in quantity, from the horizontal to a very high position, and
respecting different points of the compass. . . . A geological
map of Cantyre would have been requisite to illustrate the very
peculiar distribution of the sandstone in that district, but it is
here inadmissible : the general map which accompanies this
work will perhaps convey a sufficient idea of it for the present
purpose. It must suffice, in addition, to remark, that a continuous tract of this rock extends along the eastern shore of
that peninsula, from the harbour of Campbeltown southwards ;
and that to the north of that spot on the same shore, a few
very minute detached portions are also found. On the western
shore some independent masses of large size occur, all of them
presenting the same characters, both in composition and in
their relations to the micaceous schist on which they repose.
Indications of their existence are even found extending across
the low tract which intervenes between Campbeltown and
Machrianish Bay ; and here their nature is further proved
from their being followed by a portion of the same sandstone
and *coal* that succeed to the red sandstone in the central tract

of Scotland, which lies between the Clyde and the Forth. In describing the alluvia of Arran, it was remarked that the red sandstone was often covered by a great body of alluvial matter which appears to have arisen from its decomposition; remaining in the places in which it was formed. The same feature was then noticed as occurring in Cantyre. It is here, indeed, even more remarkable, as, independently of those alluvia which are still actually connected with subjacent bodies of the rock in this district, portions of it are to be found now unconnected with any rock; occupying the surface, without seeming to have undergone any transportation. From these several appearances it may be concluded that the red sandstone of Cantyre once formed a more continuous mass, and that its present disjunction is to be traced to those gradual operations by which extensive tracts of the surface are decomposed, and often removed. The red alluvia appear to be the last remaining indications of the parts that formerly occupied the places where they are found: and it is not difficult to foresee that in the further progress of time, the present insulated masses of that rock will terminate in that complete decomposition to which they are fast hastening, and ultimately, perhaps, disappear altogether. As the identity of this mass of sandstone, throughout its whole course through Scotland, was shown, from these considerations its original continuity is also in a great degree demonstrated; and thus the islands of the Clyde become reunited to the peninsula of Cantyre, in a geological sense, as perfectly as they have been shown to be geologically continuous with the much greater tract to the north-east of their position. . . . The association (of trap and red sandstone) will be found on the shores of Cantyre, in the vicinity of Campbeltown. Considerable masses of porphyry, of which the rock of Devar is among the most conspicuous, occur in this tract; and in every instance they appear to be connected with the red sandstone, or with the coal strata above it. Even in these cases where these masses are in contact at one part with the primary rocks, their larger portions will be found to repose on the sandstone or other secondary strata in the vicinity. . . .

" It has been shown, in describing the sandstone deposit of these Clyde islands, that it bore the marks of waste in a great degree, indications of which are found, not only in the partial occurrence of this rock in Cantyre, but in the cliffs of Arran, and in the trap veins visible in the several islands; the persistence of which remain as records of the loss of the surrounding strata. There is therefore abundant proof that the original extent of these islands was more considerable, and their intimacy of position greater than it is at present; but whether we are justified in concluding that they ever were continuous, is a question on which it is hopeless to speculate. I must here remark that no traces of the red sandstone are found within Loch Fyne, the northern limit of that rock being situated considerably to the south of its junction with the Clyde. If, therefore, the sandstone of Cantyre, Arran, Bute, and the mainland, were judged to have been once continuous, that extensive inlet must have been a fresh-water lake, discharging its waters through a channel between Bute and Arran, or between the latter island and Cantyre." (ii. 499–506.)

The distinguished geologist to whom I am indebted for the Geological Map of Cantire (which will be found much more minute and correct than Macculloch's " General Map"), has favoured me with the following note on the foregoing passages from Macculloch's work:—

" Macculloch gives a tolerably minute description of the areas occupied by the different kinds of gneiss, mica, schist, &c. &c.

There is, however, every reason to believe that all of these
metamorphic rocks in Cantyre will, when fairly analysed and
mapped, turn out to be the equivalents of the metamorphic
Lower Silurian strata that extend from the north coast of
Sutherlandshire to the Old Red Sandstone that crosses Scotland
from Stonehaven on the east to the Frith of Clyde. This is
proved by Murchison and Geikie."

NELSON'S HANDBOOK.   (Vol. II. p. 294.)

" Kyles of Bute. All its shores are beautiful, and those of
the narrowest and most curving portions present a fine succession of picturesqueness and romance."—*Nelson's Handbook to
Tourists in Scotland;* by the Rev. J. M. Wilson, p. 258. While
the last pages of " Glencreggan " were passing through the
press, I purchased a copy of the latest edition of Nelson's Handbook, which had previously escaped my notice. As I have referred (Vol. I. p. 80) to the very scanty notice bestowed upon
Cantire by the Guide-books, I think it but right to make
mention of this very excellent Handbook, which is compiled
(for the most part) upon an easily-understood and useful plan;
and is greatly increased in value by the addition of eighteen
coloured maps. It does not (like Black's Guide) pass over
Cantire, although its brief notice of the peninsula (amounting
altogether to not more than two pages out of 536) is treated in
a somewhat dislocated fashion; and the short descriptions of
Tarbert, Campbelton, and Dunaverty are imbedded in three
different sections of the book (63, 65, and 69) and are thus encountered " quite promiscuously," or have to be hunted up by
means of the Index. It is evident that the editor is of opinion
that no one would select Cantire as a touring spot, and he has
not therefore thought it worth his while to favour it with a

continuous description. Such information, however, as he has given may be relied upon for correctness; and therefore the tourist to Cantire will do well to provide himself with this Handbook, or Mr. Fyfe's Guide-book (which has the merit of cheapness, and of which I have spoken at Vol. I. p. 80), or Messrs. Anderson's Guide, to which I have referred in Vol. I. p. 85, and which is the only Guide-book containing a tolerably full account of Cantire.

From Nelson's Handbook I may add the following items of information : —

Davar Island (Vol. I. p. 67). The light-house was built in 1854.

Sanda Island (Vol. I. p. 114). A light-house stands on the island, built in 1850, showing a fixed red light, visible at the distance of 15 miles. The cliffs are above 300 feet high.

Campbelton Fisheries (Vol. I. p. 170). "It employs about 150 boats in the herring-fishery."

Kildalloig (Vol. I. p. 173), the seat of Sir L. H. D. Campbell, Bart.

Tarbert (Vol. II. p. 268). The population of East Tarbert is about 800.

INDEX.

THE END.

LONDON
PRINTED BY SPOTTISWOODE AND CO.
NEW-STREET SQUARE

BOOKS OF VOYAGES AND TRAVELS, WORKS ON NATURAL HISTORY, ETC.

THE COMPARATIVE ANATOMY and PHYSIOLOGY of the VERTEBRATE ANIMALS. By RICHARD OWEN, F.R.S., D.C.L., Superintendent of the Natural History Department, British Museum; Fullerian Professor of Physiology in the Royal Institution of Great Britain; Foreign Associate of the Institute of France, &c. In One thick Volume, 8vo. with upwards of 1,200 Engravings on Wood..[In the press.

THE SEA and ITS LIVING WONDERS. By Dr. GEORGE HARTWIG, Author of *The Life of the Tropics*. With several Hundred Woodcuts, a Physical Map, and 12 Chromo-xylographs, from Designs by H. N. HUMPHREYS. *Second Edition*.................................8vo. 18s.

THE LIFE of the TROPICS: a Popular Scientific Account of the Natural History of the Animal and Vegetable Kingdoms in Tropical Regions. By Dr. GEORGE HARTWIG, Author of *The Sea and its Living Wonders*. [In preparation.

FOREST CREATURES: 1. The Wild Boar; 2. The Roe, a New Wonder in Natural History; 3. The Red Deer; 4. The Fallow Deer; 5. The Cock of the Woods; 6. The Black Cock; 7. The Eagle; 8. Homer a Sportsman; 9. Hints. By CHARLES BONER, Author of *Chamois Hunting in the Mountains of Bavaria*. With Illustrations by Guido Hammer, of Dresden. Post 8vo. [*Just ready*.

THE NATURAL HISTORY of CEYLON: comprising Anecdotes illustrative of the Habits and Instincts of the Mammalia, Birds, Reptiles, Fishes, Insects, &c., of the Island; also a Monograph of the Elephant, and a Description of the Modes of Capturing and Training it. By Sir J. EMERSON TENNENT, K.C.S., LL.D., &c. Re-published from "*An Account of Ceylon, &c.*" with copious Additions, and new Illustrations from Original Drawings. Post 8vo. ....[*Nearly ready*.

WILD LIFE on the FJELDS of NORWAY. By FRANCIS M. WYNDHAM. With 5 Illustrations in Chromo-lithography, 2 Maps, and 5 Woodcuts.................................Post 8vo. 10s. 6d.

THE BISHOP of VICTORIA'S WORK, entitled *Ten Weeks in Japan*. With a Map and 8 Illustrations in Chromo-xylography...8vo. 14s.

ALPINE BYWAYS; or, Light Leaves gathered in 1859 and 1860. By a LADY. With Illustrations in Chromo-lithography from Original Sketches, and 4 Route Maps ....Post 8vo. 10s. 6d.

THE ALPS; or, Sketches of Life and Nature in the Mountains. By H. BERLEPSCH. Translated by the Rev. LESLIE STEPHEN, M.A. Fellow and Tutor of Trinity Hall, Cambridge. 8vo. with 17 Illustrations from Original Designs by Emil Rittmeyer.................................[*Nearly ready*.

NARRATIVE of the CANADIAN RED RIVER EXPLORING EXPEDITION of 1857, and of the ASSINNIBOINE and SASKATCHEWAN EXPLORING EXPEDITION of 1858. By HENRY YOULE HIND, M.A., F.R.G.S., &c. With 20 Chromo-xylographs, 76 Woodcuts, 3 Maps, &c.. 2 vols. 8vo. 42s.

London: LONGMAN, GREEN, and CO. Paternoster Row.

SEVEN YEARS' RESIDENCE in the GREAT DESERTS
of NORTH AMERICA. By the Abbé DOMENECH. With above Sixty
Illustrations...2 vols. 8vo. 36s.

ANAHUAC ; or, Mexico and the Mexicans, Ancient and
Modern. By EDWARD B. TYLOR. Pp. 356; with Route Map, 4 Illustrations in
Chromo-lithography, and 26 Engravings on Wood..........................8vo. 12s.

A WEEK at the LAND'S END. By J. T. BLIGHT,
Author of "Ancient Crosses and other Antiquities of Cornwall." With a Map,
geologically coloured, and 96 Illustrations drawn and engraved on the Wood by the
Author ....Square fcp. 8vo. 6s. 6d.

TWO MONTHS in the HIGHLANDS, ORCADIA, and
SKYE. By CHARLES RICHARD WELD, Barrister-at-Law. With 8 Illustrations...Post 8vo. 12s. 6d.

THE AFRICANS at HOME : being a popular Description
of Africa and the Africans condensed from the Accounts of African Travellers
from the time of Mungo Park to the Present Day. By the Rev. R. M. MACBRAIR,
M.A. With a New Map and about 70 Woodcut Illustrations..Square fcp. 8vo. 7s. 6d.

THE LAKE REGIONS of CENTRAL AFRICA. By
R. F. BURTON, Captain H.M. Indian Army. Map and Illustrations.
2 vols. 8vo. 31s. 6d.

PEAKS, PASSES, and GLACIERS. By Members of the
Alpine Club. Edited by JOHN BALL, M.R.I.A., President. Travellers' Edition,
comprising the Mountain Expeditions and the Maps printed in a condensed form.
16mo. 5s. 6d.
*** The Fourth Edition of "Peaks, Passes, and Glaciers," with 8 coloured Illustra-
tions, may still be had, in One Volume, square crown 8vo. price 21s.

THE OLD GLACIERS of NORTH WALES and SWIT-
ZERLAND. By A. C. RAMSAY, F.R.S. and G.S., Local Director of the Geological Survey of Great Britain. Reprinted from PEAKS, PASSES, AND GLACIERS ;
with Map and Woodcuts ....Fcp. 8vo. 4s. 6d.

"**T**HE EAGLE'S NEST" in the Valley of Sixt : a Summer
Home among the Alps. By ALFRED WILLS, Barrister-at-Law. *Second
Edition.* With 12 Illustrations on Stone, and 2 Maps ....Post 8vo. 12s. 6d.

SOCIAL LIFE and MANNERS in AUSTRALIA : Being
the Notes of Eight Years' Experience. By a RESIDENT ....Post 8vo. 5s.

COLONIZATION and COLONIES : Being a Series of
Lectures delivered before the University of Oxford in 1839, 40, and 41. By
HERMAN MERIVALE, M.A., Professor of Political Economy. Second Edition, with
Notes and Additions...8vo. 18s.

London: LONGMAN, GREEN, and CO. Paternoster Row.